THE THIRD ANGEL

The Third Angel

A Novel

Alice Hoffman

Chatto & Windus

LONDON

Published by Chatto & Windus 2008
First published in the United States in 2008 by
Shaye Areheart Books, an imprint of the Crown Publishing Group,
a division of Random House, Inc., New York

2 4 6 8 10 9 7 5 3 1

First published in Great Britain in 2008 by
Chatto & Windus
Random House, 20 Vauxhall Bridge Road,
London SW1V 2SA
www.rbooks.co.uk

Addresses for companies within The Random House Group Limited can be found at:
www.randomhouse.co.uk/offices.htm

The Random House Group Limited Reg. No. 954009

A CIP catalogue record for this book
is available from the British Library

ISBN 9780701182724

The Random House Group Limited supports The Forest Stewardship
Council (FSC), the leading international forest certification organisation. All our titles that
are printed on Greenpeace approved FSC certified paper carry the FSC logo.
Our paper procurement policy can be found at
www.rbooks.co.uk/environment

Mixed Sources
Product group from well-managed
forests and other controlled sources
www.fsc.org Cert no. TT-COC-2139
© 1996 Forest Stewardship Council
FSC

Printed and bound in Great Britain by
CPI Mackays, Chatham, ME5 8TD

The Third Angel

I.

The Heron's Wife

1999

MADELINE HELLER KNEW SHE WAS RECKless. She had flown to London from New York two days ahead of schedule and was now checked into her room at the Lion Park Hotel in Knightsbridge. The air was still and filled with dust motes; the windows hadn't been opened in months. Everything smelled like cedar and lavender. Maddy felt hot and exhausted from her travels but she didn't bother to turn on the air conditioner. She was madly, horribly, ridiculously in love with the wrong man and it made her want to lie there on the bed, immobilized.

Madeline wasn't stupid; she was an attorney in New York. She was thirty-four years old and had graduated from Oberlin and NYU Law School, a tall woman with long black hair. Many people thought she was beautiful and smart, but none of those people mattered. They didn't know her. They had no idea she was a traitor to her own flesh and blood. They would never have guessed she would throw her life away so easily, without thinking twice.

There was good love and there was bad love. There was the kind that helped raise a person above her failings and there was the desperate sort that struck when someone least wanted or expected it. That was what had happened to Maddy this past spring when she'd come to London to help plan her sister's wedding. Allie hadn't even asked for her help; it was their mother, Lucy, who'd told Maddy she should go to London and assist with the preparations; she was the maid of honor after all. And then when she got there, Allie had already taken care of everything, just as she always did.

Allie was older by thirteen months. She was the good sister, the perfect sister, the one who had everything. She was a writer who had published an extremely popular children's book. When she walked down the street people often recognized her, and she was always willing to sign scraps of paper for someone's child or present a fan with one of the bookplates she carried in her purse. Once a year she came back to the States to give readings for what had become a perennially popular event where children dressed up in bird costumes. There were nine- and ten-year-old cardinals and ducks and crows all waiting on line to have their copy of *The Heron's Wife* signed. Maddy sometimes accompanied her sister on tour. She couldn't believe all the fuss over a silly children's story, one Allie had pinched from a tale their mother used to tell. Technically, the story belonged to Maddy as much as it did to her sister, not that she'd felt the need to write a book or change it inside out to suit herself.

The story was one Lucy Heller would tell down by the marsh where the girls had grown up. Lucy's own mother, the girls' grandmother, had waded barefoot into a pond in Central Park to talk to a huge blue heron. She didn't care what people thought; she just went right in. She'd asked the heron to watch over Lucy and he always had. Now Lucy had asked him to protect her own girls and he had come to live in their marsh in Connecticut.

"How can a heron watch over a person?" Maddy had whispered to her sister. She didn't have much faith in stories, even though she was only eight years old. In that way, she was very much the skeptic her mother had been.

"He can have two separate lives," Allie was quick to say, as though the answer was simple, if only Maddy could unwind the mysteries of the universe. "He has his heron life up in the sky and his life down here."

"I'm glad he can help us both," Maddy said.

"Don't be ridiculous." Allie was always so definite and sure of herself. "The blue heron only has one true love."

And so it came to be in Allie's book. There was a woman who married a man she loved. The couple lived in a house that resembled the one on the marsh where the sisters had grown up. There were the same tall silver reeds. The same inky black sky. The bride and groom resided in their house made of sticks and stones for nearly a year, in happiness and peace. And then one day, when the man was out fishing for their supper, there was a knock on the door. The woman answered and there was the groom's other wife, a blue heron come to look for her missing husband.

"How can you stand all these children around?" Maddy had asked at an especially crowded reading. They had runny noses. They were germ filled, noisy, and rude. And did they have to laugh so loudly? It was earsplitting.

In Allie's book, the heron wife was wasting away. Her feathers were falling out. She hadn't eaten a mouthful since her husband had left.

One of us wins and one of us loses, but which will it be? she asked the bride at the door.

"They're my readers. I want them to laugh."

Allie was the one who always came home for visits, but at long last Maddy was to be her sister's guest. Frankly, she'd avoided coming to London; she said she was too busy, but it was more than that. She didn't need to see how perfect Allie's world was. Finally, there was no getting around it; there was a wedding to attend to, after all. A wedding where Maddy would once again be the sidekick, the bad little sister who couldn't follow rules, who even as a grown woman was still afraid of ridiculous things, thunderstorms and mice, traffic jams and airplanes. She would most likely be made to wear a horrible dress of some dreadful synthetic fabric while her sister glowed in white silk or satin. Second-rate, second-best, the dark side of everything. She never believed men who told her she was beautiful and she shied away from friendships. She did her work and kept to herself, the sort of woman who could stand idly by while children removed a butterfly's wings or buried a toad in the mud. What people did on their own time was none of her business. Cruelty, after all, was a fact of life. It wasn't up to her to set the world right. That sort of thing was her sister's concern.

Because Maddy was only in London for a long weekend that April, arriving on a Thursday and departing late Monday, she and Allie had raced directly from the airport to the dressmaker's so that Maddy could have her fitting. They'd been close as children, but had grown apart, and were now as different as sisters could be. Allie, however, had done her best to try and choose a dress that would suit Maddy: blue silk, flattering, showing off Maddy's figure. As for Maddy, she hated the dress, but she kept her mouth shut. She had decided she would try to be the agreeable sister for once in her life. She even agreed to taste potential wedding cakes when they were done with the dresses. That was why she was here. To help her sister.

They went to the baker's and tasted half a dozen confections, but the buttercream frostings were too heavy and the chocolates were too rich. Allie hadn't seemed satisfied with anything. She said she thought wedding preparations were a waste of time. In the end, she chose a plain yellow cake that had been made from her own recipe. She hadn't really needed Maddy after all.

Maddy was still in her compliant mode. "Good decision," she said. "Plain is the way to go. Less chance for anything to go wrong."

Not that she believed in that particular philosophy when it came to herself. Plain was good for Allie, not Maddy. Maddy was greedy and she always had been. She used to steal from her sister, headbands, jewelry, T-shirts. If this had been her wedding cake, she would have wanted mousse and jam and chocolate and brandied apricots and spun sugar. There was no such thing as too much for a girl who always thought she was second-best.

The day after the cake-tasting adventure, both sisters were curled up in bed with stomachaches under a comforter. They wore pajamas and socks. When they were children, they hadn't needed anyone but each other; it felt that way again for an hour or two as they sipped cups of tea. But there was no way to regain what Allie had ruined when she'd left home. When it came down to it, they really had nothing in common anymore. It had been seventeen years since Allie had gone to college in Boston. She went off to London in her junior year, returning only for a week or so at a time. She'd deserted Madeline, left her alone in the big house in Connecticut with their parents, who had reunited after several years of leading separate lives. The Hellers had no close neighbors and Maddy had no friends. She was standoffish in the way that lonely people often are. After her sister left, Maddy grew more isolated. Even when she went off to Oberlin, she was the only one who came home for Winter Term or spring break. When Allie's letters arrived, Maddy refused to read them. Instead, she went out to sit in the reeds. On days when the sky was clear she would sometimes see the blue heron who lived there. She had read that most herons live in pairs, the larger male and the more delicate female, coupled for life, but this one was alone. He was far off, across the water. She often called to him, but he didn't seem to hear her. He never once looked her way.

ALLIE'S FLAT IN Bayswater was airy but nondescript, not at all Maddy's style. Nothing to envy. Simplicity once again. Allie's wardrobe was full of wool and cashmere in shades of gray and navy and black. Practical clothes that were well tailored. Maddy knew this because she'd sneaked a look in the closet while Allie was in the shower. She felt as though there was a mystery about her sister, some essential detail that would explain her superhuman abilities to do the right thing. She didn't find any clues in all her searching, although she did discover that the single splash of color in the closet was a sheer pink blouse, a birthday present sent by Maddy last fall from Barneys. She couldn't help but notice that the store's tag was still attached.

The day after the wedding cake fiasco, they went out to lunch with the bridesmaids, even though they still had stomachaches. There was Georgia, Allie's best friend, who was the art director of the publishing company that had published Allie's book. Suzy, a transplanted Texan who had been a student along with Allie during junior year and had married an Englishman. She was now the mother of nine-year-old twin girls, so ensconced in her adopted city that she had a lilting British accent. The third friend, Hannah, taught hatha yoga and lived in the same building as Allie. Allie had been one of her students, and still took a class once a week. Hannah was very tall, and she wore white for nearly every occasion. She looked like a cat, as if she could stretch out and bend in two.

"At last, the little sister!" Georgia cried when Allie and Maddy arrived at the luncheon. Allie's friends gathered around to greet Maddy. It was a nicer restaurant than Maddy had expected; small vases of flowers with name tags marked their places at the table. The other bridesmaids told Maddy that they were jealous because she was the only one wearing sky blue silk—they were all in almond-colored linen.

"Yes, but you'll be able to wear those suits for other occasions," Allie explained when her friends complained. "That's why I chose them. Maddy likes extravagant things."

True enough. The other women had noticed that Madeline was overdressed for the occasion; she was wearing a peacock-colored silk blouse and long silver and opal earrings. Well, people could think she was vain if they wanted to; it wasn't a crime to have good taste, after all.

"Maybe that's why she's never come here to see you before," Georgia guessed. "She's been waiting for the big dress-up occasion so she can show off."

"I haven't come because I work," Maddy said.

"And the rest of us don't?" Georgia wasn't one to back down.

"I didn't say that."

"You didn't have to. So what is it you do that keeps you so busy?"

"I'm an attorney," Maddy said.

The other women exchanged a look.

"Is there something wrong with that?" Maddy asked. "Some comment you'd like to make?"

"Well, she's here now," Allie said to her friends. "That's what's important."

All the same, there was a chill at lunch after that. Allie's friends were polite to Maddy, but no more. They discussed things she didn't understand, television series she'd never heard of, books she'd never read. She was once again, by choice or design, the outsider in her sister's life.

When she went to the lavatory, Georgia and Suzy were there. Maddy swore they shut up as soon as they saw her.

"So what's Paul like?" Maddy asked of the bridegroom-to-be as she washed her hands.

She definitely wasn't imagining it: Georgia and Suzy exchanged an odd glance in the mirror.

"Decide for yourself," Suzy said. She sounded extremely Texan, someone you wouldn't want to cross.

"You're her sister," Georgia added as she reapplied some lip gloss. "I'm sure you can make your own judgments."

"THEY DIDN'T LIKE me," Maddy said to Allie after lunch. Not that it mattered. She didn't care what people thought of her. She was like her grandmother in that way. She did as she pleased, no matter the consequences. She would have waded into a pond in Central Park if need be. Maddy and Allie had decided to walk home from the restaurant. It was spring after all. They cut through Hyde Park, which was so green they couldn't help but think of home, all of those reeds in the marsh, all those places to hide.

"Of course they liked you," Allie said. "Don't be so insecure."

No one else would have guessed Maddy was insecure. But Allie knew she had been a thumb sucker, a blanket holder, a little girl who had been frightened of spiders, afraid of the dark, terrified of mice. Allie would often have to crawl into bed beside Maddy and tell her a story before she could fall asleep. It was their story, the one about the heron, the one they had shared before Allie claimed it for herself and put it into a book.

"Paul will probably hate me, too."

"You always expect the worst. Let's try to be positive. Let's expect the best."

By now Maddy knew the entire story of Allie and Paul's meeting. They'd come across each other purely by chance at Kensington Palace; that was why the wedding reception was to be held on the palace grounds at the Orangery, which had once been Queen Anne's greenhouse. Both Allie and Paul had gone there to leave flowers in Princess Diana's memory the day after the accident in Paris. Allie had brought along a bouquet of white roses. She had chosen each individual rose at her local greengrocer's, making certain there were no blemishes, no browning petals.

The whole Diana affair had made her feel so hopeless; it was as though love was impossible in such a bleak, cruel world. But then she had taken the white roses to Kensington Palace, where the bouquets reached out for hundreds of yards, and there was Paul, who had decided to come at the very last moment. His visit hadn't been planned; in fact, he'd torn up some flowers from his neighbor's garden, red things he didn't even know the name of, to lay at the palace gates, mostly because his mother was such a fan of Diana's. Paul's mum, who lived in a village near Reading, had been utterly broken up by the news and Paul thought she'd be pleased to know that he had stopped to pay his respects on her behalf.

Allie had confided to her sister that she'd been crying when she first saw Paul; she'd literally felt dizzy when she looked at him. He'd come over to ask if she was all right; she'd shaken her head no, then had been unable to speak. They went out for coffee, and that was that. It was unbelievably romantic. Love strikes when you least expect it. That's what Allie had told her. It struck and it went right through you, as invisible as ether.

When Maddy first heard the story, she'd wanted to shout, What on earth is romantic about doomed love? But she'd said nothing. Only that Diana had been a fool not to know whom she was marrying in the first place. Maddy had seen an interview in which Prince Charles had been asked if he was in love. "Whatever love is," he had said with Diana sitting right next to him. She should have gotten up and walked away then.

Maddy and Allie took a detour on the way back from their lunch with the bridesmaids so they could stop at Harvey Nichols to try on shoes. They were both shoe fanatics. They still had that in common. All through high school they had shared shoes and clothes. Everyone thought they both had fabulous wardrobes, when in fact they'd had less than most of their friends. Maddy tried on a pair of suede boots that closed with silver buttons. They were gorgeous. She was considering spending the £300. When she wanted something, she wanted it desperately. She knew that if she didn't get the boots they would nag at her and she'd regret it, so she might as well do the rash thing and buy them.

Maddy was most certainly not jealous because she was only the bridesmaid, not the bride. Not at this wedding. The off-white silk suit Allie had chosen for herself was a little sad. It was her usual practical style, something she could wear again and again, not an outfit anyone would dream of for her wedding. Maddy herself would have gone for organza and satin, some ravishing design a woman could wear only once in her life. As Allie was warning her that suede was easily ruined in the rain, Maddy paid for, then claimed, the lovely, expensive, impractical boots.

• •

THEIR MOTHER USED to sing "Row, Row, Row Your Boat" when they took a dinghy out along the cloudy Connecticut shore on those rare days when she felt well enough. That was where the heron lived, out beyond the flat water. Lucy Heller was too weak to use the oars; that was up to the girls. Lucy had been in treatment for cancer from the time Maddy and Allie were ten and eleven until they were in high school, the period when their father was gone. Lucy grew stronger as time went on, a survivor who never had another relapse, but back then the most she could manage was to carry her knitting bag. Lucy's mother's life had been claimed by cancer and although Lucy tried to keep her fears to herself, her children sensed them anyway. They came to believe she was doomed.

The girls hatched a plan should one of those boating outings ever turn dire. If the dinghy rocked over, if a sudden storm arose, they would save each other first. Even if they were warring and had had a terrible fight that very day, if Maddy had swiped a book or a bracelet, or if Allie had cleaned their room and tossed out Maddy's collection of seashells, they would still rescue each other. They would hold hands and help each other stay afloat. They always made sure to wear life jackets, so they would be ready. They checked the newspaper for weather reports.

A curse had been placed upon their mother. That was why she was so distant and sad. That was why her husband had left her during her treatment. No one rational would have done that. No one whose wife hadn't been under a spell. The girls decided that they were the only ones who could break the curse. There was only one way to combat an evil spell: blood for blood, skin for skin, ashes for ashes. They would call to the heron who was bound to watch over them. They'd make a sacrifice to his spirit. The sisters crept out to the backyard after bedtime. It was very dark, and Maddy tripped over a stone. Allie had to grab on to her to keep her from falling. They were in their nightgowns. No one had done the wash for two weeks and the hems of their nightgowns were dirty. Their feet were bare. Things in the house were falling apart. There was no food in the refrigerator and they had run out of clean clothes. No one took out the garbage and moths flitted around the boxes of pasta and rice in the cabinets. That was the way illness appeared in a house, in the corners, in between floorboards, on the hooks in the closet, along with the sweaters and coats.

Maddy hung back as they approached the end of the lawn. Curses, after all, were powerful things. It was impossible to see beyond the hedge. There seemed to be no one else alive in the world. If they went forward, would the earth still be there? If the heron came when they called to him, what would they do next? Maddy didn't even like birds. A blue heron was almost as big as she was; she knew that from reading the Audubon guide. They were territorial and would fight any interlopers.

"Come on," Allie said. "There's nothing to be afraid of."

Allie had gotten the shovel from the garage. When she started digging, the earth puddled with water. Maddy stood close to her sister. Allie smelled like soap and sweat and mud. She seemed to know exactly what she was doing.

"You're getting in the way," Allie said. "I can do this myself."

When the shoveling was done, Maddy handed Allie the razor they'd stolen from the bathroom.

"It won't hurt a bit," Allie promised. "He'll come to us then. He'll protect us."

She was always saying things wouldn't hurt in order to get Maddy to do what she didn't want to do. Sometimes it was true and sometimes it wasn't.

"The best thing to do when something hurts is to say one word over and over in your head," Allie whispered. "Something comforting." Their father was gone. Their mother might soon be in the hospital or locked into a high tower by mysterious forces or dead. The word Maddy chose to say was *rice pudding*. Technically that was two words, but it was her favorite dessert, and it always brought her comfort. Allie was quick when she dragged the razor across Maddy's hand. She'd been right about the pain. It didn't so much hurt as it burned.

"Okay," Allie said. "Good job." Once she was done with Maddy, she cut herself. One deep gash across her palm. She didn't even wince. "Now we hold our hands over the dirt."

They let their blood trickle onto the earth, then Allie shoveled the dirt back over the place where their blood had fallen. Their nightgowns were filthy by now, not that they cared. Their hair was tangled down their backs. They climbed up into the sycamore, the biggest tree for miles around.

"Something should happen," Allie said. But nothing did. They waited and waited, but not a thing changed. Allie was hugely disappointed. She was the protector, the one who made all the decisions, the dependable one. She never cried, but now it seemed she might. "He's never coming back," she said. "He can't save her."

For Maddy, the thought of Allie crying was the most terrifying part of the night. "Just because we can't see him doesn't mean he's not there."

Allie looked at her sister, surprised. Frankly, Maddy had surprised herself.

"It's dark out there," Maddy went on to explain. "And the human eye is limited." Her science class had been studying the human body, and they had just learned about the eye. The sisters looked out over the marsh. They couldn't tell where the land stopped and where the water began. The silvery reeds looked black as coal. Maddy whispered, and for once she sounded sure of herself. "I'll bet he's there right now, only he can't reveal himself. We have to just trust that he's there."

The girls' mother seemed to feel better the next day. She sat in a lawn chair in the pale sunshine with her knitting beside her. At noon she went into the kitchen and fixed Allie and Maddy their lunch. They heard her laugh later in the day. The sisters had made something happen through blood and faith. They never spoke of that night again. It seemed like a dark secret. Families such as theirs didn't believe in such nonsense. They didn't sneak out in the middle of the night and cut themselves with razor blades. Still, Maddy couldn't help but wonder if the curse hadn't somehow been shifted onto her when she lied to her sister. She continued to cut herself. She chose places no one would notice: the back of her knees, the soles of her feet, her inner arm. Her sister was right. After a while, it no longer hurt.

On Maddy's second night in London, Allie cooked an Indian curry that caused the entire flat to smell like cumin. It made sense that Allie would have learned to be a great cook. She practiced until she was perfect. She didn't give up the way Maddy did when it came to her personal life. Maddy stayed out of the kitchen. She didn't even ask if she could set the table. Surely it would never be good enough.

Paul came over at seven. Maddy had curled up on the couch, drinking a glass of wine, painting her toenails, ready to be unimpressed. Allie's friends and beaus never interested her. They were studious bookworms, not Maddy's type. Maddy was more concerned with her toenails; she had chosen a silvery color of polish that looked like gunmetal. She hated London. The shops were expensive and everyone spoke down to her, even the yoga instructor. She wished she could sneak away. She'd prefer to be in Paris by herself. She'd never even been there. She'd stay at a room at the Ritz that had green silk wallpaper and locks on all the doors. She could walk through the Tuileries, have coffee in a place where no one spoke her language. This whole wedding preparation was a joke. Maddy had heard that half of all marriages ended in divorce. It might even be 75 percent. Why would anyone take on odds like that?

Allie went to open the door when the bell rang. Maddy heard the murmur of voices. Frankly, she didn't much care what they said. Other than discussing wedding details, Allie hadn't talked about Paul. She wasn't the sort to confide in her sister. All Maddy knew was the same old story of their first meeting: Kensington Palace. Diana. White roses. He was probably the most boring man in the world. Now, at the door, Allie said something about Paul not being late for once, and he said that he was always on time, she was always early. They sounded tired and annoyed, not the lovebirds Maddy had expected.

"Here's my little sister," Allie said as she brought Paul inside.

Maddy looked up. Allie had been right about one thing— Paul was ridiculously handsome. He was tall, in his early thirties, but boyish, the sort of man who would probably always seem young. He had very short blond hair, his head was nearly shaved, and a sort of effortlessness about him that seemed both dangerous and charming. Paul came over, leaned down, and kissed Maddy on either cheek. She could tell he'd already had a drink. Strike one. She didn't trust people who drank alone, even though she often went to bars by herself after work, just to relax and calm down from her day.

"Welcome to the family," Paul said.

"Shouldn't I be saying that to you?" Maddy also didn't trust good-looking men. She'd been through quite a few of her own.

"Either way. We're family. Now that's a bad color for you," he said of her nail polish. "You look like an android. You're far too pretty for that."

"Don't listen to him," Allie said as she dragged Paul into the kitchen to taste the curry. It was shrimp with coconut milk. When they'd gone, Maddy looked down at her toes. Paul happened to be right. Anyone would think she was made of titanium or steel. They would guess she had no feelings at all.

Dinner was fine. The curry was excellent, not too spicy. Allie was flushed from the heat of the kitchen. Maddy was surprised to see her sister have several whisky and sodas. Allie wasn't much of a drinker and she certainly wasn't a cheerful drunk. With every whisky she grew more silent and moody.

Forget running off to Paris. Maddy wished she was back in her apartment in New York, eating a yogurt out of a container for her supper, joyfully and blessedly alone.

"So what do you do?" Paul asked.

"Not this again," Maddy said. "Is this all people talk about in this country?"

"I told you," Allie reminded Paul. "Maddy is an attorney, an important one. She works for an investment firm in Manhattan. She specializes in real estate."

"Right. You make money." Paul was actually sneering. He seemed angry, ready to argue about anything.

"Is that a crime?" Maddy felt her back go up. So she invested money for rich people; was she supposed to apologize for being good at what she did?

"Who am I to judge?" Paul said.

"Exactly." Maddy poured herself another glass of wine. She would need it. She saw now why Allie was drinking. This was a difficult man. "You're nobody."

Paul stared at her, taking her in, then he grinned. Maddy had the distinct impression that for some odd reason he thought he knew exactly who she was; that he might even know something she didn't.

"He's not exactly a nobody. He's a film editor," Allie said. "He's the one who told the film company about *The Heron's Wife*. I told you that, too, Maddy. You both don't listen. You have that in common."

Allie cleared the plates and refused any help. They could hear her washing up in the kitchen.

"She always does it all on her own, doesn't she?" Paul said. "Never needs the least bit of help."

"Of course. She has to control everything. No one else can do it as well as she does, can they?"

Paul finished his wine and poured them both some more. "I don't know why your sister is marrying me. I'm not sure what she's told you, but she's making a terrible mistake. Has she talked about me much?"

"I'm sure you'll make her delirious with joy. And you can relax. She doesn't talk about you at all, so you're safe from my prying." Maddy was dismissive. She'd known his type before, and was surprised that her sister, usually so practical and smart, had fallen for him. One of those too-handsome men who always thought he was the most important person in the room. Someone who had to be coddled, the center of attention; most likely he had very few friends.

"She hasn't told you anything?"

"Is there something to tell?"

"There's always something to tell, my girl. Everyone has a story."

Maddy looked him over more carefully. He wasn't quite what she expected. Once he dropped the arrogant attitude he was surprisingly nice.

"I'll probably ruin everything," he said humbly, which further surprised Maddy. "I haven't been very successful at this."

"I didn't know you'd been married before."

"Not marriage. Love. I was raised to be self-centered, not that I fault my mum. She's the best, really. I'm just a selfish bastard. It must be in my DNA. What's in yours other than beauty?"

Madeline felt something go through her. Just like that, sitting there at the table. Attraction was a very strange thing; it had a life of its own. Paul was looking at her very oddly, considering who they were and what was happening.

"I'm selfish, too. I'm the opposite of Allie." Maddy could feel herself flush. This wasn't supposed to be about her. "I'm sure you'll do just fine by my sister."

"Right," Paul said. "We'll live happily after ever. What are the odds of that?"

For some reason they both laughed. Maybe they could tell they had an equal disability in the love department, losers both. Maddy hadn't managed to keep a boyfriend for more than a year. She grew bored easily and she was demanding. She told people she'd been ruined by her placement in the family. She'd always been babied, always followed Allie's lead.

"I'm glad you're getting along," Allie said when she came in with dessert. There were berries and ice cream and a bowl of Cream Chantilly, along with a bottle of cherry brandy.

They could have answered in many different ways. Instead they looked at each other across the table. That was when Madeline knew there'd be trouble. The moment of doubt, the thud of the pulse, the quick image of the disaster to come. It was all right there, laid down like a road map across the tabletop. Spoon, fork, knife, heartbreak.

"Did you make this whipped cream yourself?" Maddy asked her sister. "It's delicious."

But she wasn't thinking any of that. She couldn't care less about the sundae. She didn't even like desserts anymore. She was thinking of a time when she was seven years old and was terrified of a storm; she'd run down to the cellar to hide. She remembered what it was like to hear the rest of her family looking for her, calling her name, frantic in their search, and how it felt not to answer. For once she had power over them. She who was no one, Miss Second-Best. She felt that way now. As though she was the only one in the room who truly knew what was going on. She looked at Paul again, just to make sure she wasn't imagining this. He was staring right at her.

She wasn't imagining anything.

That night Maddy brushed her teeth in her sister's small, cluttered bathroom. She wanted to go straight to bed and stop thinking. Her heart was pounding like mad. Too much wine. Too much caffeine. She was only in London for a few days and wouldn't be back until the wedding at the end of August, so how much damage could she actually do? It was just a game, nothing more. A little flirting behind Allie's back, minor misbehavior she equated with stealing the hair ribbons and trinkets that Allie had never even noticed were missing. Once, on impulse, Maddy had poured a glass of milk over Allie's bed. It was so mean she couldn't believe she'd actually done it. She never confessed. She acted surprised when the room started to smell.

Maddy didn't understand her own envy, it was so deep inside her. Their mother said it must have been mold that caused the odor; the house was damp, after all, surrounded by the saltwater marsh. Lucy spent an entire day washing their clothes, along with the sheets and blankets. She hung everything out on the line. Maddy saw her mother in the yard at the end of the day, sitting beneath the sycamore tree, exhausted from her work. There were still piles of more laundry to do, most of it clean. Maddy could have stepped in then; she could have said there'd been an accident and saved her mother all

that trouble. But she didn't. She stood by the reeds without saying a word.

MADDY WAS A fool for checking into the Lion Park at the
height of summer. The rooms were stifling, there was no room
service, and the plumbing was ancient. Her mother had had a
white ceramic ashtray decorated with a green lion from this
hotel that she kept on her night table for years. "It was once my
favorite place in the world," Lucy told the girls. "I was twelve
and I thought it was so elegant."

Maddy had always imagined a real live lion in a hotel room,
and maybe that was why she'd made the reservation. Her
mother had seemed so fond of the place. But the hotel was
second-rate. As for the lion, it was made of stone; it sat out in
the courtyard, covered with moss.

"Oh, that," the desk clerk said of the lion when Maddy had
checked in. "It was taken from a monastery in France and it's
been in the garden for several hundred years. It was there before
the hotel was built. There's a crack running down his back and
we don't know what we'll do if he ever splits apart. We'll have to
find a new name!"

There was only one person who knew Maddy had arrived
early, and she was actually counting the minutes until he
appeared. She'd sent him a registered letter and he'd signed
for it, so he clearly was well aware that she expected him to
show up. There were pigeons on the window ledge and Maddy
could hear the traffic from Brompton Road. The rest of the
family, Maddy and Allie's parents, Lucy and Bob, the aunts and
uncles and first cousins, along with several of Allie's friends

from the States, would all be staying a few blocks away at the Mandarin Oriental. Maddy had told her parents her firm had an arrangement with the smaller hotel around the corner; she would practically be staying for nothing. She said she was writing a brief for a client who might have to do jail time because of his potentially shady investments and she needed peace and quiet. Her hotel had no cable or movies to rent; it had no fancy spa, only a small lounge where guests could have dinner and drinks.

The Lion Park was seven floors tall, but squat; it took up most of a block. It was not the sort of place from which Maddy would have expected her mother to keep a memento. The hallways were long, with door after door painted blue, each with a room number embossed in gold and a fluted glass knob. Every floor looked the same; it was possible to get thoroughly lost because the hallways followed the angle of the street outside and bent back upon themselves. Very confusing for most guests.

The lift fit only four people and the staircase curved upward with smaller and smaller stairs, until at the very top one had to take baby steps or risk a fall. Maddy's room was at the far end of the hotel, on the street side. Inside there was a bed with a white bedspread, a dresser, a television that received four grainy channels, and an air conditioner on a stand, vented through the window via a plastic hose, a contraption that actually seemed to make the room hotter. All through the hotel the carpet was wool, a dark murky green. The bathroom was small, with a dreadful tub that only had a handheld showerhead; the sink was in the room itself. There was an overhead light and one lamp on an old-fashioned desk. Maddy didn't really mind; all she had cared about since her visit in the spring was coming back. She wished that her stay was for fifteen days, or thirty, or more. Ten thousand days would not be long enough. When he didn't arrive that afternoon, she called him and left a message on his answering machine.

You'd better show up. You owe me that at least. You owe me more, as a matter of fact.

That night, Maddy fell into a fitful sleep. She dreamed she was in the backyard in Connecticut. There was the sycamore tree with a thousand bones tied to its branches. Red flowers grew instead of leaves. Maddy went to pick a flower, but she sliced open her hand. The flowers were made of glass. She remembered what it felt like to cut herself. She remembered that she thought it was the only way to feel anything. Inside her dream Maddy heard a man shouting. She opened her eyes and he was still shouting. The clock on her bedside table read ten-thirty P.M. All of a sudden she was completely awake. She had never heard such impassioned shouting. An Englishman, and for an instant she thought Paul, but it wasn't Paul's voice. The ruckus was in the hall, in the doorway of the room directly across from hers: 707. Maddy got up and went to peek out, but there was no keyhole, no way of seeing what was happening outside. She thought for a moment of opening her door, but the unseen man was shouting so terribly that Maddy felt she might stumble into a confrontation that was none of her business. Instead, she put her ear against the door. She couldn't make out very much, only stray words. "Every time," she heard him say. "Unbelievable."

Maddy slipped back under the covers and put her hands over her ears. She stayed there, shivering, until she stopped thinking, until all she could remember was the sycamore tree.

She remembered sharing a bed with her sister and how afraid she'd been of the dark.

He had returned to the flat the morning following the curry dinner, after Allie had gone off to a meeting with the director of the film adaptation of *The Heron's Wife*. They were tweaking the final edits of the screenplay. Georgia was to be the set designer and she came by and picked up Allie. They'd be at it all day. Maddy was supposed to amuse herself, then join Allie at the dress shop. It was the final fitting for the wedding suit and the maid of honor's dress, which was being taken in at the waist. When tailored, it would fit Maddy perfectly. "You'll look like a flower," Allie had said. "An iris. Don't forget to meet me at five."

Allie left breakfast on the table, the way she had when they were girls. There were croissants and cereal and jam, but all Maddy wanted was black coffee. Instead of bothering with breakfast, she fixed herself some strong coffee and had a ciga-rette even though she knew Allie didn't like anyone to smoke in her flat. One more rule to be broken. She sat by the window and waved the plume of smoke out into the air. Allie would never know. She'd never been the suspicious type. Really, for someone so smart and so sure of herself, she'd always been quite easy to fool.

Allie had been at her meeting for nearly an hour when the buzzer sounded. Right away, Maddy had the strangest feeling that it was Paul. She had been thinking about him all night. She was despicable for being attracted to her sister's fiancé, but it was all in her mind, after all, and she wasn't responsible for what went on inside her head. It wasn't as though she planned to act on any of it. Yes, she had always stolen things from Allie, but a man wasn't a velvet skirt or a pair of boots. Even Maddy knew that. Love wasn't something you could borrow and then return.

Maddy went to the intercom. "Heller Residence." She was wearing a T-shirt and underpants and one of Allie's robes. Her hair smelled like smoke and she knew she'd have to shampoo it before she met up with Allie.

"I know where I am," Paul said through the intercom.

So that was it. The moment before the disaster. Maddy could push the button and let him up, or she could step away and go back to bed. She could pretend she hadn't heard him; perhaps a deliveryman had rung up and she'd decided to ignore his arrival.

"Why should I let you in?" was what she said. She thought she knew the answer, but she wasn't sure.

"Because you want to," Paul told her.

When Maddy pressed the buzzer to unlock the door to the downstairs vestibule, she could feel the vibration through the bones of her hand, up along her arm, into her shoulder. She had a breathless, giddy feeling, as though she were about to dive off the high board into a pool. She thought about the way he'd looked at her at the dinner table. Imagining him, she felt flushed again, overwhelmed with desire. She didn't think of herself as a liar or a cheat, but sometimes the truth was mutable, wasn't it?

Maddy could have changed her mind while Paul took the lift up, but she didn't. He knocked on the door and she told herself nothing bad was about to happen. He is coming for a scarf he forgot, or to leave a gift for Allie, or to grab a bottle of wine in the fridge. I am opening the door to him for that reason, because he needs something he accidentally left behind.

She was lying to herself. She was good at that. She hadn't bothered to tie the sash of her robe.

"So what's the decision? Are you letting me in?" Paul stood just outside the door. He was the sort of man who usually got his way. But now he seemed to hesitate.

"You sound like the big bad wolf," Maddy said.

"Oh, no," Paul said. "Slam the door in my face and I swear I won't howl. I'll slink away. You, my girl, will never have to see me again."

It was so easy. She opened the door for him and the rest was like disappearing into the dark night to a place where no one could find you. No footsteps, no fingerprints, no evidence of any kind.

SHE WAS TWENTY minutes late to the dress shop.

"I got so lost," Maddy said as she rushed into the fitting rooms where Allie was trying on her suit. "I thought I'd never find this place."

Allie laughed. "You look a mess."

Maddy's hair was pinned up and she hadn't bothered with any makeup. She was wearing jeans, a sweater, and boots. She still felt him all over her. She had showered but she felt rank, as though she'd just crawled up from the sewer. She couldn't believe what she had done. Such things weren't quite as real if you didn't think about them, and that was what Maddy planned to do.

She tore off her clothes and slipped on her maid of honor

dress. The tailor lowered his eyes. Maddy thought she might be giving off the odor of sour milk. She thought of the time she'd ruined her sister's bed. What on earth had made her do such a vile thing?

"You're supposed to go behind the curtain to undress!" Allie said. "You exhibitionist!"

"Oh, who cares!"

Maybe she deserved to be punished, set out on the street with no clothes for people to jeer at. When she let him into her sister's flat she hadn't been thinking. Maybe Paul hadn't either. He seemed angry afterward, even though he was the one to begin it. Fuck it all, he'd said. That's what my future's worth. Might as well live even if you ruin everything before you drop out of this world, right? Maddy had a fleeting thought: Maybe he hadn't so much been desperate for her; maybe he was simply desperate. The truth was, she didn't know him at all.

"It fits like a dream," Allie said of the blue dress.

"It does," Maddy agreed.

Allie turned to stare at herself in the mirror. She did not look pleased. She looked like a woman who wanted to run. "Am I doing the wrong thing?"

"Wearing a suit when you could have chosen a gorgeous gown?"

Maddy felt sick. She hadn't had breakfast or lunch. She hadn't had time. She was too busy ruining things, right there in her sister's flat. She made up the bed after he'd left. She couldn't help but think, He didn't even help me clean up. He'd been right about himself. He was selfish and thoughtless and yet she wanted to see him again. She liked the idea of leaving no evidence, of having a secret no one would ever guess. She wondered if she had a monster inside her, one that had outgrown its bounds.

"You know what I mean, Maddy. Should I call off the wedding?"

Maddy stared at her sister, stunned. Allie stared back at her in the mirror. Was it possible her sister knew she had been betrayed by the look on her face? Could she pick up the scent of duplicity? Maddy wished they could both walk through the mirror to the other side, to the day before this one, when there was so much less to hide. But she had to have what she wanted, didn't she?

"Are you serious?" Hopefully her voice gave nothing away. "Are you considering calling it off?"

"I'm the one who's always expected to keep my promises." Allie took off her suit jacket; all she wore underneath was a white slip. It was prettier than her wedding outfit. "Isn't that right? Isn't that what you all want from me?"

MADDY CALLED PAUL the next day, but his mobile had been turned off and no one answered his home phone. While Allie went out to run errands, Maddy snooped around on the Internet. She found that Paul had been the film editor on several TV programs for the BBC. Although he hadn't seemed to have worked very much in the past year, Maddy did manage to find out a huge amount of information—his school records, sports record, facts about his parents who lived near Reading where his father was a professor of chemistry and his mother, who'd been a nurse, was chairwoman of the local horticultural society. She quickly became an expert on the details of Paul's life. He came over that night for a drink, and while Allie was getting the ice he said to Maddy, "Let's forget it ever happened." As if she had been the one who had come after him. He was standing very close and he'd taken her arm. She thought he was even more of a liar than she could have first guessed. She wanted to get him back some way. She had the nerve to kiss him then, right in her sister's living room. He backed away and said, "Good-bye, little sister," as though it was over between them.

She didn't have much time. She'd be in New York in a matter of hours. Allie was working the next day, and Maddy assured her she'd manage to entertain herself. She'd go see Buckingham Palace. She insisted that she'd be perfectly happy to wander around like a tourist. Instead, she looked up Paul's address and went out to hail a taxi. When she pulled up in front of his flat, she didn't know what to do next. Most likely he wouldn't answer the door if he realized it was Maddy.

"Did you want to get out?" the driver asked.

"If I did I would. I'm waiting for someone."

They sat in the parked cab without speaking. At noon, Paul came out and signaled for a taxi of his own.

"Follow him and don't let yourself be seen," Maddy told her driver.

Paul's taxi deposited him outside one of the old grand houses in Kensington. It reminded Maddy of a wedding cake. There was a little park across from it where children were playing under the trees. Maddy should have guessed she wasn't the only one Paul was cheating with. She sank back into the cab. Cheaters cheat and liars lie. That was what was in their DNA.

"Are you getting out now, miss?" the driver said.

She watched Paul go up the steps and ring the bell. The door opened and he went inside. Maddy paid the driver and got out; her face was hot and flushed. Paul was surely betraying Allie, yet Maddy was the one who felt violated. She waited a while, then went up to the town house. A maid came to answer the bell.

"I'm expected," Maddy announced.

"They're having lunch outside," the maid replied. "I wasn't told there was a third."

"Well, there is," Maddy said.

She sounded sure of herself, so the maid let her in. The house was enormous and cool and elegant. After the sunlight it was somewhat difficult for Maddy to focus in the shadowed interior. There was a great deal of woodwork and a huge stair-case. The entryway floor was patterned in black-and-white marble.

"I'll find my way," Maddy assured the maid. "I'm fine on my own."

"If you say so."

Maddy could hear voices, and all she needed was to follow the sound. She went through the front hall, into the parlor. The walls were painted red and gold and the floor was ebony. Maddy continued on through a French door that led to a con-servatory. Beyond that was the garden. Paul wore linen slacks and a pale blue shirt. A tree was in bloom and there were dozens of rosebushes along a high stone wall. The garden was deep, dark green, almost black in the shadows. The paths were made of slate and brick and stone. There were birds in the trees. Paul had taken his jacket off. He'd been pruning the roses, but now he came to sit at the table, across from his lunch partner, a woman Maddy could only see from the back, and who wore a large straw summer hat. Paul was laughing at something his companion was saying. "If you want to hire me to be your gardener, I'll take the job in a minute," he said happily. "Of course you can't pay me a cent. And with my handiwork, I'll probably kill everything."

Maddy moved closer; the tall hedge beside the path trembled as the birds in it took flight. Paul looked up. When he saw Maddy he froze.

"Are you all right, Paul?" his companion asked.

"Probably not," he answered.

"You have got to be kidding me," Maddy called from the stone path. "This is why you couldn't take my phone calls?"

Paul excused himself from the table. "I'll be right back," he said to his lunch date. He walked toward Maddy, furious. "Are you insane? Did you follow me?"

"Does she pay you for services other than gardening?"

"Mrs. Ridge is a family friend. She's been like a grandmother to me. So keep your voice down."

The woman had turned to look and Maddy saw that she was an elderly woman, a very beautiful English lady, hardly a rival.

Mrs. Ridge began to rise from her chair, concerned. Paul grinned and waved. "This will just take a minute," he assured her.

He took Maddy's arm and led her back through the conservatory. There were yellow and brown orchids in a row and majolica pots filled with ferns.

"Mrs. Ridge has been responsible for a great deal in my life, including my education. She's part of our family. She has no children of her own and she dotes on me. I'm crazy about her as well. I don't expect to be followed to my visit with her."

"I didn't know," Maddy said.

"You know very little," Paul said dismissively.

Maddy turned and ran. What had she done? He wasn't even worth caring about. He was selfish and horrid, just as he'd warned. She ran out of the house, twisting her ankle on her way down the steps. She walked all the way to the park, limping, and paused by the side of the road. When Paul came by in a taxi she was in tears.

"Get in," he called through the window. They stared at each other. "Get in and don't make a fucking scene."

Maddy climbed into the taxi and closed the door.

"I told Mrs. Ridge you were a lunatic business associate," Paul said. "She suggested I fire you."

"Great. Lovely."

"We did something desperate, my girl. Agreed?"

Paul seemed exhausted. Maddy noticed he had a terrible cough; he'd probably been sick when they were together. She would surely come down with whatever he had. She deserved it.

Paul leaned in close. He smelled like soap. "We made a stupid mistake. I know why I came over that morning, but I never thought you'd open the door for me. I was a little surprised how ready you were to betray her."

"To hell with you. You were a party to it."

"I felt sure you'd turn me down and then go running to Allie and tell her I'd propositioned you."

"You wanted me to say no?" Maddy was mortified. She didn't understand.

Paul's shirt was wrinkled now; the fabric was linen, the color of the sky, pale and fresh and new. He'd left his suit jacket behind. "Look, I'm sorry. I shouldn't have involved you. I truly apologize."

They'd reached their destination and had pulled over to the curb. Maddy didn't notice they had arrived until there was a tap on the taxi window. She nearly jumped out of her skin. Paul rolled down the window. It was Georgia, just leaving after dropping Allie at her flat.

"What do you know," Georgia said thoughtfully.

"I saw her on the street and thought I'd give the poor girl a ride." Paul opened the door. "Go on," he said to Maddy. "Your chariot has brought you back. Good to see you, Georgia." He shut the door and the taxi pulled away and that was it. He was finished with her. She had served her purpose, whatever it was.

"I detest him," Georgia said.

"Really?" Maddy turned to go inside. For once they agreed. "So do I."

AFTER SHE GOT back to New York she said nothing about what had happened. When she spoke to Allie on the phone, she questioned her about Paul. She hated him in some strange, greedy way. She couldn't stop thinking about their single encounter. Maybe she would stand up at the wedding and announce what had happened. Why shouldn't she? She'd be doing both Allie and herself a favor. It would be best to reveal him to one and all, even if that meant she'd have to reveal herself as well.

Maddy grew depressed. Her work suffered and one of the partners asked if she'd had a death in the family. Usually she was busy all weekend; now she slept till noon and avoided going out. When her parents came into the city and stopped at her apartment one Sunday, their knock at her door woke her even though it was two in the afternoon.

Lucy pulled her aside. "What's wrong?"

"There's nothing wrong! Why do you always think the worst of me?"

"I know when something's wrong," Lucy Heller told her daughter.

"Really? Then you should have known it throughout my childhood. You didn't seem to care back then. You didn't seem to even notice me."

Her mother was taken aback.

"How can you say that? Of course I noticed you," Lucy said. "I noticed how much alike we were. Haven't you?"

Maddy thought about the time she had run away from home after her parents split up. She'd worn a raincoat and her winter boots; it was spring and everything was damp. It was so easy to run away. She opened the door and walked into the dark. She knew exactly where she was going. She went through the yard, past the sycamore tree. Allie had told her that the blue heron would come for the one he truly loved. The grass was wet and spongy and Maddy sank into it. The mud covered her boots. There were no stars and the moon sat behind the clouds, but it was enough to light her way.

It didn't take very long to get down to the marshes. Once she was there she slipped between the reeds. They were tall and feathery, silver gray. Everything smelled foul. Maddy's boots made a sloshing sound as she walked along the shore. She could hear things that were alive: snails, nesting birds, the rising wind. There were probably spiders and leeches as well; there were most likely bats in the trees. Maddy was the sister who was always afraid, who cried when she was left alone, who pouted, who didn't know how to cook or clean or even button her heavy winter coat. She was nervous about the thornbushes in the marsh and the crabs that might bite your toes, but for once she didn't think about these things. It took a while, but at last she found it, the place where her mother said the blue heron lived. She made her way through the brambles and there was the nest, up in a willow tree.

Maddy wore a blue nightgown under her coat. She slipped off her rain boots. She was good at climbing trees; she was light and much stronger than she looked. She was breathing hard when she got up to the nest. She thought it would be made of long grass and moss, but it was made of sticks. Some were silver and some were black. The heron wasn't there, so Maddy crept into the nest. It could have crashed and then she would have fallen to the ground and broken every bone. But the sticks held her weight. Maddy wanted to see if what her mother said was true, if the heron would watch over her. Herons had no choice but to be loyal, her mother had said, it was in their nature.

When Maddy woke up, her legs were cramping from sleeping in the tree. There were red bug bites on her elbows and knees. The sky was breaking with the first streaks of light. She heard water and what sounded like her sister's voice. Maddy looked down at the marsh and there was Allie, standing in the shallow water with the blue heron. Anyone would guess that a heron would be afraid of a girl and that a girl would be afraid as well, but that didn't seem to be the case. Allie got so close she was almost touching him before he flew away. She turned to wave at the sky and when she did she saw Maddy, up in the tree. Allie's pale hair was the color of the reeds. Of course he had chosen her.

PAUL DIDN'T COME to the Lion Park the next day, even though she had left a message on his answering machine making it clear she would consider phoning Allie to tell her everything. She had resorted to threats. She didn't care how low she'd sunk. Maddy had left word at the desk that she was expecting a visitor; they could ring her room when he arrived. She had the impulse to say it was her husband she was waiting for, but even she couldn't tell a lie that big.

She sat in the hot room until she felt dizzy, then she went out and walked around London. When she returned, she ate her dinner in her room, still waiting, at least for a phone call. She drank a bottle of wine and fell asleep while it was still light. She didn't wake until she heard something out in the hall. Another argument; a man's raised voice. When the shouting stopped, she took a shower and found there was only cold water, with intermittent bursts of warmth. The soap was grainy and smelled like Lysol. Maddy got out and wrapped a towel around herself, then flopped onto the bed. It was nearly eleven when he finally arrived. The front desk hadn't bothered to call Maddy to let her know she had a guest; they just let him up. He could have been anyone, a madman out for revenge, a serial killer. Paul knocked on the door and called out her name. For a moment Maddy forced herself to remain still. She didn't want to reveal herself as desperate, not even to herself. Let him suffer. Let him wait.

He knocked again. Maddy went to open the door. She had only the towel wrapped around her.

"Jesus," Paul said, "who were you expecting?" He laughed. "Hello, little sister."

He had shaven his head and had lost weight. He looked all skin and bones. Good, Maddy thought. She hoped he was miserable, just as she was. She hoped he was regretting this marriage he'd committed himself to.

"You didn't write, you didn't call," Maddy said, trying to be lighthearted. It didn't come out that way. It sounded pathetic. Just what she didn't want. But he didn't seem to notice; he was blank and distracted. His eyes looked filmy, as though he had conjunctivitis.

"We were never anything to each other, Maddy. You knew that. Let's leave it at that. If you call me again, I won't call you back."

Maddy had hung up her silk dress over the window and a weird azure light came into the room.

"I feel sorry for Allie," she said. "I really do."

"So do I," Paul agreed.

"Are you always such a selfish egomaniac?"

"Are you?"

"If I tell her, she won't understand. She won't forgive you."

"She shouldn't," Paul said. "Neither should you."

"Maybe I won't," Maddy said.

He left without saying anything more. She wasn't even worth that much to him. Maddy got dressed. She felt used and bitter. She went down to the hotel restaurant and sat in a booth in the bar. There was an elderly gentleman having a drink and a couple laughing and sharing dessert. The waitress came over. It was closing time, but Maddy explained that she had recently arrived from the States and her schedule was off. The waitress brought her a salad and a piece of quiche along with a glass of Pinot Grigio. It was a little cooler in the restaurant, but she was still burning.

"Quiche all right?" the waitress asked.

It happened to have no taste whatsoever, but the salad was fine, and the wine even better.

"Not bad," Maddy said.

She sat there for nearly an hour drinking wine. When she finally got up to go, only the old man and the bartender were left. The couple and even the waitress had gone. Maddy took the lift to the seventh floor and promptly got lost in the hall. At last she found her way to 708. She unlocked her door and wondered if anyone else was staying on her floor. She hadn't seen another person since leaving the bar. She turned off the malfunctioning air conditioner and opened her window, even though soot and the sound of traffic came into the room. Then she curled up on the bed in her clothes.

THEIR FATHER LEFT when Maddy and Allie were eleven and twelve, while their mother was still in treatment. He moved into a house in town, about three miles inland. Their mother said not to blame him. She told them some people couldn't deal with illness; the very thought of a hospital made them dizzy with fear and grief. Allie and Maddy didn't believe her. If their father was dizzy with anything, it was with his own selfish desires. The girls rode their bikes past the house he'd moved into, but no one ever seemed to be home. When they telephoned, a woman answered. Allie said it was probably a friend or a housekeeper. Maddy may have been younger, but she knew better. Secretly, she had begun to make little cuts on her arms and legs. She didn't know if she wanted to hurt herself or somebody else. She began calling the woman their father was living with every night. Revenge was an acquired taste, but it was addictive if you didn't watch out. Maddy was the mystery avenger. She didn't even tell her sister. Even at that age she knew that revenge was a private act.

Then one day the girls' father reappeared. He parked in the driveway and called Maddy and Allie out to the lawn. He was angry, as if he were the wronged party.

"You are terrorizing an innocent woman. You are never to call her again," he told them. "If you do I'll have my number changed. She's just my landlady, you know. She's nothing more than that."

Allie knew nothing about the phone calls. But she didn't blame Maddy. She stood up to her father.

"Instead of changing your number, you should come back. We need you here."

"Did your mother put you up to this?" he wanted to know.

"Our mother wouldn't stoop to that," Allie said.

Maddy hung her head. She didn't say a word.

Their father got back into the car. Allie went after him. He was crying and he wouldn't roll down his window. He drove away. He went through a stop sign and didn't look back.

Later, up in their room, the sisters lay in one bed, their heads on the same pillow, holding hands.

"I feel bad for him," Allie said.

"Don't," Maddy told her. "He doesn't deserve it. He left us with a sick woman."

"He was crying."

"Crocodile tears. Crocodile father."

"Do you really call every day?" Allie wanted to know.

"At least twice."

"Do you think she's really his landlady?"

"Do you think he's really a crocodile?"

They both laughed. Allie was surprised that Maddy could keep a secret so well.

"There's a lot about me you don't know," Maddy said. "You should hear what I say to her."

Allie had become the one who went to all the doctor's appointments with their mother. She could be relied on to sit in the chemo room for hours, pouring glasses of ginger ale, looking for saltines at the nurses' station, reading aloud from magazines. Back then, there was some talk that Allie would be a doctor. As for Maddy, she already knew what she would be best at: betrayal and revenge.

"I say I'm going to kill her and hang her bones out to dry in our backyard," Maddy told her sister. Their knees were touching. "I'm going to make soup out of them."

Allie was shocked. "Maddy!"

"I tell her I'm going to drink her blood and put a hundred

needles in her eyes. If she really is just his landlady, she'll kick him out." The woman on the phone hadn't sounded like a landlady. She sounded like somebody's flustered girlfriend.

"You probably shouldn't do it anymore," Allie told her. "You'll get us both in trouble and Mom and Dad will be mad."

"Who cares? I hate them both." Their mother didn't seem to notice anything—the razor cuts on Maddy's arms and legs, the phone calls she made in the middle of the night. "Maybe they'll disappear and we can live alone in this house," Maddy said. "Maybe the blue heron will come and we can go and live with him."

"We can't," Allie said. "The police would come for us and there'd be a social worker who would put us in foster homes. And anyway, who would take care of Mom?"

"Somebody else," Maddy had said stubbornly. "Not me."

THE GROOM'S DINNER was crowded. It was held at a French restaurant where they were seated at an enormously long table so it was nearly impossible to talk to anyone. So much the better. When the bride- and the groom-to-be arrived, quite late, actually, which was not Allie's style, everyone stood and applauded. The first course had already been served, a cold pâté with garlic toast. Paul's parents, Frieda and Bill, seemed nice enough, and there were several other relations and friends from Reading. Maddy recognized Mrs. Ridge, the older woman who lived in Kensington. She wore a black Chanel suit, and again, a hat; from certain angles she appeared ageless. Thankfully, she hadn't seen Maddy close up on that unfortunate day in April.

"Hey," Allie said when she found her sister in the crowd.

"Hey, yourself."

"You're not staying at the Mandarin?"

"I'm just around the corner. At that place Mom used to talk about."

"Well, I'm glad you're here." Allie looked exhausted. She'd lost weight. Maddy wondered if her wedding suit would still fit. "Paul hates this kind of thing. I think he's made his escape." She nodded toward the bar. "God, maybe I should take off as well. Permanently."

"What's that supposed to mean?" Maddy asked. When Allie didn't answer, she pressed on. "You're not happy?"

Allie wasn't wearing any makeup. She looked especially pale, run-down. "Do I seem happy?"

Allie was scooped up by her friends, who wanted to know all about the celebrations to come, so she waved and went off with them. There was only one way to get through this event; Maddy drank too much. Enough so that her father noticed.

"What's wrong with you?" Bob Heller asked.

"Why does everyone always assume there's something wrong with me? I'm fine," Maddy told him.

As soon as she could, she sneaked into the bar. Paul was there, drinking a scotch. The lamplight was yellow and fell in little moon-shaped pools. His eyes seemed weirdly large.

"She knows about us," Maddy said. "She said she's not happy."

Paul looked at her blankly, almost as though he didn't recognize her.

"I'm serious." Maddy began to realize just how drunk

she was. "She knows, doesn't she? Are you glad that you've hurt her?"

"I did everything in my power to get her to leave me. Only she wouldn't. She's not disloyal. I don't think she'd know how to be." Paul looked drained. "So we're getting married. You really should congratulate me."

"Just tell me. Why me? Why couldn't you have cheated with someone else?"

"You were there. You were willing. You would have hurt her the most."

"You really are a sick bastard."

"I am. Precisely. I thought you knew."

Maddy stood and left the bar. She thought he would try to stop her, but he didn't. She made her way downstairs to the exit. If she fell and broke her neck no one would care. The younger sister who has nothing. Compare and contrast: the dark and the light, the full and the empty, the lost and the found.

She took a taxi back to her hotel. Before going up to her room, she stopped by the bar. There were a few more people than usual, some businessmen, the same young couple as the night before and the older man at the end of the bar with both a whisky and a coffee in front of him.

"I'll have what he's having," Maddy said.

"Teddy Healy?" the bartender said. "He's here every night, you know. He's cut back on his drinking. One coffee for every two whiskies."

Maddy raised her glass, then drained her whisky. She took the lift up and made her way to her room. Later, she didn't remember how she'd gotten there. She had never drunk as much as she had in London. Betrayals bred betrayals. She hadn't meant to hurt anyone, and she'd wound up hurting everyone, including herself. She got up and went to the window. From this vantage point all she could see were the angles of brick buildings and a series of rooftops and chimneys. She could barely see the sky. She leaned her head out. The air was sultry. She could spy the main road now and the traffic roaring by, streaks of white and red.

Maddy thought about the sycamore tree in their backyard. She and Allie would stay there for hours, hidden in the branches. Once their mother came out to the lawn and sank down to the grass, where she began to cry. They knew she was waiting for the heron; Allie watched the sky, but Maddy was certain he'd never come back. She was afraid of heights and of the taste of her own disappointment. Her fear must have shown through her skin.

You don't have to look, Allie had whispered. Just keep your eyes closed. I'll let you know when he's here.

MADDY WAS ASLEEP when she heard the man across the hall, shouting. She looked at the clock: ten-thirty again. She went to the door. It sounded like the same fight every night. Maybe all lovers' quarrels were the same hurts repeated over and over again. Maddy put her hand on the doorknob. She could hear her own raspy breathing as she listened to the couple's dispute. It sounded as if it was the end of something.

She sat down cross-legged on the floor, her ear against the door.

"How could you do this?" the man said.

Maddy started to cry even though the quarrel had nothing

to do with her. She should have opened her eyes when she was up in that sycamore tree. Maybe then she would have loved her mother. Maybe her mother would have loved her back.

She fell asleep on the carpet, curled up by the door. In the morning, her bones ached. On her way to breakfast she stopped at the desk to complain about her noisy neighbors to a young woman named Kara Atkins who seemed to be in charge of guest services, however limited such services were at the Lion Park.

"The people across from me are making a huge racket. They're ridiculous, the way they go at it. I can't sleep."

"I'm so sorry. Let me check." Miss Atkins went to the registry and looked up Maddy's room. "Oh, you're on the seventh floor, 708."

"They're at it every night. It's endless fighting. I know it's none of my business, but it's very disturbing."

The hotel management would be happy to move Maddy to another floor, Miss Atkins said, but Maddy told her not to bother. Paul might come looking for her; she didn't want to chance not being there.

When she went in to have her breakfast there was Teddy Healy, asleep in one of the booths. He was curled up like a mouse, snoring lightly. He'd been there all night. The hotel management treated him kindly; he was their oldest customer and they seemed to take care of him. Seeing him like that, Maddy decided to pull herself together. Then and there. She did not want to end up drunk in some hotel bar. She was not going to waste away like the heron's wife.

She had coffee and toast and jam and went back upstairs to

collect her dress. It was time for the bridesmaids' prewedding fitting. On her way back to her room, she noticed that the door of 707 was open. She peeked in. Hopefully the fighting couple was at last checking out.

The room was empty. Not only were there no guests, there was no furniture. No dresser. No bed. Several mattresses were stored up against the wall. It was freezing. When Maddy exhaled, her breath turned to smoky air. Maddy remembered that her mother's bedroom was always cold. She never wanted to go in there; she was afraid. Maybe she was like her father, ready to run at the first hint of a crisis. Allie had to take her by the hand and pull her past the door. It's just Mom, you silly, she would say. She won't bite.

Maddy went downstairs to the front desk.

"It turns out I don't have neighbors," Maddy told Miss Atkins. "There's no one in that room where all the fighting's been going on. There's not even a bed in there."

"Well, they say it's Michael Macklin," Kara Atkins explained sheepishly.

"Is he famous or something? Am I supposed to know who he is?"

"He's a ghost," Miss Atkins explained. "Or at least that's what people say. You understand, I don't believe in such things."

"That's great," Maddy replied. "I'm glad he's moved."

"Oh, he didn't move. There hasn't been furniture in there for over twenty years and that hasn't stopped him. Ghosts go wherever they like. They don't need a bureau or a desk."

"I thought you didn't believe in such things?"

"I don't," Kara said. "But I've actually heard this one."

"You're not serious."

Maddy saw the expression in Kara's eyes.

"Good lord, you are," she said.

"The incident took place in 1952, which is fairly modern in terms of a haunting, if there is a haunting."

"Not that you believe," Maddy said.

"Exactly. One of the participants in the actual event comes to the bar every night. Probably reliving what happened. But he won't discuss it."

"Teddy Healy? The older gentleman?"

"That's him."

"Are you telling me that's what I'm hearing at ten-thirty every night?"

"I'm just telling you a story," Kara said. "You can decide the rest."

MADDY HAD BEEN planning to take a cab to her sister's, but now she thought she might walk. She didn't like talk of ghosts and of love gone wrong. It was a good thing she'd decided to stop drinking. She was going to get on with her life. She carried the maid of honor dress over her shoulder. In the sunlight it looked even more brilliant as it floated behind her. When she turned into the park everything was dreamy and green. Today, she didn't hate London, even though the weather was still hot. There was the scent of something that reminded her of the marsh at home. It had a spicy, fragrant odor. The Serpentine was ahead. There were model boats in the water. The leaves on the trees were green, but the edges were yellow. She entered a garden where huge white roses grew—white saucers that seemed carved out of ice, except that they moved with the breeze.

Maddy was going to be late, but she didn't care. She had done everything wrong so she might as well be the last to arrive at her sister's. She stopped at a kiosk for a fizzy lemonade. She could see why somebody might want to haunt this park, walk down this path again and again, smell the same roses forever after. That would be a nice loop to be doomed to repeat if you had to be a ghost, if you believed in such things. Ghosts didn't need furniture, so maybe they didn't need love either. Maybe they slept in nests in the trees, looking down at the stupid things human beings did.

Maddy made her way to Bayswater. When she entered Allie's flat, the other bridesmaids were already there in their creamy suits. They stood around in silence; it seemed more like a wake than a fitting for a joyous event.

"Couldn't you be on time this once?" Georgia said.

"Not that it's any of your business," Maddy said, "but I got lost." It was almost true, after all. "Where's my sister?"

"Why don't you find her yourself?"

Allie was in the kitchen, crying.

"Look, I'm sorry," Maddy said. She tossed her dress over a kitchen chair and went to put her arms around her sister. "I'm an idiot and I'm late. There are no excuses for the stupid things I do. Your friend Georgia has already informed me of that, and I can't argue with her. I am so sorry, Allie. I think you should disown me."

Allie leaned in close. "He's ill, Maddy. He has been all year. I didn't want to burden you, and Paul didn't want anyone to know. He's been so angry. Now he's taken a turn for the worse."

Maddy could hear how noisy the fridge was in this apartment. She hadn't noticed it before. She hadn't noticed, either, that her sister looked so drained. She had never seemed excited about her wedding, only dutiful.

"He was diagnosed with non-Hodgkin's lymphoma last year, stage four when we found it. I found it. He'd been sweating at night and he'd lost his appetite. We were in the shower together when I felt it. A lump under his arm. We thought it was nothing, a bug bite that had become infected, something like that, but that wasn't it. It turned out to be cancer. It was everywhere. He didn't want me to talk about it. The thing is— I was going to break up with him before he became ill."

Maddy went to the sink for some glasses of water. That way Allie couldn't see her face.

"He was a lousy boyfriend. I don't know if I ever really was in love with him or if it was just time to settle down when he proposed. We were both wrong for each other, but there we were. I had to see him through treatment, didn't I? I'm not the sort of person who leaves, but it was horrible. Much worse than Mom. He was so sick from the chemo, they didn't know if he'd survive it. He lost thirty pounds, he lost his hair. I had to stay."

Maddy brought the water to the table. "Of course you did."

"He was enraged. Why him? Why us? Why anything. Well, I wasn't going to do what Dad did, was I? I wasn't going to leave in the midst of a crisis. Then he went into remission in the winter. He didn't need a bone marrow transplant. He was getting stronger. In March, I told him that it was over and he got so mad again. God, he was furious. We had pretty much broken up right before you came to visit in April. I was just going through the motions; you must have guessed at that cake tasting. I was going to cancel. And then it came back and everything changed."

Neither sister could drink her water.

"It was too late for the transplant," Allie said.

"He'll get better."

"You're not listening to me, Maddy. There is no better. There's probably not even a tomorrow. He was admitted back into the hospital after the dinner. It's happening so fast. He's lost his vision. He can't move his legs. It's up and down his spine."

Maddy needed to sit down. "I didn't think this could happen so fast."

"I'm sorry to tell you like this. I told the others when they arrived today. Georgia and Hannah knew, but no one else. Oh, and Mom. She's always known."

"Mom?" Maddy could barely swallow. "You told her and you didn't tell me?"

"I wanted to protect you."

"Of course. I'm so weak. I couldn't be any help to anyone!"

Allie looked wounded. "I didn't mean that at all."

"Why can't you ever treat me like I'm an equal?" Maddy took out her pack of cigarettes and lit one. Allie didn't even tell her to put it out. Here was Maddy, once again thinking of her own hurt first. She took one drag, then stubbed the cigarette out in a plate. "I'm an idiot," Maddy said. "I'm sorry."

"We'll have the wedding in the hospital. I wish we could have it under the sycamore tree. We could tie bells and bows to all the branches." That was what the heron wife had done to call her husband home when he strayed in Allie's book. "We'll have to pay off the Orangery—the caterers and the flowers and everything—we always knew that was a possibility. That's why I wouldn't let Mom and Dad pay for anything."

"Dad knows? God, Allie, the whole world knew and I didn't?"

"Paul didn't want you to know."

"Did he single me out? Did he say, Don't tell Maddy?"

"No, of course not. He's just so headstrong. He's the kind of person who will refuse to see our closest friends, then take some lonely old lady out to the theater or to dinner. He didn't want to ruin my life with his illness. He did everything he could to make me dump him. I thought it was just because he was so angry at me. Now I understand he wanted to set me free."

"Are you telling me that he's dying?" Maddy didn't quite sound like herself.

Allie was wearing her wedding suit. She'd lost so much weight she was down two sizes. "He is," she said.

Georgia peeked around the doorway, then came into the kitchen. "Everything all right?" Georgia linked her arm through Allie's and gazed over at Maddy. "You told her?" Allie nodded. "We don't have to go on with the fitting," Georgia suggested. "We can send the tailor home."

"Hell, no," Allie said. "I'm going to make sure everything's moving right along."

When Allie went into the parlor to see about her brides-maids, Maddy turned to Georgia. "What hospital is he in?"

"Bart's," Georgia said. "St. Bartholomew's Hospital. That's where he was in the autumn. Hannah and I took turns staying with Allie back then."

"I had no idea," Maddy said.

"Did you ever ask?"

"Don't make this my fault. Allie can never accept any help."

"Well, your mum has been back and forth all spring and summer. She's been helping out all the while."

Maddy felt stricken.

"I'm surprised he didn't tell you himself," Georgia said. Here it was; the reason for her dislike. "Did you think I didn't know when I saw you together in the taxi? You both looked so guilty. Let's just hope Allie never finds out."

Maddy escaped into the parlor and slipped on the blue silk dress. None of the bridesmaids was speaking. Only the tailor and his helper were chattering away. Maddy's dress didn't need to be taken in at all. "Perfect," the tailor said.

"You look gorgeous," Allie agreed. "The dresses have already been paid for, so they may as well fit correctly. You can all wear them for some other occasion."

The tailor and his helper began to pack up their packets of needles and pins.

"Do you want me to stay?" Maddy asked her sister. She knew what the answer would be.

"I'll call you if I need you," Allie vowed, even though they both knew she never would.

Maddy took a taxi back to her hotel, left the dress at the front desk, then returned to the waiting taxi and continued on to the hospital. There was a great deal of traffic and it was nearly dinnertime when she got there. The hospital was like a labyrinth, crowded and confusing. She hated hospitals. No one seemed to have any information, but at last Maddy found Paul's room. A nurse stopped her and insisted she put on a blue mask.

Maddy went in, eyes averted so she wouldn't be imposing on the first occupant in the room, who was in bed and breathing with great difficultly. Already she felt like crying. Paul was in the second bed, ashen, half-asleep, hooked up to an IV. Paul strained to see.

"Allie?" he said.

His optic nerves had been affected and all he could see were shadows. Maddy should have realized that at the groom's dinner. She'd been too busy hating him to really notice what was going on. He was desperately ill.

"No. It's me," Maddy said.

"The little sister." Paul grinned. He looked his age. Not so boyish now. "You're supposed to bring flowers and grapes on hospital visits."

"I can't believe you're such a good liar." Maddy sat on a hard-backed chair beside his bed. She took his hand. It was limp, cold. "You should have told me."

"Told you what? That I must have fucked up in the eyes of God or the angels? That my life was ruined and that I was ruining Allie's life? I was so damn angry at her."

His dinner was on a tray, uneaten. Soup, some flat soda, toast with a pale coating of butter. Paul's lips looked dry and sore.

"She didn't love me," Paul said.

"Would you like a drink?" Maddy asked.

"Scotch and soda. A double."

Maddy held the paper cup up and Paul sipped from the straw. Ginger ale.

"We had the dress fitting today," Maddy said. "She looked pretty."

"Maybe you should get her a vat and some black dye. She deserved better."

Maddy tried to get him to drink some more, but he waved her away.

"Do you know why I'm really mad? Because I knew this would happen and it has. I can't move my legs, little sister. I can't see you."

Maddy put the drink down, and took up the watery soup. "You should eat."

"That's enough," Paul said after three spoonfuls. "I'm throwing up blood."

Maddy put the tray away and came to sit beside him on the bed; she leaned her head against his chest. There was his heart, still beating.

"Poor Allie," Paul told Maddy. "Her childhood repeated all over again. A life spent in someone's sickroom. I wound up doing exactly what I vowed I'd never do to her. She's fucking terrified."

"Allie was never terrified of anything," Maddy said.

Paul laughed and then began to cough. "You don't know her as well as you think you do. She's terrified all right."

"Stop talking. You need to rest up."

"I don't have to rest up to die. And don't tell me I'll be well again." Paul closed his eyes. "Let me have one person who's honest with me."

"The way you were honest with me?"

"I never lied. You lied to yourself. If you're going to be here in my last hours, the least you can do is entertain me."

Why did she not hate him anymore? If anything she hated herself for being stupid, for being duped, for betraying Allie.

There was a blue vein across Paul's skull that Maddy had never even noticed. "Here's a true story," she began. "There's a ghost in my hotel."

Paul laughed again, then turned his head toward her, interested. His eyes were leaking fluid.

"Seriously," Maddy went on. "He's haunting a fellow who spends all his time in the bar."

"Dear Maddy. You are so innocent. You believe anything anyone tells you. Next thing you'll tell me the devil is beside me."

The man in the first bed had started to moan.

"Close the fucking curtain," Paul told her. "People are so damned noisy when they're dying. You'd think they'd give the rest of us some peace."

Maddy went and drew the curtain more tightly; in the process she glimpsed an old man doubled up in pain. A shiver went through her. She turned back to Paul. On the other side of his bed there was a curtain as well. She couldn't see the patient behind the curtain, just a stream of light filtering through the fabric. Paul was curled knees to chest. It was almost as though she could see through him. It wasn't until that moment that she realized Paul truly was dying. He was half there and half not.

She'd never been good at dealing with illness. She'd always wanted to run away when it got anywhere near this point. Maddy thought of the horrible things she'd said to her mother when she was younger—if it wasn't cancer, it wasn't considered a problem. It was nothing. She had never hated herself as much as she did at this moment. Paul didn't look like the same person as the man she'd slept with in the spring. She didn't even know him. She would have liked to have gone out into the hall. She could have kept on going, out the door, continuing on until she reached the white rose garden in the park. Instead, she forced herself to pull a chair close to the bed. She was afraid she might hurt him or spill something.

"I think after what happened between us, I should be the one to take care of you," she said.

Paul laughed, a short dry laugh that quickly faded. "Are you mad? I'm a desperate fucking narcissist in the jaws of death. You don't want me."

He had to stop talking; he began to struggle for air. He turned his head from Maddy; his body was limp, as though his muscles were no longer connected. The cancer was along his spine. When the end came, it was ridiculously fast. The bones were like lace now, beautifully destroyed. "She's the one I love. You knew that."

He lay there quietly. Maddy thought she heard him crying.

"We had a huge tree in our backyard," Maddy whispered. "If you climbed it you could reach the sky. We tied bells and bows around it to call the birds to us. But they only answered the sound of Allie's voice. They never even heard me."

"Right." Paul's eyes were still closed, but he was nearly smiling. "There's my girl. Entertain me. I knew I could count on you for that. I knew you could tell a good story. Tell me more about her."

WHEN SHE RETURNED to the Lion Park, Maddy was informed that she had a guest. Her mother was waiting for her in the restaurant. Maddy wanted to go upstairs and lie down; instead she went to join her mother.

Lucy had ordered a glass of white wine even though what she really wanted was a whisky. A plate of melted ice was beside her glass. The temperature had risen. The hotel was air-conditioned in its public rooms, but it was still stuffy. She remembered that about it.

"The place looks the same. Just older."

For the past several nights, Lucy had walked past the hotel. This was where she first began to understand that a person could lose herself if she wasn't careful.

"I came here because I remembered you talking about it," Maddy said. "And you had the ashtray. I thought it was going to be nicer."

"It was the first time I'd been to London. The first time I'd been anywhere, really. I was here for a wedding then, too. I see they still have the old stone lion."

"So tell me, Mother, was I the last person in the world to know Paul was so ill?"

"He's a very private man. And he was in terrible shape. Allie told me she didn't want to go ahead with the marriage before his diagnosis, but she stood by him. That's the way she is."

"Fake?"

"Loyal."

"Right. It's always Allie. The good one, the loyal one. She always gets everything."

Lucy laughed until she saw that her daughter was serious. "What she has is a terminally ill man."

"I could help," Maddy said. "I could do my part and see him through."

Lucy reached across the table and took her daughter's hand.

Maddy had always believed her mother never loved her, not the way she loved Allie. The proof of it was when Maddy went into her mother's bedroom one day to find the shades pulled down and all the lights shut off. Lucy's eyes were closed. She sensed someone in the room, and she had opened her eyes and was startled to see Maddy standing by the door. Her mother said, I can't, just like that, and Maddy had run. She was sure of what it meant: I can't take care of you. I can't love you. Now she wondered if perhaps she'd been mistaken. Maybe her mother had meant, I can't have you see me this way. I love you far too much for that.

"There's nothing to take care of, Maddy. It's over. This is their business. This man is going to be Allie's husband, whether or not he's dying. She's the only one who can see him through."

Maddy pulled away and covered her face. Her hands smelled like hospital soap, clean and sharp. She certainly didn't want her mother to see her cry. Lucy ordered another glass of wine. This was the daughter who didn't feel anything; the one she could never reach.

"You can't make someone love you, you know. I learned that with your father. I didn't want him if he didn't want me. I saw what that could do to a person."

"I did something terrible," Maddy said. "I can't ever be forgiven."

"Trust me," Lucy said. "You can."

After Maddy went up to her room to lie down, Lucy remained at the bar. She called for a whisky and soda. She knew she hadn't been a very good mother, especially to Maddy. She thought it would be better if she kept her distance. Her daughters wouldn't miss her so terribly if anything happened to her. They wouldn't be devastated if they were already on their own.

When she'd first heard that Maddy was staying at the Lion Park, Lucy had phoned over. She hadn't even been sure Teddy Healy would still be alive. But the girl at the front desk who'd answered her call assured her that he was, and then Maddy herself mentioned him. Maybe it was fate or perhaps it was only circumstance; either way it seemed time for Lucy to go back. There were several elderly customers at the bar, but it wasn't until a gentleman came in late in the evening and spoke to the bartender that she was certain it was Teddy. She remembered his voice. His features looked familiar, even after all this time. As for Teddy, he didn't seem to recognize her at all. Lucy, after all, was a woman in her fifties and he was an old man.

Over the years Teddy had been a reliable godfather to his brother's three children. He always remembered birthdays and had been at every graduation ceremony. But drinking was the only thing that he'd taken seriously for a good part of his life. Some of the women at the bank where he'd worked had made it clear they were available, but Teddy was wary. If he wanted female companionship when he was younger, he phoned a business that offered those services. It was easy enough; an attractive woman would come up to his place, and they'd have sex and he'd pay her, and then he would go to the Lion Park and get drunk. That was the constant in his life. The bar at the hotel. The hour when he went upstairs and relived what had happened to him.

One night, many years ago, Teddy had gotten so inebriated that the porter at the Lion Park had tossed him out on the street. It was the sixties, a time of wild goings-on; drugs were everywhere and yet Teddy was the one thrown out on his ear.

A girl had come over and said something to him. She was stern and very pretty. Things were different back then; young women talked to strangers. This one helped him into a taxi and told him he'd kill himself with loss of liver function if he didn't quit drinking. She told him to think of someone other than himself. You never knew who you were helping, she'd said. It's your duty as a human being, after all.

Teddy began to sober up after that. He started to travel, to Africa and the Middle East, places where the landscape was huge, where life had gone on forever and his pitiful existence seemed completely unimportant. He still drank, but it wasn't the same. He wasn't obliterating himself. He gave most of his money away, to schools in the countries he visited, to children whose tuition he paid. He also took care of his nephews' university educations. He visited elderly people in homes and read to them. He had a beautiful reading voice, people said. He went on to make recordings for unsighted readers. He thought if he did enough good in the world, perhaps that young woman he'd once met might be right; what he'd lost on the night of the accident might come back to him.

Teddy did have liver problems and emphysema, just as that young woman had once predicted, but he still went to Africa once a year, to Nigeria. He had been involved in building a school there, and was helping to raise money for a girls' dormitory, so they could attend classes as well. But he still came back to the lounge at the Lion Park, and not simply because it was a pleasant place to be. This was the place where his life had gone wrong.

Lucy was surprised by how fragile he looked, a man who needed his nap in the afternoon.

"Teddy Healy. Is it really you?"

Teddy raised his coffee cup to her. He rarely had more than a drink or two these days. "Here's to you," he said, clearly having no idea who she was.

"I'm Lucy Green. Lucy Heller now."

Teddy Healy stared at her. An attractive dark-haired woman. A total stranger. Then she did something with her face, a sort of half smile, and he saw the girl she had been years ago when she had stayed here.

"Lucy," he said. "Yes."

"I tried to write to you at this address, here at the hotel, when I returned to the States, but the letters came back to me."

"Myself and letters were never a good match."

"I've thought about you often, Mr. Healy."

"Well, God bless you," he said. "Thank you."

"My daughter lives in London. One of them. She's about to be married, but her fiancé is very ill. They don't expect him to survive."

"Stay away from letters and marriage," Teddy Healy said. "That's my best advice."

"Right," Lucy said. She knew the pain such things had caused him.

"I'm sorry for your daughter's troubles," Teddy added. "That's a very sad thing."

"Thank you. I was sorry for yours. I should have come back here years ago. I meant to, but I got caught up in my own life. I made more mistakes than I could begin to count."

Teddy Healy shrugged. He called for another coffee and one for Lucy as well. "To hell with the past," he said.

"My daughter says the place is still haunted."

"So I've heard." Teddy glanced up and saw she wasn't going to let it go at that. "You don't believe in that nonsense, do you?"

"I saw it once," Lucy said. "I wasn't much of a witness. I fell and hit my head."

"You've got a good, long memory," Teddy said. And that was unfortunate; that was what he always worried about. That he'd ruined her life as well as his own. "I suppose you remember I was a coward."

"I remember I thought everything that had happened was my fault."

"Well, that's a foolish idea. It was mine. I took away your childhood. There's no way to make amends for that. I can assure you."

"Is that what you think? If anything, you gave my childhood back to me."

Teddy laughed. "That I don't believe."

"You did. My father married a woman he met over here, and we lived together in New York. I walked my dog through Central Park every day, and I was happy, something I never thought I'd be again. What I saw up on the seventh floor of this hotel was an innocent man. I definitely remember that. Come with me and we'll see."

"To tell you the truth I don't go upstairs anymore. Not since I cut down on the drinking." The barman brought over their coffees. "Put that on my tab." Teddy looked up at the clock. It was nearly ten-thirty, that dreadful time.

"I think we should go upstairs and be done with it, Mr. Healy." She'd already stood up.

"I won't get rid of you until I do, will I, Lucy?"

She shook her head. He recalled that she'd been stubborn then, too.

They took the lift up. She hadn't remembered it to be so small or so creaky. They got out on the top floor. Seven. There had been some work done along the molding where the pet rabbit who'd lived in the hotel back when Lucy was a girl had torn off strips of wallpaper. But most everything seemed very dim, in need of repair.

"My daughter's staying on this floor."

"She could have found a better place to stay," Teddy said.

"We all could have done that."

Teddy chuckled. He looked quite pale.

When they got to 707, Lucy knocked, then opened the door. The room was empty and cold. Some extra mattresses were stored against one wall. Lucy left the door open and she and Teddy stood in the hallway, looking in. Teddy glanced at her once and she felt his uncertainty. They both remembered everything. They might not recall what they'd had for breakfast, but they assuredly recalled exactly what had happened in this room.

It was now ten-thirty. When Lucy's husband had left, she had often thought about Teddy Healy. She knew that love wasn't something you could bargain for. She remembered the girl she had been; in many ways, she was still that girl. She had lost her faith in people when she was young, long before she'd come to London.

They could hear some guests down on the sixth floor, a little tipsy, laughing. It was ten-thirty and then ten thirty-five and then it was a quarter to eleven. There was no evidence of a ghost, or whatever the thing had been.

"What happened to it?" Teddy Healy asked.

Lucy leaned in close to him. "You're a good man. Maybe that's all you needed to know. You always were. You were good to me."

"What I did for you was nothing."

"You couldn't be more wrong, Mr. Healy. It was everything to me."

MADDY SPENT THE next day alone. It was nothing new to her. But this day was different. Today she wished she was with the rest of her family. She went out wearing jeans and flip-flops and the T-shirt she had slept in. The heat wave hadn't eased and many restaurants had run out of ice and cold drinks.

Maddy had her hotel key and some money in her pocket. She felt homeless and lost. She found her way to the garden in the park with the huge white roses, where she sat on a bench. A man was sleeping on the bench directly across from hers. It was quiet in the garden. Maddy couldn't hear the traffic on Brompton Road. Time seemed to have slowed down. For once she thought about the things she had done and she wasn't pleased. When the man began to moan in his sleep, Maddy got up. She walked for miles. By the end of the day her feet hurt; she went into a pub in the late afternoon where she drank a warm Coke. No one bothered her. A few people glanced at her, then looked away. A pretty woman in bad shape. She hadn't washed her hair, only pinned it up. Her clothes were rumpled and she looked on edge, as though she'd had better days in some other place and time.

Maddy tried to phone her mother's hotel room several times

to check in and see how Paul was doing, but Lucy was never in. She left six messages with the front desk. She phoned the hospital, but when the switchboard answered and asked who it was she'd like to speak to, she hung up.

It was nearly dark when Maddy made her way out of the pub. She had wasted the entire day with soda and chips. The air was ashy and deep. There was a rosebush growing by a garden gate around the block from the hotel, with flowers that appeared almost blood red in the gathering dark. That night underneath the sycamore tree when they cut themselves, Maddy realized that if she decided not to feel any pain, nothing could hurt her. She let her sister be the one with hope, while she believed in nothing. She was more like her mother than she would ever have imagined.

Maddy ate her dinner in the hotel restaurant that night. She sat at the bar.

"You're here more than Teddy is," the barman said. "A regular. He's even been getting his post here." He held up an envelope. Inside was an old snapshot of a girl and a dog sitting on a bench. The barman had peeked. Someone had written WITH GRATITUDE on the back of the photograph.

"Well, I won't be a regular after this week," Maddy assured him. "I'll be going home." She ordered soup and wine, but she drank just the wine. The soup was watery with thinly cut vegetables floating on top. She had no appetite anyway.

"I hear we're rid of our ghost," the barman went on. "I have no idea how it was done, but it's a miracle. Teddy himself tried to shoot him once, but the bullet went right through him. As far as I can tell, ghosts are the essence of a person filtered down to the basics. A circle of vibrant illumination. That's what we're supposedly all made of."

"You sound like a believer," Maddy said.

"I saw him on occasion," the barman confided. "Wandering the hallway. Lost as a mouse. Poor fellow. I guess he finally went on to his just reward."

When Maddy went upstairs she ran her hand along the wall to feel for the bullet hole in the plaster outside the door to 708. She went into her room, took off all her clothes, and put on her blue dress. She had to stand on the desk chair to get a look since the mirror was small. The dress suited her; Allie had chosen well. She knew Maddy. The color was perfect.

Maddy had seemed not to need anyone, but inside she was broken, made of bones and black ribbons, blood and darkness. She fell asleep in the hot, sticky room with the desk lamp switched on, still wearing the bridesmaid's dress. She heard a whisper in her dream; a man was speaking, and she was guided by his voice. There was a trail of stones, and she followed them until she saw Paul. He was wrapped in white tape and his eyes were white as well. He said, Bury me under the sycamore tree. In her dream, Maddy was barefoot and standing on stones; her feet had begun to bleed. She wanted to say, Of course, I'll do anything you ask, but she couldn't speak. She was falling into pieces. A hand, an arm, a leg. She wondered if she could put herself together again with red thread and needles. She wondered if she would have the strength to lift the shovel and dig the grave he'd asked her for. There were white roses growing, but she couldn't see them in the dark. She'd simply have to believe they were there.

◆ ◆

ALLIE WAS BY his bedside when it happened. It was 5:22 A.M.
She noticed the clock, the way people notice odd, practical
things just at the moment when everything seems so unreal.
There was the table. There was a water glass with a straw. It
was that silver-colored time between night and morning, when
the sky is still dark, but lights are flicking on all over the city. It
was quiet, the way it is in winter when snow first begins to fall.
But it was the fifteenth of August, the morning after her wedding day. She had been married a week ahead of schedule.

On the day of her marriage, the doctor had called Allie into
his office to say that he thought Paul would not last twenty-four
hours. He might not even last the day. His vital signs were slipping and he was unresponsive; his dosage of morphine was so
high it was toxic. Allie thanked the doctor and sat there unable
to move.

"You don't have to thank me," the doctor said. His name
was Crane. He had a huge heart and probably shouldn't have
been a doctor. "You can hit me if you want to."

All Allie wanted to do was use his phone. She called Paul's
parents to tell them to drive up to London immediately. His
mother would fall to pieces. All through the autumn, when Paul
had been having the chemo that made him so desperately ill, he
had wanted to go home on the weekends. And then early that
summer, when it came back so quickly, he looked forward to
those visits more than ever. It was a tiring trip, but he didn't care.
Allie often had to drive. Paul had never allowed himself to be a
passenger before, but now he dozed on the way. That was when

she first began to understand what was happening. That was when she began to fall in love with him.

She hadn't lied to Maddy; she'd hadn't loved him before. When she accepted his proposal of marriage she had done so because it appeared to be the next step. It had seemed the right time, if not the right man. Paul was indeed difficult and self-centered. He always had his defenses up. The charm that had attracted her at first had worn thin. Allie had wanted out so badly, she didn't even care that he had prowled around when he was at his angriest. And then this summer, after the recurrence, when she least expected it, everything had changed.

On those trips to Reading, Paul would often vomit out the window, or they'd have to stop by the side of the road or at a tea shop because he was so nauseated he couldn't stand the movement of the car. But as soon as he got to the village where he'd grown up, he was happy. The house was called Lilac House and had been in the family for years, nothing very elaborate, just a small pretty country house with a little cottage in the rear of the property that was surrounded by boxwood. There was indeed a row of huge old lilacs in the garden. Some were purple, some violet, some were the color of cream. In the summertime, however, they were just a hedge of green, heart-shaped leaves.

Paul was a bird-watcher, something Allie hadn't known about him till then. As it turned out, there was a great deal she didn't know. That he was kind, for instance. He went out of his way to speak to old people whenever they stopped for tea on their travels, taking time to discuss the weather and state of the world. He liked to go to a fruit stand and bring his mother a basket of apples when they came to visit. "Get the good ones," he'd call to Allie when he could no longer step out of the car to choose the fruit himself.

"Absolute best apples in the universe," he would insist when she came back to the car. "I was a vegetarian when I was ten," he told her.

"Were you?" Allie was surprised. He liked his roasts and stews.

"My grandfather was one and I wanted to please him. He was quite the old guy. A doctor. I admired the hell out of him. Whatever he did, I did."

"What else did you do when you were ten?" Allie asked. Paul was already having difficulty with his eyes.

"I dreamed of you," he said.

"Bullshit." She'd laughed.

"Football," he said. "Cooking."

"No."

"Oh, yes. Jam pancakes and puddings and apple tarts. Vegetable stews. I was good at it. And I did dream of you," he added. "Whether or not you believe it, it's true."

Once they'd arrived, Paul would sit on the lawn of Lilac House bundled up in a sweater, a wool blanket covering him. He could identify almost any bird from its song. He was a fan of the underdog, birds other people thought of as pests: ravens, magpies, kestrels. On the other hand, he could be sentimental; he adored mourning doves and said they had the sweetest voices of all. At Lilac House, he spread out seed and bread crumbs and sat there on the lawn, still as could be, as birds gathered around him.

"He has perfect pitch," Frieda told Allie one evening as they were fixing dinner together in the kitchen.

"I didn't know that," Allie said.

Although the house wasn't fancy, it was quite lovely, with the details of another era when workmen were artists. There were intricate moldings and fireplace mantels framed by carved owls; there was an old earthenware sink in the kitchen and a stove with six burners. On the pine table sat a huge pot of cut flowers from the kitchen garden. Everything smelled sweet.

"He should have been a musician really," Paul's mother said.

She had been scraping vegetables into the sink. Then suddenly she stopped; she seemed withdrawn into silence. Frieda bent over, no longer speaking, felled by despair. She was sobbing without any noise or any tears as the tap water ran.

Allie went to Paul's mother and embraced her. She felt no one could understand this except the two of them. Only they knew how it felt to be watching Paul on the lawn, slipping away.

"This cannot happen to him," Frieda had said.

There were bits of onion and carrot in the sink. When Allie half shut her eyes and gazed across the room, past the bunch of cut lilacs, everything looked purple.

"I'm so, so sorry," Allie said.

"How can I live without him in the world?" Frieda had said. "He's not like other people, you know. He hides his true self because he's so easily hurt. And now this is the end. There is no way back."

They stood there crying, then they pulled themselves together and went back to fixing dinner. They were similar in that way; women who made the best of things, even their own mistakes. That night, they cooked some of Paul's favorite dishes.

Beef stew, which he couldn't even take a bite of. Too heavy, but his favorite all the same. He loved the scent and called from the parlor, "Thank God I'm not a vegetarian, ladies." But sometimes the essence of a thing was enough; he could never have digested the stew. Frieda had also cooked peas and creamed them. That would be better. He might manage a little. Saffron rice. He loved the color and was a huge fan of Indian cuisine. A strawberry mousse with cream. Just the sight of the dessert would suffice. Paul's father helped him back inside the house; he was too weak to sit at the table in the dining room, so he went to the couch in the sitting room and stretched out there, exhausted from the trip across the room.

"Mother, I can't believe you did all this specially!" Allie heard him say when Frieda brought him his dinner on a tray. She adored him for that, for the way he appreciated his parents and older people in general, for kindnesses she'd never even known about, for the way he lit up when he talked about football and his grandfather and this house where he'd grown up. She loved him at last, when it was too late. He hadn't even the energy to get off the sofa. "You don't have to be this good to me," he said to his mother. "I don't deserve it."

On those visits they would sleep together in the single bed in the guest room. It had been Paul's room once, and all his belongings were still displayed, trophies and plaques. He always asked for the window to be left open so that he could listen to the birds.

"This is where I dreamed of you," he told Allie when they got into bed.

"Liar," she said. She wrapped her arms around him, carefully.

"I spent all my years here looking out the window, wanting to escape, and now all I want is to be here again."

ALLIE HAD NO doubt that Frieda would know the time of his passing was near. She had been an oncology nurse, and her father a country doctor. She'd known recovery would be difficult as soon as they'd told her the diagnosis. Frieda didn't question the fact that Allie and Paul were getting married that very day. She only asked what she could do. Allie suggested she bring flowers. Frieda wished it was still lilac season; she wished they had more time. But she was practical and always had been. She woke her husband from his nap and said, "This is it. We have to say good-bye."

Allie phoned the superintendant registrar who was to marry them and apologized for needing him to appear on such short notice. Then she called her mother at her hotel and asked her parents to come over as quickly as possible.

"Don't bring anyone else," Allie had told her mother. "I can't deal with anyone else."

When she was done with her calls, Dr. Crane came and sat next to her and took her hand. He knew this was the day.

"I'd have to be stupid not to know," Allie said. "I mean, his mother was a nurse and she told me the situation was dire. I brought my wedding outfit anyway. But I didn't get a dress with a veil and all that lace. That would have been foolish."

"Love has nothing to do with the here and now," Dr. Crane said.

Allie looked up at him, surprised. Had she said she loved Paul or did he just know? It was a funny thing for a doctor to say. Maybe she'd misheard him. She hadn't slept all night. She was wearing tan slacks and a black T-shirt and sandals. It was hot, but Allie was wearing a gray sweater thrown on over her shirt. Whenever she was tired like this, she grew cold. Her pale hair was tied back in a ponytail. She'd lost fifteen pounds without trying. That had never happened to her before. This had never happened, the way she felt.

"But I'm in the here and now," she said to the doctor.

They sat together for a while, then they went back to Paul's room so Dr. Crane could check his vital signs. The doctor put a hand on Allie's shoulder before he left and she almost lost it then.

"Thank you," she managed to say.

She rushed out to use the ladies' room. She didn't want to leave Paul alone for any amount of time, so she quickly peed and washed up, then hurried back to his room. There was no real night or day in the hospital, but this was the time between shifts so it was quiet. The hallway felt like a world in outer space, somewhere between universes. Allie stopped outside of Paul's room, the way she used to stop at the door to her mother's room on her way to bed. She would close her eyes and recite a secret spell she'd invented, one she'd never even told Maddy about, to allay her fears. She was terrified that someone would die on her watch. She had dreams about Death, and sometimes she heard him speak. He would wake her from her sleep and on those nights her skin was cold. She would creep out of bed and go peek inside her mother's bedroom to make sure she was still alive. Perhaps it was more of a prayer than a spell that she whispered.

I will do anything, I will give up anything. Just don't let anyone die today.

When Allie got back to the room, Paul was tossing and turning, agitated, in pain. Sometimes the end was so fast it was shocking, that's what Paul's mother had told Allie. And Dr. Crane had warned her not to have any expectations when the cancer returned. The illness was like that, mysterious, headstrong, making its own rules. Just when you thought it might edge along forever, everything exploded. There was no longer any need to wear a mask; there was nothing to protect him from.

Paul was burning up with a fever. He looked beautiful, alight from inside. A falling star. Allie got a wet washcloth and held it to his forehead. She could feel the heat through the folded cloth.

Don't let him die today.

"Dear Allie," Paul said when he realized she was there. "Go home. Just leave me."

Allie sat on the edge of the bed. "We're getting married," she said.

"You can walk away," Paul said. "You served your time. I'm a bad man."

"Yes, I know. But I like you that way."

He didn't laugh as she'd hoped. "Really bad, Allie. I did something I can't tell you about just to hurt you. We can't get married."

She had known when she saw her sister in the dress shop; she could always read Maddy when other people couldn't.

"It doesn't matter what you've done. We're getting married today."

"I thought we were getting married on the twentieth."

Allie said nothing.

"I see," Paul said. "My darling girl."

The man in the bed next to Paul, the one visitors had to pass by in order to reach Paul's bed, had died. The other man behind the curtain, the one near the window, had had surgery to remove his leg. He was an American and young, a graduate student from New Jersey, whose family would soon arrive. But for now he had no visitors. When Paul closed his eyes, Allie went to look in on his roommate, Rob Rosenbloom. Rob was awake. He had a morphine drip, too.

"Hey," he said. "How's our boyo?"

Rob was in his midtwenties. He was long and lanky, with wild dark hair and blue eyes. He'd been studying at the London School of Economics when he felt the lump in his leg. He'd been a crew fanatic and had joined up with a London Borough team, so he thought the bump was a pulled muscle. It wasn't.

Now he told Allie that Paul talked to himself all the time. He was tormented, but Rob didn't tell her that part. Paul cried in the night and Rob had to lie there and listen.

"We're getting married this morning," Allie said. "Here. In this room. It's such an imposition. I hope you don't mind."

"Of course I don't."

"Yes, well, there won't be many of us, so it shouldn't be too noisy. Just his mom and dad and my parents. We'll just inconvenience the hell out of you while you're recuperating."

"He's sorry for all the things he's done," Rob said. Rob had an athlete's body, except for the leg of course, and a clear, open face. He looked even younger than he was. He worked for a firm in Manhattan that had let him take six months to live in London and accept the fellowship he'd been offered. "He doesn't think he's worthy of you."

"Are you a mind reader?" Allie asked. "How do you know all this about Paul? He never says a word about how he feels."

"I listen to him." Rob was looking at her as though he knew her. "He is so sorry, Allie."

"Should I get you your breakfast? I can ring the nurse. They have excellent porridge, although I don't recommend the eggs."

"I'm fine," Rob said.

"Yeah, sure. So am I." Allie laughed. "We're both fine." Her nose was running for no reason. "I didn't think I'd ever fall in love. I didn't think I was capable of it."

"It's a good day for a wedding," Rob said. "I'd offer to stand up for him, if I had two legs."

Allie felt stricken. She went to Rob, then leaned down and kissed his forehead. He smelled like a boy, like someone who shouldn't be in a hospital bed.

"He's so sorry you can't even believe it," Rob said.

When Allie stood up her nose and eyes were running like mad. "I hope you don't mind." She blew her nose. "I'm falling apart."

Rob laughed. "I think I'm the one falling apart."

"Oh. I'm sorry."

"Don't be," Rob said. "It's nice to have a beautiful woman around."

Allie buzzed for the nurse to bring Rob's breakfast.

"Paul's asleep," she told the nurse. The nurse had brought a tray for Paul as well, which she then stored on a shelf. It was a token meal of applesauce and a soft-boiled egg. Paul had stopped eating when he'd been admitted to the hospital. His body shut down haphazardly, Dr. Crane had said: eyes, digestive system, muscles, bones, respiratory system, brain.

It wasn't a real sleep, however. Allie realized this as she got into bed beside him. It was a drugged sleep, a faraway sleep. His eyes were open. It was the last kind of sleep; when you're no longer fully awake, and won't be again. They were face-to-face. Paul said something but Allie couldn't hear him, not even when she put her ear up to his mouth. She thought it was something about a mockingbird. She hadn't wanted to fall in love, but she had. Just the tiny bit of information about him, his preference for mourning doves, for example, now seemed the most important fact on earth. She wanted to remember it always. She wanted to study doves, their habits, their bone structure.

"This is our day," Allie told Paul. There was a ridiculous lump in her throat. Like a golf ball or a round bit of bone.

Her parents arrived first. They looked terrible. Allie's mom hadn't slept and her father's face appeared bloated and red. Bob Heller was so guarded and unemotional. If he started to cry, Allie would be undone. She couldn't think about other people now. That was why she hadn't invited her sister. She wanted things kept simple. It was the only way she could get through this. One minute at a time.

Lucy had stopped at her daughter's flat to pick up the bride's wedding suit. She'd brought along a strand of turquoise beads for Allie that had belonged to her own mother, something borrowed, blue, and old all in one. What was new was a pair of flats Lucy had bought on the way, darting into The French Sole since Allie hadn't had time to pick up the shoes she'd ordered.

"I wasn't planning on dressing up. I was just going to wear

this," Allie said of her slacks and sweater. "Who really gives a damn? We don't have to wear masks in here anymore. It's beyond that now."

"Wear the wedding suit," Rob called from behind the curtain. He really couldn't help eavesdropping. He was less than a foot away.

"Who the hell is that?" Allie's father wanted to know.

"Rob Rosenbloom. He's from New Jersey. He doesn't know it's not polite to shout things out in a hospital room. Do you, Rob? We Americans have no manners."

"I'm only trying to be helpful," Rob said. The Hellers went around to introduce themselves and apologize for commandeering the room.

Allie decided to take Rob's suggestion; he was an outside observer, after all, and most likely had a more rational view of what seemed to Allie like insane behavior. A wedding in a hospital—who did that? A conversation with her parents as if this was any other day and they were arguing about her wardrobe instead of sobbing at Paul's bedside. Allie went to the ladies' lounge. She took off her clothes and stared at herself in the mirror. A woman came in and stopped in her tracks.

"I'm getting married," Allie said.

She was wearing a bra and underwear and heavy socks. She looked too disheveled to be anyone's bride. Her white suit was on the lounge sofa. The woman came over and hugged her. Being in the hospital together was like being on the front line; you didn't need to be privy to everything about someone to know them. The facts of a person's life were made up of medicine, pots of tea from the lunchroom, sorrow, disaster. That was enough.

"God bless you," the woman said.

"Thank you," Allie said as she stepped back.

The other woman went on to use the toilet while Allie proceeded. When she came back out to wash her hands, Allie was dressed. She had even combed her hair. The woman nodded her approval. "Very pretty."

Allie thanked her and gathered her worn clothes together. Every little piece of kindness felt huge. She went back to Paul's room. Paul's parents had arrived while Allie was dressing. Frieda sat on a chair beside the bed. Bill was speaking quietly with Allie's dad. Before this summer, Allie hadn't even known that Paul phoned his parents every Sunday. He could tell the difference between the trill of a warbler and the song of a lark because Frieda had taught him the difference. He was spoiled and selfish, but he was also a dutiful son who loved his mother and always wanted to go home to Lilac House. He had known how to love someone, and she hadn't.

"You'll never find another man like Paul," Frieda had said to Allie during one of those weekends when Paul was no longer in remission. "Love can be complicated or it can be simple," she'd told Allie.

Allie had laughed. "Paul's such a complicated person."

"But loving him is simple," Frieda had said.

Allie had listened to what her mother-in-law-to-be told her. To love someone so complicated you had to be committed to a single emotion—the way you loved him—no matter what. In that way, it was indeed simple.

"Then that's what I'll do," Allie had decided. Paul's mother, who had seemed distant when they'd first met, a cautious woman who'd seen scores of Paul's girlfriends, had thrown her arms around her.

"Sorry about that," Frieda had said afterward, embarrassed by her emotional display. "I swear I'll never cry in front of you again."

She hadn't, until now. Seeing Frieda break down was too much. Allie left Paul's room and went back into the hall before anyone saw her. She composed herself. She told herself she was in a play and she had a part and she was sticking with it. She was not going to become hysterical or run away or do anything that might hurt Paul's parents. She stopped at a phone booth and called Georgia and asked her to be a witness.

"I'll be there in ten minutes," Georgia said.

When Allie went back to the room Frieda was blowing her nose. "Darling girl," she said. Frieda had brought along a bouquet of white roses. She came to embrace Allie. "Lovely suit," Frieda said. "Perfect."

"Silk," Allie said. Having a normal conversation seemed utterly mad.

"Think of all those silkworms working away somewhere. Now you're getting married. Paul will be a married man."

The thought of what was happening was overwhelming to Frieda; she dissolved yet again. She seemed delirious. She whispered to her husband that there was someone standing against the wall. She'd seen it all before in childhood. Her father had been a doctor, after all, going from house to house. Frieda was convinced it was the Angel of Death.

"We don't believe in that, darling," her husband said softly. "We believe in the hereafter."

The nurse came in and shooed everyone out so she could see to Paul.

"I'm a nurse," Frieda said. "I can stay."

"Not with your own son," the nurse told her. "It's not a good idea. You can come back as soon as I'm done. I'll be quick about it. I promise."

Frieda was not easily convinced to leave.

"Come on, we'll get a quick cup of tea," her husband said. "We'll get take-away cups and bring it back and she'll be done by then."

Before Frieda left she turned to Allie. "They're probably right. I don't think you want to see this on your wedding day. Come with us, Allie."

"I'm fine," Allie said.

Allie had seen terrible things before, after all. She had seen her mother after her surgery, unable to get out of bed. She had seen the fragile blue veins on her scalp when she took off her wig. There was no way to be embarrassed or repulsed. Allie had never been squeamish; it had been weaned out of her. When the others left, she stayed. She sat beside Paul and held his hand.

"Hello," he said.

"Hello," Allie said back to him.

The nurse was changing his bedsheets first. For several days he had been defecating in the bed. It was so difficult to move him they no longer bothered and a diaper chafed against his skin, plus, Allie wouldn't let them do that to him. No diapers. Even if he didn't know or didn't have the strength to care, she cared for him. He hadn't eaten all week, so there wasn't much left to him, only a tiny dropping, like that of a fox.

She meant to tell him it was over in their suite at the Hotel Pulitzer in Amsterdam in the fall. Mrs. Ridge had paid for their trip. Because of that they'd gone first class. Allie had the words in her mouth. She was ready to say good-bye, and then all of a sudden a heron was on the lamppost beside them.

"He knows you've written about him," Paul said. "He's come to pay his respects."

Paul loved the Dutch attitude toward herons. People left their windows open, welcoming them into their homes. Have a heron in your house and your luck will change. Feed it milk and bread and beer and it will be forever grateful.

"Maybe we should move here," Paul had said. "We'd be happy in Amsterdam. We'd live by the river. We'd leave all the windows open and let the herons fly through our flat. It would be your book come to life."

ALLIE LOOKED RIGHT into Paul's eyes. This was their life now. The nurse bathed him a bit, then dealt with his catheter. Paul made a face; utter pain.

"Fuck that woman," he said.

Allie smiled. "You'd probably try if you could."

"You should go." Paul's eyes were open.

Was he truly awake? Allie always vowed she would marry a man with blue eyes, then she'd found Paul. He must have told his mother about the roses she'd brought to Kensington Palace. He must have said, When I marry this woman she has to have white roses.

"I'll bet it's summer," Paul said. "Leave if you know what's good for you."

"I think I'll stay a while. We're getting married you know."

"Go and don't feel guilty."

"I can't," Allie said. "I fell in love with you."

"All done," the nurse said. She checked the IV and let him have some more morphine. Paul's eyes closed.

The superintendant registrar arrived and promised to make the service brief. When Georgia came in, she hugged Allie, then held the bouquet of flowers while Allie edged into bed with Paul so that they could be close while the ceremony was performed. When the superintendant registrar made the pronouncement that they were both free to lawfully marry, Allie signed her name to the marriage contract. Paul's father held his hand and tried to help him make an *X,* but in the end Bill had to sign Paul's name. Lucy and Bill then signed as witnesses. Frieda needed to sit down; she bowed her head.

And then it was done; two married people.

"I'm happy you were the girl he fell in love with," Frieda said when she regained her composure. "Have I told you that? I should have told you before."

On the other side of the curtain, Rob Rosenbloom was quietly crying, but they pretended not to hear him. Allie slipped on the twenty-two-karat gold wedding band they had chosen, and then did the same with Paul's band. The ring was too big, so she put it on his middle finger. He was the one who'd chosen twenty-two karat. "The real thing," Paul had said at the jeweler's. "None of this eighteen-karat crap for you."

Georgia leaned in to give Allie a hug once Allie and Paul were officially husband and wife. She was still holding on to Allie's white roses. "I unofficially caught the bouquet. Which means I'm next."

Rob had asked a nurse to order a cake from a local bakery. The cake was delivered in thin slices on plastic plates from the cafeteria. The family opened the curtain so Rob could join in.

"I didn't know there was somebody gorgeous hiding there," Georgia said.

Rob grinned and accepted his cake. His nose and eyes were red. He had an IV in his arm. Sometimes he woke in the night convinced that his leg was still there and that it had fallen asleep. Everyone praised the cake he'd ordered. It was a yellow cake frosted with white spun sugar. Simple, just what Allie had wanted.

"How did you know?" Allie asked Rob.

"Psychic," he said, but he'd heard all about the things that she wanted, late at night when Paul talked through his pain and his sleep.

Allie took a single bite of the cake, and then Paul moaned and raised his knees.

Allie thought about the night when she followed her sister into the marsh. She had walked right into the water when she spied the blue heron. Take me away from here, she had whispered. They had looked at each other for a very long time, and for those moments Allie believed he would take her with him. But when he took flight he had left her there, standing in the water, freezing.

"I think we could all use some rest," Lucy Heller said. "I've gotten you a room at our hotel," she told Paul's parents, who were grateful but said they were perfectly fine. Their dear friend Daisy Ridge had a house in Kensington and had invited them to stay, but frankly they would prefer to sleep in the hospital lounge. Frieda was not about to leave her son.

"What if he needs me?" she said to Allie. She sounded like a little girl.

"Of course you'll stay. The nurses will give you blankets and anything else you need."

Allie's parents kissed her good-bye. Her father-in-law, for that's who Bill was to her now, suggested that perhaps she should go home and sleep for a few hours, but Allie couldn't do that. Frieda understood.

"Go and get some tea, that won't take long. Or some soup." Frieda had brought a little recorder and a tape of birdsongs to play. "I thought he might like this."

Allie embraced her mother-in-law. She didn't want to go, but Georgia insisted.

"Just for a few minutes," Georgia promised.

Allie went to the lunchroom, guided by Georgia; she let Frieda take over the watch, for that's what it was now. Minute by minute. The wedding lunch they were to have at the Orangery was to be a cold salmon with cream sauce, salad with raspberries and walnuts with a vinaigrette dressing, tureens of roasted vegetables, sliced lamb and tiny potatoes. Now Georgia ordered a pot of tea and two stale buns with drizzled frosting, a bowl of veggie soup, and wheat crackers.

They ignored the soup and stuck with the tea and the dreadful sugary buns. Allie had two bites. Georgia offered to stay through the night. During those times Paul was in the hospital for treatment, Georgia would often get into bed with Allie and wrap her arms around her friend while she cried. Sometimes Georgia would cry right along with her. She was the only one who'd known that Allie had decided to break it off with

Paul before he was diagnosed. Afterward, all conversation about how she wanted to leave him ended.

There were times when Georgia considered warning Allie about her sister. She'd seen Paul and Maddy in the taxi together. She'd seen the look on Maddy's face, and she'd known. Frankly, Georgia had never been a huge fan of Paul's. She'd thought him superficial, too handsome, too self-involved. Paul had never once asked Georgia a single question about herself; she doubted whether he knew what she did at her publishing house, or if he was even aware that she had worked with Allie on *The Heron's Wife*. She'd been the art director on many children's books, and had won several awards, but *The Heron's Wife* was her favorite. Part of the charm of the artwork was the beautiful layout Georgia had created. It was possible to read the story two ways: Front to back, the heron returned to his heron wife and the world of the sky. Back to front, he stayed with his one true love on earth.

"Maybe I should spend the night with you here," Georgia offered.

"You don't have to. Really. I'll have the in-laws."

They both laughed at that. In-laws, after all. As much as she respected Frieda, Allie knew she would have to defer to Paul's mother on certain issues. Frieda wanted Paul buried with the rest of the family, in the village, and Allie would never challenge that, even though he would be terribly far away. She couldn't even think about how far away it was.

"Now I'll have in-law problems without the husband." Allie tried to joke, but she was near tears.

"Darling," Georgia said. "Frieda adores you. And with good reason."

"Don't say anything nice to me," Allie warned. "I'll break down if you do."

They said their good-byes in the hallway. "Give him a kiss for me," Georgia said.

"You've never wanted to kiss Paul in your life."

"I meant the neighbor with one leg. Rob. He's a doll." Georgia hesitated. "Should I really go?"

"I can do this," Allie said. "I don't have a choice."

"Well, it's not as if you loved him," Georgia said. "Right?"

Allie put her arms around her friend. She didn't let go.

"But I do," she said.

"Jesus, Allie. I had no idea." Georgia was stunned. "You didn't tell me, darling."

"I didn't know."

"Fucking love," Georgia said.

"Just my luck."

Allie took the stairs back to Paul's room. Once everyone had gone, Paul's mother had collapsed. The nurse had given her an antianxiety medication. The birdsong tape had been turned on. Allie thought of sitting in the grass with Paul outside Lilac House. It now seemed the most important thing they had ever done together.

"Frieda," Allie said.

"I'm so sorry," Frieda was saying. "I'm just a wreck."

"She hasn't slept in two days," Paul's father explained.

The in-laws went off to the visitors' lounge to lie down for a bit. There were blankets and pillows set aside for people keeping vigil. The nurses were incredibly kind. It was the hour when the minutes slowed down. Allie switched off the birdsong tape. On the other side of the curtain, Rob had fallen asleep. The sound of his morphine pump and the pump attached to Paul were in alternating rhythms, but somehow soothing. Allie removed her shoes, the ones that her mother had picked up for her that morning at The French Sole. She took off her jacket so that she was wearing only a camisole and her skirt, then she climbed onto the bed. Paul was curled up, breathing very slowly.

"Shall I tell you the story of the heron and his wife?" Allie whispered.

"I know it by heart."

"But you don't know what happened when he left his wife on earth for his heron wife. When he flew into the sky, high above the trees."

She tried to put her arms around him, but he moaned from the contact, so she simply stayed close.

"She glued feathers all over her body. She taught herself to fly. She followed him so that she could see him one last time. Nothing could stop her. She had to say good-bye. She loved him beyond all time and reason even though it was too late."

Allie had begun to cry. She didn't want to disturb Rob in the next bed; she didn't want to make a mess. She tried to slow her breathing to match Paul's. Earlier, the doctor had said Paul wouldn't last much longer. How was it that doctors knew things like that? Or was it that the morphine drip was set at such a high level because of his intense pain that no one could survive the amount of chemicals that were being poured into his body?

"I will never let you go," she said to Paul.

"Go," she thought she heard him say.

Allie got as close to Paul as she dared without touching him. They didn't need to touch anymore; they were twined together now. She fell asleep beside him. She dreamed she was in a white dress and that it was her wedding. She could see the marsh and there was mud all over her bare feet. It was time, she knew that, right now.

She woke up freezing, in the dark. Allie didn't know where she was, but she knew who was beside her. She got out of bed and went around to the other side. She sat on a hard plastic chair. She saw that Paul's wedding ring had fallen off. His eyes were open but unfocused. She didn't even realize that it was happening until it did. There were birds outside, even in the heart of the city. He made a noise in his throat, and the sound went right through Allie in some deep, wrenching way. This was the here and now. This exact moment. Paul opened his mouth and a strange breath came out, as if his spirit was leaving him. Allie reached up to catch it, but it slipped through her fingers. It was so fine, it was like trying to catch light within a pair of clumsy hands or sift running water in the dark.

THE CEMETERY WAS a mile down the road from Lilac House. Everyone in the Rice and Lewis families had been buried there. It was possible to see the fields of yellow rapeseed and the low hills where Frieda and her father had walked until the week of his death. Frieda felt comforted that Paul's grave would be right next to his grandfather's. Odd the strange things that could console you.

"Listen to that," Frieda said to Allie, who was now her daughter-in-law. There was the low cooing of doves in the trees. "He would have loved that."

Allie was wearing a black dress she'd borrowed from Georgia. She'd lost so much weight she had to pin it together on the inside, along the back seam. Allie and the Rices had agreed upon a small ceremony held at the graveside. Allie stood between her parents. She had told her friends and Paul's not to come up from London and she'd sent a note to Maddy explaining that the ceremony would be private. Paul had been so discreet about his illness; she wanted to give him that still. There was one family friend, Daisy Ridge, along with her companion, a nurse who helped her navigate the hilly ground. Because Mrs. Ridge had no heirs, she'd thought of Paul as her grandchild. It was a terrible day for her; halfway through the service she had to compose herself on a nearby bench.

"We shouldn't have let Daisy come," Bill Rice said. "It's too much for her."

Allie went to sit beside the old woman. They held hands and listened to the minister and the doves in the trees.

"Lovely, lovely boy," Mrs. Ridge said. "The light of his mother's life."

Allie bowed her head. She was such a fool; she had wasted so much time.

There were two drivers waiting to take the families back to the house. Mrs. Ridge went up to the guest room to have a nap before she was driven back to London. Paul's football trophies were still on the bookshelf. There were several photographs of him with the various teams on which he'd played. Allie helped the nurse, whose name was Bernadette. They both looped their arms under Mrs. Ridge's and guided her into bed.

"He never let me pay when we went out for lunch," Mrs. Ridge said. "He phoned me twice a week. He used to say, Guess who this is? like a little boy, as if I didn't know his voice."

Allie stayed there while Mrs. Ridge fell asleep so the nurse could go and have a bite to eat. It was a long day. It was hot and muggy. The trip from London had been tiring and the trip back would be worse. By then evening would be falling and the road would seem endless and dark. Allie looked at the photographs of Paul when he was a boy. He had the same smile he'd always had, a bit sneaky and very charming. She stood by the window and looked at the fields he used to see in the mornings when he got out of bed.

Mrs. Ridge was asleep. She had willed her entire estate to Paul and now she would have to change it. She would leave it to the girls' school the women in her family had always attended. She would have gardens planted and the names of all the women in the Ridge family would be engraved on a bronze plaque mounted on a stone wall. She would also have a garden in memory of Paul, one that was filled with plants that birds were drawn to: sunflowers, gooseberry, plum trees.

Mrs. Ridge was so quiet Allie leaned down to make sure she was still breathing. She was, only very softly. Her skin was paper-thin and she looked so pale against the blue blanket. Mrs. Ridge needed her rest. Allie went downstairs, but she couldn't bring herself to go into the parlor where everyone was having lunch. She went outside, then walked down the road. She felt as though she could go for miles. Maybe if she did she'd walk backward in time, the way her book could go backward if you started on the very last page. That was the way a reader could wind up with a happy ending. It had been a secret, although most of her readers knew about it now. She walked and she walked, but it was still the same road, the same trees and sky and yellow fields.

After a while, Allie started back. Nothing had changed. She was still in the here and now. A passing car honked its horn and someone waved at her, but Allie didn't know anyone but the Rices in Reading.

Her mother was waiting at the turn into Lilac House.

"It's a beautiful spot," Lucy said. "Did you know there's a house out back? A little place called The Hedges where Frieda and Bill lived when they were first married."

"Paul wanted us to move there." Allie had come to stand beside her mother. "He said it would be the perfect place to write. I told him he was crazy. I could never live all the way out here."

They walked across the lawn to The Hedges and peeked in the windows. It was a darling place. They went around the house to where there was a twisted pear tree.

"I should have been a better mother," Lucy said.

"Mother, nothing you did would have pleased Maddy. She has a contrary nature."

"I don't mean to Maddy. To you. I didn't want you to need me and then be destroyed the way I was when I lost my mother. You became too independent. You were so capable. She was always so jealous of that. She was just like me. Vulnerable. Unable to show how hurt she was."

"You want me to forgive her?" Allie said. "Do you know what she did?"

"Does it matter?" Lucy said. "My guess is that she hurt herself more than she could ever hurt you. She's holed up in that hotel room of hers, devastated. She needs you to need her. That's what she's always wanted."

They went to look into the kitchen window. There was an

old soapstone sink. The floors were made of planed chestnut, the planks worn down by so many years of footsteps. Allie thought Paul was right; they could have been happy here.

"You are a good mother," Allie said.

Lucy slipped her arm around her daughter's waist. She hadn't been, but she had tried. "I would have done anything for you."

"I knew that," Allie said.

"Maddy didn't."

Allie turned away from the kitchen window. She could see their life inside, the way it might have been. She understood regret. There were birds in the hedges; she couldn't see them, but she could hear them chattering. This is what happened when you fell in love with someone. You stood in the garden and listened to birdsongs. You looked through the window.

"Frieda will be wondering where we've gone off to," Lucy said.

They walked over the grass, arms linked.

"I could have lived here," Allie said.

Frieda was standing at the back door of Lilac House. She waved to them and they waved back. She wore a blue apron over her black mourning dress. She'd stayed up all night to make a roast so that no one would go hungry.

"How do I do this?" Allie asked her mother.

"You do the best you can," Lucy said. "There's nothing more than that."

EVERYONE LEFT BEFORE dark, including Allie's parents, who rode back to London with Mrs. Ridge and her nurse in a chauffeured car. Allie was in the garden, where the lilacs were so tall it was impossible to see the road. The leaves were dusty, the way they always were in August when the weather turned hot. Bill had gone off to bed, but Allie and Frieda didn't want to go inside; they sat on wooden chairs, listening to the birds call. There were still patches of blue sky, even though it was nearly ten o'clock. The air was so heavy and thick that every second seemed to linger.

"My father told me there were three angels," Frieda said. "He was a very serious, lovely, practical man. He was always on time. He was someone you could depend upon. He said there was the Angel of Life, the Angel of Death, and then there was the Third Angel."

"I've heard of the two," Allie said.

"It was either the Angel of Life or the Angel of Death who would ride in the back of the car when my father went on house calls, but he never knew which one it was until he arrived at his destination. Even then he said he was often surprised. It was hard to tell the difference between the two sometimes."

They were drinking iced tea that Frieda had fixed. Allie could see the chimney of The Hedges, the house she and Paul should have been living in right now.

"And the third one?"

"Well, he's the most curious. You can't even tell if he's an angel or not. You think you're doing him a kindness, you think you're the one taking care of him, while all the while, he's the one who's saving your life."

Allie began to cry. She wished she was in the kitchen of The Hedges, trying her best to make a plum pie or cutting up apples for a tart. She wished Paul was on the couch, calling to her, making fun of her baking.

"We can't imagine the half of it," Frieda said. "The way he'll find us when we least expect it. The way he'll change our life."

"No, we can't," Allie said.

"I'm glad you decided to stay the night."

They went inside together; they washed the dishes, dried them, then put them away. Allie waited until she heard Frieda go up to her bedroom, then she turned off the lights. The birds were still singing at this late hour, confused by the long summer days. Allie waited at the window, hoping he would walk past on his way to wherever he was going. But she fell asleep in the chair, and when she woke the next morning and looked out across the yellow fields across the road, he was gone.

SHE STOOD ON the steps to the Orangery. It was her wedding day, the one they should have had. The gates to Kensington Palace had been opened, but the restaurant was still closed. Allie was wearing the white silk suit. There were a couple of robins on the grass. The hedges were so green they looked black. The sky was a pale summer blue with only a few high clouds. Their wedding day had seemed so distant once; now it was here. She had never canceled the reservations at the Ritz in Paris. They had train tickets for that afternoon. The tickets were in Allie's purse, along with her passport. Despite what she'd said and what she'd told herself, she'd been hopeful till the very end, just like the heron bride in the marsh, waiting for her beloved, convinced he would come back. Allie couldn't stop thinking of the way he'd looked in the hospital bed, curled up, so thin, under a white sheet and a hospital blanket. Today, the air was still and humid. The day would be brighter later on, but that didn't seem to matter. She was a widow.

Tourists had begun to arrive at the palace. There was a display of Diana's dresses, all of those beautiful clothes she'd worn. The inky blue silk dress she had danced in one night with a movie star as her partner. The pink bolero jacket covered with little mir-rored charms that she'd worn to India. A groundskeeper collect-ing trash stared rudely at Allie, puzzled to find her sitting on the patio of the shuttered restaurant in her silk suit, but he didn't say anything. Allie was trying to decide what to do next. The door to her life had closed. She was in her own future, alone. Nothing had turned out as she had expected.

She looked behind the hedges to the lawn. There was a woman walking toward her. Allie had telephoned and left a message at the desk of the Lion Park. She'd said she wanted her sister to come to the Orangery wearing her maid of honor dress. It was a good choice. It was the perfect dress. Maddy had walked all the way through the park. She sat down beside Allie. She didn't know what to say. She was shivering in the blue silk dress that she felt she had no right to wear.

"The view from here is beautiful, isn't it?" Allie said. They looked out over the lawn. At the end of her story, the heron was shot by poachers who thought he was nothing but a crow. His heron wife and his wife on earth mourned their husband together. Neither one could bear to be alone.

"I'm sorry," Maddy said. Tears were falling on her dress; she knew that once silk was wet it was ruined, but there was nothing she could do. "I'm so sorry. I did everything wrong."

There was a line forming at the entrance to Kensington Palace. The hedges gave off a peppery scent. Allie thought about the roses she had bought for Diana on the morning she met Paul, how perfect they'd been even in the summer heat. She thought of the day when she and Maddy tried to break the curse that was upon their mother. She'd never told Maddy that her secret word had been her sister's name.

"How do people go on living?" Allie said. "That's what I can't figure out."

"You're the one with courage."

"Me? Don't be an idiot. It was you. You were the one who climbed into that nest up in the tree. You were the one who did as you pleased. You telephoned that woman Dad was living with. I always did what I thought I was supposed to. Until it was too late."

"We should go look at Diana's dresses," Maddy suggested. "That would be a distraction."

"I've seen them," Allie said. "I know what they look like. I have a better idea."

They would visit Paris instead. Allie couldn't be talked out of it. They stopped at Maddy's hotel so she could get her passport and luggage, then went directly to Waterloo. In the taxi, Allie leaned her head back. She would buy clothes in Paris. Nothing that belonged to her seemed irreplaceable. If it was indeed true that you could read something backward or forward, she had chosen her direction. Both her mother and Paul's would understand.

"Are you sure you don't want to change your mind?" Maddy said when they got to the station. "I wouldn't blame you."

Allie remembered what the doctor in the hospital had told her. Love had nothing to do with the here and now. That's what Frieda meant when she said it was simple to love Paul, no matter how complicated he might be. You didn't have to think about it, you just did it.

"You're the only one who understands how I feel," she told her sister.

At Waterloo, Allie settled herself on a bench while Maddy went to call her parents' hotel. They were leaving that afternoon and Maddy had planned to travel home with them. She'd bought her ticket to New York and it was nonrefundable. She'd never get her money back now. Not that it mattered.

"Do you know how frightened we've been?" Lucy said when she answered. "We've been beside ourselves. We're supposed to leave for the airport in an hour and we couldn't find either one of you girls. We phoned the police."

"Don't worry," Maddy said. She had to shout to be heard. "We're safe. As soon as we're through traveling, we'll come home."

And then it was time to leave. There was a crush of people; the weekend was going to be lovely and no one wanted to miss the opportunity to spend the last few summer days in France. Luckily a porter helped Allie and Maddy find their seats just as the train left the station. In no time they were going more than 250 kilometers an hour. Through the window there were streaks of landscape in blue and black and green. They could see the blur of London that they were leaving behind.

They were comfortable in their wedding clothes. Silk was perfect for any sort of weather; it wore well for traveling. They didn't dwell on the past; instead they talked about people who were on their train. They made up stories about them, and once they started they simply couldn't stop. They guessed who was in love and whose heart had been broken, who had committed murder, and who had saved a life.

11.

Lion Park

1966

Everything was yellow in the park. When it rained, leaves came swirling down. When it was sunny everything looked golden. Frieda Lewis was nineteen and had been working for four months at the Lion Park Hotel in Knightsbridge. Her favorite rooms to clean were the ones on the seventh floor. From there, she could look out the windows in the back and see the little courtyard park with its stone lion. From the front rooms she could see the tops of the trees in Hyde Park. Once she climbed onto the ledge and stood there for a moment, above the traffic and the fumes, mesmerized by the movement of the trees and of the clouds in the sky. Brompton Road seemed as if it was part of a child's game, with tiny cars set out in a row. Then all at once, Frieda felt light-headed and she had to back in through the window. Her head was pounding, but she felt exhilarated, too. She had the feeling that something special was in store for her, a miracle of some sort, something amazing and unexpected. She might be working as a maid in a London hotel, but that wasn't who she was inside.

She was a headstrong girl whose parents believed that she had ruined her chances at life. She had passed her A-levels but had decided that she wanted a real life, and by that she didn't mean marriage and babies. She didn't want anything ordinary. And she certainly didn't want the life her father planned for her. He was a doctor in Reading, and he thought he knew what was best for everyone. If anything, she wanted the opposite, a life that would make her father cringe, that would hurt him. She had even considered that poetry might be her calling. She had something inside her no one understood, that much was certain, and that sort of isolation often led to a poet's life.

Frieda had broken up with her sweetheart, Bill, who had assumed she would marry him. Well, everyone made assumptions, didn't they? Everyone thought they knew her when they knew nothing at all. She had wanted a bigger life, something spectacular, and now here she was in London, much to her parents' dismay down in Reading. She was a small-town girl who desperately wanted a big-city life. That's the story of a mouse, her father had told her. Not of a bright, talented woman who should be in university.

Frieda's parents might think she was wild, but she was

nothing compared to most of the girls at the Lion Park. Everyone was young and wanted to have a good time. They all wore thick black eyeliner and looked like a horde of Cleopatras when they went out en masse. They dressed in miniskirts or blue jeans with hoop earrings and high boots and they all smoked too much. The girls who worked at the hotel were given rooms on the second floor; the worst rooms had three or four girls crowded into them, but even those were fine. They held impromptu parties every night and went to concerts and clubs in a lovely, giddy group. They frequented the restaurant Cassarole on the King's Road and went to the Chelsea Antiques Market looking for old silk underwear and Victorian blouses ribbed with satin. They traded clothes. Nearly all of the girls had worn Frieda's black dress, bought for eighteen hard-earned pounds at Biba in Kensington, a dress so short you had to hold it down with both hands when exiting a taxi. Katy Horace had managed to snag Mick Jagger for a night while wearing that dress—well, maybe it was only an hour or so, but all the same it was Mick, or so she said, and it was the dress that had got to him.

The Lion Park was known for its reckless clientele—people in the music world, poets with bad reputations, men in love with other men, women who had left their husbands, drummers on tour who practiced all night and drove people mad by pounding on the furniture, girls who were thinking about suicide, couples who couldn't decide if they loved each other or wanted to kill each other. The hotel was a bit seedy—the furniture was scuffed, the carpet was worn—but it was possible to have privacy here. They said the Lion Park was much like the Chelsea Hotel in New York; as long as you didn't outright murder anyone in your room, anything went. You could be a vampire, for all the management cared, as long as you paid your tab on time.

On nights when a famous guest was in residence, there were often dozens of girls waiting outside, screaming at the sight of any long-haired young man. The neighbors complained about the groupies, but what could they do? Freedom of speech included freedom to scream, didn't it? When the noise got bad, and the fans spilled onto the street, the authorities were called, but mostly the night porter, Jack Henry, took care of the crowds. Jack Henry joked that he'd had more sex by promising groupies he'd get them in to see some other man than he'd had in all the rest of his life. The girls who worked at the Lion Park thought him a dirty old man, though he was probably not much more than thirty. Jack surely had his flaws, but he could be depended on to keep his mouth shut. For the right tip, he could get a guest most anything: a gorgeous woman, a doctor who wouldn't report a drug overdose, bottles of absinthe or Seconals, and, most importantly, discretion.

For instance, no one, not even the girls who worked at the hotel, knew that Jamie Dunn was staying on the seventh floor. But of course not many people had heard of him yet. He wasn't much of anything, not really famous, just an American singer who had signed a record deal. He had come to the U.K. for a few concert dates, all of which had been a disaster. He had a reedy, angelic voice and people complained they couldn't hear him. Audiences wanted electricity; even Dylan had gone for it. Jamie knew he had to get a band together and make some noise. And he needed his own material. That's what the executives had told him at his record company, or at least they were his company at the moment, if he gave them what they wanted, if they didn't ax him the way they did a thousand other talented, hopeful young men.

Now Jamie was holed up in room 708, trying, and failing, to write. After two days he stopped eating and started in on some serious drinking; that was how his binges always began. Like Rimbaud, he had to burn to create, but he burned without brilliance and he knew it. He just got drunker. He was six foot three and only 165 pounds, so in a matter of days he looked gaunt. His hotel room was a mess. Overflowing ashtrays, cups of coffee, dirty laundry on the floor. He'd stopped showering while he tried to write—even soap and water were possible distractions. He had his long hair tied back with a leather band. He had great bone structure thanks to a heritage that included a Cree Indian and Ukrainian grandmother along with a half-Irish, half-Italian grandfather. His mother was a Polish Jew. His was a New York City heritage, a little of everything. He hadn't cut his hair for four years. He made women swoon without even saying anything. He believed in signs, symbols, luck, fortune—all of it. His bad leg? It meant he was made for something different. The pain he always had? Proof that ordinary life was not for him. If not for his leg, he'd be in Vietnam. He'd probably be dead and gone by now.

Most of all, he believed in vows. Now he made a pact with himself that if he could write one perfect song, he'd cut off his hair. He'd make a sacrifice of himself and burn his hair on the hotplate he'd had housekeeping bring up. He'd annihilate the part of him that was so weak he often went to bed for weeks at a time when he couldn't create, when the world was just too much for him to bear.

He'd been weak as a boy, born with a defect in his hip, and had had several operations before the time he was twelve. He'd grown up in pain, spending months at a time in Queens County Hospital; even when he was discharged, he wore a metal brace that had been strapped on so tightly he still had the marks on his skin. When he ran his hand over his leg he felt a line of indentations reminding him of what he had suffered and what he now deserved as reparation. Other boys had made his life hell at school. He hated his own flesh and blood and bones. Most of all, he hated the pain. He'd taken Demerol and morphine all through his youth, then had progressed to street drugs in high school. He favored heroin, and he looked forward to shooting up more than anything. He was in love with the moment before and the moment during. He had his best ideas then, if only he could remember them. His notebooks were filled with scribbles he couldn't understand. Thank God he could function in a vacuum and was able to ignore the noise in the hotel, trained to do so by a childhood spent with three brothers who were endlessly fighting. On his first night in London, there had been a brawl out in the hallway just as he was getting down to work. It felt like home. No problem. Jamie ignored it, exactly as he had ignored his brothers. He'd always been his mother's favorite, set apart; he didn't feel much of anything watching his brothers beat each other. He didn't even take sides.

When it got to be too much he yelled, "Shut the fuck up." He pounded on the wall behind his bed and soon enough the racket had stopped.

It had happened again the next night. It sounded like the same exact argument, but then his brothers had fought over the same things for years. Jamie happened to be drunker that night so he raced into the hall with a lamp he'd grabbed to use as a weapon. But once he was standing there wearing only his torn jeans, Jamie didn't find anyone out there but a startled maid who'd been turning down the beds in the rooms. The girl had long brown hair and huge eyes and she looked like an angel out there in the hall. She was so pure and beautiful it was difficult to look at her and not feel humble. It was one of those moments Jamie would have liked to write about, if only he could write.

"Sorry," Jamie said. He realized he might look quite threatening, unwashed and tall, limping around and holding the lamp like a spear. He might, in fact, appear to be a lunatic. "I'm hearing things. I think I'm going insane."

"We have a ghost," the girl said. "Or so they say."

It was Frieda. The other girls had all warned her about room 707. Guests hardly ever stayed through the night there; they usually checked out and demanded their money back. Supposedly, someone had killed his rival in that room. No one knew the whole story, but it was definitely cold in there when you turned down the bed. Occasionally there'd be a guest who'd specifically request 707, usually a writer looking for inspiration, or a guitarist or drummer who wanted to prove his courage by spending the night in a haunted room while getting good and drunk.

"Not that I believe in ghosts," Frieda went on to say, "although it's possible that some sort of vibration could emanate from the ether."

Jamie laughed. "Well that explains everything. Just my luck. I'm fucking haunted."

"It's the hotel, not you." Frieda could see behind Jamie

when she peered through his door, which had been left ajar. His room was in bad shape. She'd noticed the Do Not Disturb sign on for several days. If Frieda wasn't mistaken she saw a plume of smoke. She hoped he wasn't about to burn the hotel down to the ground. "Do you want your bed turned down?"

"My room is turned upside down already. That ghost ruined my concentration, damn it. Come have a drink. I need some company. Alive company."

Frieda laughed. "What, now?"

"You might work here, but they don't own you, do they? You're not a fucking slave, are you?"

That was the sort of challenge that always got to Frieda. It was weird that this fellow sensed her antiauthoritarian streak. Not many people knew that about her. She looked like a proper Goody Two-shoes; in fact, she was anything but. She had turned in one of her teachers at school for using stray cats for their biology lab, then had gone back, climbed in through the window of the schoolhouse, and set all the cats free. Several of them had followed her home; that was how she'd been caught and given a week's suspension from classes. The headmaster had driven by and spied the cats lounging in the grass outside her house. "We didn't think you were that sort of girl," the headmaster had told her, but she was then and she still was now.

Frieda followed Jamie inside precisely because she shouldn't. He went to open the window first thing. The room was acrid and smoky.

"I know it stinks in here. Sorry. Whisky all right?" Jamie pulled on a T-shirt. He was extremely handsome, better looking than Mick Jagger. There was a purple suede jacket thrown over the bureau and several pairs of socks littered about. A half-eaten order of fish and chips had leaked grease onto the bureau. Frieda's mother had been a cleanliness fanatic; if she saw this room she'd probably have a stroke. Mrs. Lewis had spent her whole life making their house perfect, cooking lovely dinners, not letting a dish sit in the sink, and what had it gotten her? Absolutely nothing, in Frieda's opinion.

Frieda nodded. "Whisky's fine." She had been in nasty rooms before, but this really was the worst. Not that she minded. "Did you have a riot in here?" she asked.

"Sorry. I've been working round the clock. I seriously don't know what day it is. Am I saying 'sorry' a lot?"

Jamie quickly made up the bed. He wasn't very good at it. He threw a blanket over everything.

"Working at what?" Frieda said as he handed her a glass of whisky. The glass wasn't particularly clean but Frieda had read that alcohol killed all germs. You could pour it on a wound, for instance, if you had no other antiseptic. Frieda was a very quick drunk, one drink and kerplunk, she could easily find herself on the floor. So she took a tiny sip. She shivered as the whisky burned her throat. She felt very daring and grown-up.

"I'm a songwriter," Jamie said. "When I write I make a mess. I forget the outside world."

Poets were known for such things, and Frieda didn't count any of it as a mark against Jamie. He had more important matters to think about than the details of the corporeal world. She noticed the guitar propped up against the wall. There was sheet music scattered around. She knew famous people stayed at the Lion Park, but unlike Katy and some of the other girls, she'd never actually met one in the flesh. The odd thing about Jamie was that she felt as though she'd known him for a long time. She wasn't uncomfortable with him at all. It was probably the poet inside her that bonded them.

"Sing something," Frieda said.

"What'll you give me in return?" Jamie grinned at her. He couldn't help himself with women; seduction came easily to him. He thought it was from those years in the hospital, flirting with nurses as a boy, needing their kindness so desperately. He was charming, he knew, and he used his charm to his benefit. Otherwise he'd still be at home in Queens. He had one brother who worked as a cook in a diner, another who was in the army serving in Vietnam, and the third lived in his mother's basement and took odd jobs, or so he said. No one had actually seen him work. They all resented Jamie. The called him a lucky bastard and a selfish prick, not that Jamie cared. If someone wanted to fault him for using what he had, they could go right ahead. He wasn't going to sit still and let the world walk over him when all he had to do was smile to get what he wanted. Smile and come up with a song.

"I'll give you a song title," Frieda said. She had a million ideas. She didn't even have to try; ideas just came to her. She was always thinking up movie plots and stories for books and ads for TV. Her old boyfriend, Bill, had called her a dreamer, but Frieda couldn't stop thinking. Her head was filled with ideas. "Once you have a title, the rest is supposed to flow. Or so I've read."

Jamie poured himself another drink. He knew what he had been missing. A muse. Someone who could inspire him. That was why he was in a rut and couldn't write a damn thing. Frieda was wearing the white smock all the maids wore while on duty. It made Jamie think of snow and of purity. She looked like a nurse, a hot one. She looked like an angel on his bed. She wasn't his type, but she was very sweet and honest. The opposite of Jamie.

Jamie himself had done some evil things, but not on purpose. He'd been driven to self-interest by his desire for fame, and, of course, by drugs. When he was a boy, he thought about ways he would get out. Not just out of the hospital; he wanted a way out of his life. His mother always said that she had known as soon as he could walk, he'd be through the door. He would lie, steal, cheat, he would put himself above all others, but he would get out.

"All right," Jamie said to Frieda. He found her fresh and interesting. Most girls were tongue-tied around him. When they did manage to speak, he found they didn't have much to say. "Fine. Let's see if it works that way. What's your title?"

Frieda didn't even have to think. Her ideas came to her fully formed.

"'The Ghost of Michael Macklin.'"

Jamie laughed. "That's a far-out title."

"He's the ghost across the hall. The one you think you hear. He died of love. I don't know how exactly, but love was allegedly the cause."

"'The Ghost of Michael Macklin.'" Jamie let it roll around in his head.

"'It's a great title and you know it. Now you owe me! Just one song. You have to sing!'"

Jamie sang to her then, not his own composition, none of those were ready yet—they really weren't very good—but a song he knew most women were suckers for: "Greensleeves."

He didn't know why that song spoke to women so deeply, but it did; several women had fallen in love with him when he sang it. It was something about the desperation of it all; being done wrong was romantic in some weird way that made a woman melt. He could see that it was happening right now in the way that Frieda was looking at him. Her open mouth; her utter concentration. It was so easy to win a woman over, it gave him a charge. Plus she was pretty, and different, and smart. Jamie felt a little awkward because he had a girlfriend. Well, actually a serious girlfriend. That was the other reason he was in London. He sometimes forgot about that. He was getting married.

When he was done, Frieda applauded. "Well, I don't know about your songs, but you have an amazing voice. An absolute ten."

"Really?" Jamie was surprised by her no-nonsense ways. He was full of himself, but he was vulnerable and filled with self-hate as well. He often felt like chucking it all and wondered if everything he did was crap. Somehow when this girl said something, he believed it.

"Totally gorgeous. Soulful. Better than Mick Jagger."

"You don't know Jagger," Jamie said.

"Let's just say that he couldn't say no to my black dress the other night."

She felt insane to be saying a thing like that. She'd merely wanted to seem desirable to Jamie. She had no experience with anyone resembling a rock star in any way. Frieda's ex-boyfriend, Bill, was nothing like Mick Jagger, other than the fact that they were both human beings. Bill was at university in Reading studying chemistry. He worked part-time in a lab researching cancer cells. But Frieda didn't feel anything she was saying to

Jamie was a lie. She felt different being with him here in his room drinking whisky and sitting on his bed, like the wild girl her parents thought she was. Someone Mick Jagger might have made a pass at.

"Really? Mick, huh?" Jamie didn't believe her for a second. She wasn't the sort of girl who would have slept with one of the Rolling Stones. She was the type to fall into everlasting love. Jamie knew she was hoping to impress him. He tried not to laugh. He had an uncanny way of knowing the truth about someone, even though he often didn't know the truth about himself.

"Well, I wasn't the one wearing the dress," Frieda admitted. "But I've worn it since."

"Sex by association." Jamie grinned. She certainly wasn't the typical maid. She seemed more like a college student. "If I want to catch up to Mick, I've got to start writing songs— otherwise my deal with the record company means crap. I've got to at least give them an A side and a B side for a single, pronto."

"All you need is a little help, and your songs will pour out of you. You've got a great title already. That's half of it, isn't it?"

Frieda finished her drink and got ready to leave. She had gulped her whisky a little more quickly than she'd planned; now she was tipsy. She still had a dozen or more beds to turn down.

"Wait a minute," Jamie said. "What about my song? I thought you were going to help me?"

"I dare you to finish it by the morning," Frieda said. She knew that some people responded to ultimatums and challenges. She did, after all. Tell her she couldn't do something, and she'd have it accomplished in no time. Just like those cats she'd set free from the biology classroom; because of that there were now dozens of cats wandering around the house where she grew up. They lived out in the fields and were decimating the rabbit population. Sometimes she forgot about consequences.

"Okay. Fine." Jamie saluted her. He seemed lit up by the challenge; it was as though no one had ever dared him to work hard at something before. Frieda saw what people meant by charisma, it was almost as if he had no control over it. He was the sort of person who drew you in; she felt sure that as soon as she walked away from him everything would be much darker and less interesting.

"You really think I can do it?" Jamie said.

It was the real him for an instant, and Frieda felt more drawn in, more bonded, poet to poet.

"How about if I come back tomorrow night and if you haven't finished, I get that purple jacket. Then you'll have something at stake."

"Fine," Jamie agreed. "You're on. But what do I get if I win?"

"A song," Frieda said. "A brilliant side A or B."

Jamie turned on the look that had always gotten him what he wanted from the nurses. "More," he said.

"Not enough?" Frieda was flustered. "A kiss," she threw in. "Maybe," she added, even though she realized she was dying to kiss him.

Jamie might have written the song he'd promised her, but at eleven o'clock Stella phoned him, and he could never say no to a woman, especially one he was set to marry. He grabbed his jacket and pulled on his boots and went down to the lobby. The porter called him a taxi. He'd written two lines before Stella had called. *When I'm with you, I'm always yours. I belong to you.* It sounded like a lie to him.

"Don't do anything I wouldn't do," the porter, Jack Henry, said as Jamie got into the cab. Jamie thought he must look suspicious.

The taxi took him to Kensington, where Stella's parents lived. They were off somewhere on a holiday, so Stella and her sister, Marianne, had the place to themselves. How anyone could trust them, Jamie had no idea. Even he was more trustworthy than those two girls. They were the wildest of the wild, always together, always in trouble. Jamie could have been staying in Kensington right along with the sisters, living in luxury instead of in a third-rate hotel with no room service, but he and Stella fought so often he knew he wouldn't be able to write in the Kensington house. He probably should have stayed at the Lion Park that night as well and gotten to work on his song and won his kiss from Frieda, but instead he knocked on Stella's parents' door. The Ridge family was rich, extremely so, and Stella was beautiful. She was everything a man could want, particularly if a man was looking to self-destruct. She was all wrong for Jamie. They were too much alike. Fire and fire. Not a good mix. The kind of thing that led to immolation and disaster. Stella was definitely no one's muse. She was too self-centered, and needy, and gorgeous. And there was one other thing about Stella that was an utter negative: She was addicted to heroin.

"You're always at that crappy hotel," Stella said when she opened the door for him. "Maybe you're having an affair.

Maybe that's why you're spending so much time there. We're getting married. We should be together."

"Shut up. I'm over there trying to write. It's not any fun."

"Shouldn't it be?" Stella asked. "I thought you were supposed to enjoy the creative act. And you shut up."

"Since you know so much about creative acts, why don't you do something?"

"I am a creative act in and of myself." Stella smiled beautifully.

They went into the parlor together. Marianne and her boyfriend Nick were in there, snorting heroin. They were all rich except for Jamie. Jamie was the odd man out, and that's why they adored him. They thought he was real and they thought he was funny and when he was famous he'd get them invited to parties in Hollywood. They probably wouldn't have cared if they knew he took money from their wallets and purses, which he did on a regular basis. Money meant nothing to them and quite a lot to him.

Jamie often thought about his mother, who always worried about him and was probably sitting in her apartment in Astoria, Queens, worrying about him right now. She used to make him wear a hat and gloves to school even though everyone already made fun of him because of the brace on his leg. He looked like a monster; he actually scared some of the little kids as he clumped down the halls of the school. He thought about the way his mom had sat by his bedside during his recoveries. She loved him and he'd been a thankless child, except for one thing: His mom's dream was for him to be ambitious, and that he was. She dreamed he would succeed, and he sure as hell wasn't going to fail.

Stella and Marianne's mother, on the other hand, had never changed a diaper. Stella had told him that one night; she'd actually had tears in her eyes, and Stella was most certainly not a crier. Their mother had been depressed and she'd traveled most of the time. That early neglect was probably the reason the girls now felt they were entitled to anything they wanted. Jamie felt sorry for Stella even though she had everything; he understood why she tried her best to be a bitch.

The first time Jamie had come to the house it was to be introduced to the parents, Daisy and Hamlin Ridge. He hadn't understood he'd been invited in order to torment them, but he realized that soon enough, as soon as Mrs. Ridge looked at him. She was a tall, elegant woman and she instantly despised him.

"This is your boyfriend?" she said. "He doesn't look famous to me."

"Nice to meet you, too," Jamie countered. He liked to disarm people, come up from behind and win them over, but that didn't seem to be happening with Daisy Ridge. She was made of stern stuff.

The father, Hamlin, had wandered off to read the paper.

"She's only with you because she knows I won't approve," Mrs. Ridge told Jamie. "You realize that."

"I appreciate your honesty," Jamie said.

"How rude can you be?" Stella said to her mother.

Daisy shrugged. "At least he appreciates my honesty. Whisky?" she asked Jamie.

"Definitely." He nodded.

"You are not taking anything she offers you," Stella told Jamie.

"Let's go," Marianne had called from the hall. The sisters

always protected each other and Marianne especially hated scenes. She knew how upset Stella could get. "Nick's expecting us."

"Nick's fine because he has money and he isn't a Jew," Stella said to her mother. "Isn't that true?"

Hamlin looked up from his paper, mildly interested.

"Good for you. You managed to snag your father's attention with the Jew comment," Daisy said to her daughter. She handed Jamie his whisky. "Do you think you'll be good for my daughter?"

"Let's just get out of here," Stella had said to Jamie, who would have preferred to finish his drink. "She doesn't give a damn about Marianne or me. Never has, never will."

"Let's go, let's go," Marianne called. She had the driver waiting for them. She was wearing a pale lemon-colored fur coat.

Mrs. Ridge grabbed Jamie's arm as he went to leave. Surprised, he turned to her.

"Don't hurt her," she said, for his ears alone. "I mean it."

In the back of the car, Stella had snorted some heroin that was laid out in a line on a magazine balanced on her knees. "I don't think our mother ever even touched us. She had better things to do. More important things."

"She was damaged," Marianne put in. "Very fucked-up history. Love and death. That kind of thing."

"Everyone's damaged. That's no excuse," Stella countered. "Look at Jamie," she teased. "How much more fucked-up can you get?"

He pinched her and Stella grinned at him. Of course he would hurt her. That was the point.

"Our mother lost her twin sister," Marianne explained. "She was in love, and she killed herself because the fellow didn't love her back, and the fellow was actually Dad if you can believe it."

"Wasn't Mum lucky?" Stella said. "She won the prize. Hamlin Ridge."

Stella's father had business in New York, and that's where Jamie and Stella had first met, at a party. It was ridiculous that they knew the same person, but then again that person dealt drugs, so maybe it all made sense. Everyone was equal in the eyes of his or her drug dealer; a dollar sign and nothing more.

Stella had been back to New York twice after their first meeting, staying at Jamie's tiny apartment in Chelsea. She loved New York. She was a city girl. She could score drugs wherever she went. When it turned out the guy they both knew who'd had the party got busted, Stella assured Jamie there was nothing to worry about. They took a taxi to East Tenth Street and Jamie waited in the cab while she scored. That was their official first date, and his first time shooting heroin. He'd only snorted or smoked it before. It was like Demerol, but faster, better, clearer somehow. Using made them fall in love with each other. Blood mixed with blood, they became one person. They started to talk about what life would be like when they were married. Then they started to talk about wedding dates, even though Stella's parents would have a fit. Maybe because of it. Jamie was a musician, a Catholic, and a Jew. Add heroin addict to that and Stella had found the man who would cause her parents the most distress. He was the perfect nightmare, a drug-addicted musician who did not eat meat on Friday and had the genetics of the ghetto. What could be better, more delicious, more powerfully painful? They would tell her she was throwing her life away, which is precisely what they did, but it was her life and she could destroy it any way she wanted to. Besides, Stella loved showing Jamie off; he was so beautiful and so on the edge of ruin. Everything she wasn't supposed to have, all in one dish.

On the evening when the Ridges were away and the town house was fair game, Jamie sat down on the rug after saying hello to Marianne and her boyfriend. He leaned his head down and snorted the line of heroin Nick had set out for him. He felt so much better here than he did at the crappy Lion Park Hotel, where he couldn't write even a single verse. What the hell was he thinking? He could write a song in half an hour if he wanted to; sometime the next week would surely be soon enough. Even his hip felt good now that he was here and getting high, or it felt nothing, which was the same as good. Better.

Stella lay down on the floor with her head in his lap. She had very blond hair. She was almost invisible she was so blond. She was like a hot piece of snow. Gorgeous and hard to hold on to. She felt unloved and angry and sometimes she cried in her sleep. Jamie felt as though they had been brought together by fate, even though they would probably drive each other crazy in the end. He thought about the maid in the hotel telling him he could write a song if he worked all night. Stella would never tell him anything like that. She'd never had to work at anything and she didn't think he should either. In so many ways, it was a relief to be with her.

"Let's have a bath," Stella said. "You stink."

"Yeah, sure. You run it," Jamie said. "Put in bubbles."

"You do it," Stella said. "I'm not your geisha, you bastard."

"Spoiled brat." Jamie grinned.

Since it was true, and since calling her on such matters was the reason she was with him in the first place, Stella stood up and pulled Jamie to his feet. All her other boyfriends had done exactly what she told them to do. They were boring. Sometimes she thought she could drive Jamie to hit her if he found out about some of the things she did when he wasn't around. She wasn't about to drop all of the men in her life until she was actually married. She wasn't about to end up like her mother, stuck with somebody who didn't even look up from the paper when she spoke to him. A battle was better than that; someone willing to fight.

Stella and Jamie went upstairs, up the curvy staircase with the chestnut newel posts and banisters. Even the ceiling was wood. They went to the bedroom and pushed open the engraved gold-and-white door. There was more woodwork in the house than Jamie had ever seen.

Jamie lay on the big bed while Stella ran a bath. There was a feather quilt and so many pillows that the whole bed seemed made of feathers. Jamie could smell citrus and jasmine; Stella smelled like that. It was a perfume she ordered from France. There was a green-tinted light coming in through the arched windows that faced a small park across the street. Lying there in the pillow bed, surrounded by feathers and jasmine, Jamie had a moment of total well-being. No pain whatsoever. He wondered if this was what it was like to be dead and gone. He almost rose out of his body; he could feel his spirit pulling away, but he willed himself back before he nodded out. He watched the shadows of the ivy outside that were cast across the ceiling. He was so happy not to be in the life he used to have.

Jamie was asleep when Stella came out to get him, so she

took her bath alone. She stayed in the hot, oily water until it was cold, so cold she was shivering, and the ends of her blond hair had turned green from the bath salts. She was the difficult sister and Marianne was the easygoing one; it had always been that way, their mother had said, as if she knew the first thing about Stella. Jamie was still asleep when Stella got into bed, which meant she didn't have to have sex with him. It meant she could pretend he was everything that she wanted and she was everything that he needed, that in the long run it was going to all turn out perfectly.

AT MIDNIGHT FRIEDA woke in her room on the second floor. She shared a room with two other girls who also worked at the hotel—Lennie Watt and Katy Horace—but they were still asleep. A fight was going on out on the street and the raised voices of drunken men had awoken her. Frieda went to the window. There was Jack Henry tossing out one of the regulars. Frieda noticed that Jack was going through the other man's wallet, taking out the cash before replacing the wallet in the gentleman's coat. Jack Henry was a rat, just as Frieda suspected. She was a good judge of character. Well, usually, at any rate. One of her roommates, that sharp girl named Lennie, had woken, too. Lennie's mum had worked in the hotel when she was a girl, and Lennie's older sister, Meg, managed the front desk. It was wise to be on Meg Watt's good side, as she made up the maids' schedules and assigned hours. She favored her sister and now she favored Frieda as well.

"That's Teddy Healy," Lennie said of the man passed out on

the pavement. "You don't want to have anything to do with him. I heard he killed somebody once."

Frieda sniffed. "I don't believe that."

"Well, he was responsible for something awful. Meg told me."

"Even so, we can't just leave him out there, can we?"

Perhaps because she'd often gone with her father on his visits to patients, Frieda had inherited some of his concern for those in need. She and Lennie decided to sneak downstairs to see if the poor fellow on the pavement was conscious. That was the least a person could do. They pulled raincoats on over their nightgowns and crept down the stairs. They felt like schoolgirls out on a lark and they couldn't stop giggling. If they got caught they'd be in trouble—the management fined girls who broke the rules and the manager, a Greek fellow named Ajax, had no sense of humor—but luckily that dreadful Jack Henry was having a cigarette as the barman closed up the lounge. They wouldn't have to bribe him in return for his silence.

"You keep watch," Frieda said.

She went outside while Lennie remained in the doorway. Teddy Healy was in a heap beside the building. The night was surprisingly cold. Frieda hunkered down.

"Hello?" she said softly. There was no answer. "I'm going to take your pulse," she said.

Frieda reached for Mr. Healy's wrist, somewhat surprised that she knew what she was doing. She had, after all, seen her father do this countless times. Frieda counted for a minute. Seventy. That was acceptable. There was some blood on Healy's head, but no real wounds. When Frieda had gone on house calls with her father she'd been his helper; she'd looked forward to it. She had loved him dearly until he'd left her mother. She'd been a daddy's girl, she'd had no time for her mother, but he'd left them both for some other woman. When she thought about the ways in which she had disappointed her father she got a little teary, but he'd disappointed her first. That was the start of it all, the way her life had changed around. One day she'd decided she was going to London. She was not going to consider his feelings anymore.

What do we have here? That's what her father would say whenever he walked into a patient's home, no matter the circumstances, be it a terminal illness or a broken arm or a case of gastric flu. Dr. Lewis wore two wristwatches, so he would never be late. People who are ill don't have time to wait around, he'd told Frieda. If his patient was a child, he often let them play with one of the watches during the examination. Now you've got a handle on time, he would say.

"Sir, can you hear me?" Frieda asked the man on the sidewalk. "I'm going to call an ambulance for you if you don't answer." Always make sure the individual is conscious. Ask them their name and the date. "Sir, do you know what today is?"

Teddy Healy muttered something. At least he was alive.

"Do you hear me?" Frieda repeated. "You need to answer me, sir."

"Go away," Teddy Healy said. "Leave me the hell alone."

"The date?"

"Friday, damn it."

"Good enough. Stand up," Frieda said. "I'll help."

He was a man in his forties, Frieda's father's age, and Frieda felt a little foolish helping him to his feet. What do we have here? her father would have said. A drunk on a bender? A man who's lost? A case of liver damage?

"Hurry up," Lennie hissed from the doorway. "We're going to get caught."

Frieda signaled to a passing taxi, then helped Teddy over when the cab pulled up.

"Do you know where you live?" she asked.

"Very funny," Teddy Healy said. "Who said I'm alive?"

"You seem alive. Your pulse is fine, but you'll give yourself serious liver damage if you keep up the drinking."

"I wish I could change places with that ghost."

Frieda felt a chill. Lennie said he was murderer. Maybe she'd been right. "What ghost?" she asked.

Teddy Healy opened his eyes. When he looked at her, Frieda saw something a young girl shouldn't see. Pure panic. Maybe he was a murderer or maybe he wasn't; either way he was a desperate man. All of a sudden Frieda felt frightened of what was inside this person. She wondered how her father managed to deal with his patients' fears and their secrets. Perhaps he tried his best to avoid such things and treat only the matter at hand—the broken bone, the aching back—leaving the darker areas for someone else, a teacher or a therapist or a priest.

The taxi driver helped Frieda get Teddy into the cab. Frieda looked through his wallet and found his address. She also found a photograph of a woman with blond hair who stared straight into the camera. She looked washed out, faded; she was disappearing even though she was beautiful.

There was no cash. Frieda took what little she had in her coat pocket and handed it over.

"I'll get him home," the driver promised. "No worries."

Frieda ran back into the hotel. Then she and Lennie raced back upstairs, laughing, holding hands.

"You're crazy," Lennie said. "How could you touch him?"

"My father's a doctor," Frieda said. "I've seen lots worse."

"Well, that explains how you dealt with him. It just doesn't explain what you're doing at the Lion Park."

The third girl in their room, Katy, had never woken up. She'd been the one who had borrowed Frieda's dress, who'd supposedly snagged Mick Jagger. They called her Mrs. Jagger behind her back, or Mick's girl; nobody really believed her.

"I saw what you did and you shouldn't have paid for his taxi," Lennie said. "You're a soft touch."

"You would have done the same," Frieda said.

"Like hell I would." Lennie pulled back her blanket and got into bed. "I take care of number one. That's me and no one else."

Frieda got into bed as well, but she didn't go to sleep. She took a pen and a notepad from her night-table drawer. Frieda jotted down some random words. Then she looked at them, crossed out a few, and began writing some more. She could hear Lennie's breathing grow slow as she fell asleep; she could hear Katy turning to the wall. As she listened to them, Frieda wrote about a man in a black coat walking down a long, endless hallway, and a beautiful woman with long, pale hair. She wrote about a hotel where guests never left and about the kind of love that lasted long after death. She wrote for hours without knowing time had passed. She was perspiring so much her nightgown had turned damp. Her scalp and her hair were soaked. Her heart was racing. She needed more paper so she could go on writing; she went to the bureau for a piece of the cream-colored stationery she used for writing letters. At the top of the page she printed THE GHOST OF MICHAEL MACKLIN, then she rewrote the messy crossed-out thing she'd begun on the notepad.

At last, exhausted, Frieda stored what she had written in her night-table drawer. She lay down in bed, but she couldn't close her eyes. She was far too excited. She felt as though the words had come through her; poetry at last. Something, a force of some sort, had made her write them down and had strung them together and she had merely been a conduit. While her roommates slept, Frieda had been somewhere else entirely. She had left and come back, and no one had noticed that she'd been gone.

IN THE MORNING there was a hum in the hotel, the kind that occurred when someone famous was around. Supposedly John Lennon had checked in. People said he wanted a place to escape to; therefore, if anyone saw him they were supposed to act like he wasn't there. Ajax, the hotel manager, gave the girls a stern lecture; they were employees, serious people, not screaming fans like the hordes of girls posted outside. Maids were not to speak unless spoken to, at the risk of being fired. That was what the Lion Park was all about, after all. Privacy. Double fines were in place.

Frieda wasn't working till the evening, so she went out for a walk. It was good to get away from the groupies who were making such a racket. Frieda hadn't had much sleep; she kept thinking about the drunk man on the concrete and about her poem. She supposed she had written a song. It was probably no good at all, and yet it made her feel the way "Greensleeves" did. That must mean something. She was wearing her black dress and black boots and she'd made up her eyes with Lennie's eyeliner. She felt like crying for Michael Macklin, the character in her song, yet she didn't know the first thing about him. She'd sort of made him up, after all.

Frieda sat down on a wooden bench in a small garden. She loved the way London smelled; the air trembled and seemed alive. Although the leaves were yellow, the weather was still fine. It was an enclosed garden she'd stumbled upon, the sort that made a person imagine she was truly in the countryside. Country girls were sometimes drawn to country spaces, despite their desire for a taste of city life. Frieda could barely hear the traffic through the hedges even though she was so close to Brompton Road that the bench she sat upon rattled with the vibrations from the passing traffic. She should be sitting in lectures at the university in Reading right now. The truth was, her father had always thought she would make a good doctor. She had what it took, Dr. Lewis said. Blood and illness didn't frighten her. And she asked questions whenever she went on house calls with him. That was a good sign. A questioning mind. She didn't even seem to be afraid of death. She accepted it as a natural part of our lives. That was the only way to manage a life in medicine. No hysterics, no regrets, just acceptance that all things end, if not now, then at some point in time.

One night when Frieda was fifteen her father had been called to a home in a nearby village. They'd gone over a little toll bridge where they'd had to pay the toll man two shillings.

There were willow trees all along the river, their branches grazing the water. Darkness was falling, and the hedges were so tall it was difficult to see any of the houses. Frieda loved riding in the car with her father. She had absolutely no fear of the dark.

When we ride we ride with the Angel of Death or the Angel of Life, Dr. Lewis said. Sometimes one gets out of the car. Sometimes one follows you inside.

The doctor believed there were three angels. The Angel of Life, who rode along with them most nights. The Angel of Death, who appeared wearing his funeral clothes on those visits when there was no hope. And then there was the Third Angel. The one who walked among us, who sometimes lay sick in bed, begging for human compassion.

"It's not up to us to help the angels," Frieda had said.

"Isn't it?" the doctor said.

Frieda thought this over. She wondered if he was telling her that it was her duty to help the ill and the downtrodden; perhaps she would never know if she was coming to the aid of an angel in disguise. The doctor discussed subjects other people might think she was too young to hear; she was included in all of the important aspects of his life. Frieda was the only one who knew that the doctor secretly smoked cigars. She thought he was the smartest, kindest man in the world. He rolled down the car window and sang and puffed away. He was a huge Frank Sinatra fan, and he sang "Fly Me to the Moon" that night. After they went over the bridge, they drove along the river, past willow trees. They came to a little house with horses in a meadow.

"You can stay in the car on this one, miss," Frieda's father said. "This is one where a doctor isn't really necessary. They need an angel and not the fellow in the dark coat, if you know what I mean."

"I'll go," Frieda had said. "I want to go."

She could see the sheen of two white horses, standing in the soft darkness. She didn't want to be afraid of anything, but she was afraid of them. It was a funny fear to have. Frieda didn't actually think they would hurt her, or that they were dangerous. It was more that she had the urge to run with them; to run far away, right through the grass. She loved her home and her family, but once she started running with the horses, she might never come back.

Frieda carried her father's doctor's bag. She liked to do that for him. Her father knew everything about nature. He was a bird-watcher and he was on a committee to eradicate foxhunting, which he thought barbaric. He had once brought home a rabbit, which they had kept as a pet through the cold winter months, but when spring arrived Frieda's father convinced her it would be best to set the rabbit free. They'd watched it hop away into the hedges, and Frieda had agreed that it seemed right for the rabbit to be out in the field, running so far it was soon enough a dot on the horizon. She never even thought to ask her father where he'd found that rabbit. He'd come home from a conference in London and there it was in the backseat of his car, curled up on his black winter coat.

It's a hotel rabbit, he told Frieda. You don't find those too often.

That animal is not living in my house, Frieda's mother had said. Rabbits are dirty. And they turn on you.

Frieda had never paid much attention to her mother, whose

name was Violet, an old-fashioned name belonging to an old-fashioned woman who stayed in the background. Her word hadn't counted for much. Of course, the hotel rabbit had stayed. The doctor built a hutch in the kitchen and there the rabbit remained all through the winter, eating carrots, lettuce, and peas.

Don't marry a man who always has to have his own way, Frieda's mother had told her. Marry someone who gives a damn about what you have to say. But Frieda had believed her father's way to be the right way, so she paid no attention to her mother's complaints.

At the house with the white horses, a woman opened the door. She was a pretty, dark woman, but she looked worn out. She'd been crying. "He's already gone," she said. "He's left me."

Frieda noticed everything that night. The way the clock sounded, the green woolen carpet, the wooden mantel over the fireplace. They left her in the living room while they went into the bedroom. She could hear the clock and the woman crying and the low sound of her father's voice. She felt nothing bad could happen if her father was around, not then and not ever. She realized that she still had his bag so Frieda went down the hall. She saw her father with his arms around the woman he called Jenny, leaning against him, sobbing. She saw the dead man in the bed. The room smelled foul, a mix of shit and blood. The bedsheets were stained brown. The man looked like a person and yet he didn't, a wax figure without his soul or spirit or whatever it was. No life force. No wonder this woman was sobbing. Frieda's father spied her then.

"Why don't you sit with Mrs. Foley while I call for an ambulance to come round," he said to her. "We can't have Jim staying here like this."

Frieda looked at her father. He usually referred to the deceased as the body. He never used a person's name once they were gone, not until now. Somehow this night seemed different. Frieda was not the least afraid to be in a room with the dead. It was only a body. If anything, it was the dead man's wife she was afraid of, all those tears, all that emotion.

"Thank you, Frieda," the woman said to her. She'd known her name. "I couldn't be alone."

In the car, driving home, Frieda's father sang "Fly Me to the Moon" again, but now it sounded sadder. There was no moon, in fact, well maybe a little one, hidden by the trees.

"I'm proud of the way you acted," the doctor said as they drove back across the bridge. "You have something special. You're willing to examine things and see what they really are instead of just reacting, screaming like you've seen a mouse the way most people would do when confronted with death."

"I like mice," Frieda had said.

"Exactly!" her father had said proudly. "You like mice. That is not typical for a teenaged girl. The things that distress and frighten other people don't scare you. I'm not sure you realize how rare that is."

Now, sitting in the park in her black dress, Frieda thought her father would disapprove of her. She hadn't turned out the way he had expected; nothing had. Well, everything changed in this world, Frieda and her father included. There wasn't much to be proud of anymore. A maid, not a university student. A girl wearing black eyeliner. Although Frieda still liked mice. At the hotel they were supposed to set out poison, under the beds and the bureaus, but Frieda never did. Secretly, she left out a bit of cheese every now and then in the corner of her room near the heater. It was always gone by morning.

At the far bench in the park, there was a young man asleep. He had long hair and he was out cold, breathing with slow raspy breaths. Drugs or alcohol, Frieda surmised. Possibly an overdose; possibly mild pneumonia. Frieda restrained herself from butting in; she would not allow herself to go over and check to see if the fellow was conscious. The world didn't always have to be her responsibility. Maybe the man on the bench was the Third Angel and maybe he was a homeless drunk. It was not up to Frieda to speculate. She was young and she wanted to live like she was young. She didn't want to think about dead bodies and meningitis and concussions and liver damage and the Angel of Death. She wanted to think about true love that would never die, she wanted to hear music, she wanted to balance along a window ledge on the seventh floor, arms out, and not be afraid of falling or have her mind be taken up with the many ways in which bones could shatter.

Frieda walked back to the hotel the long way around, through little side streets. She loved to look in windows and imagine what it might be like to live another life. She stopped at the coffee shop and sat at a table by the window and ordered a pot of tea and a cheese sandwich. She kept a few scraps in a napkin to take home for the mice. She was thinking about her song; it was as though it was a part of her. The fellow at the next table tried to flirt with her, offering her the jug of milk, then the sugar bowl, for her tea, but Frieda wasn't interested. He tried conversation then.

"I hear John Lennon's staying right down the street," he said, trying to impress her.

"You heard wrong," Frieda said. "John Lennon would never stay around here."

She went back to the hotel, elbowing her way through the crowd of girls outside. Jack Henry let her through the door.

"A total madhouse," he said, happy as could be, certain he'd score with one of the girls whom he promised to get up to the room where Lennon was allegedly secreted away.

Frieda thought about Jack Henry going through a drunken man's wallet; she didn't like the way he was staring at her black dress. If he'd been Mick Jagger that would have been one thing, but he wasn't.

Frieda went up to her room and took out her verse and rewrote it again, changing words as she went along. When she was done, it looked perfect. She'd used a pen she'd borrowed from the front desk and real India ink. Lennie came in from working all day, exhausted. She'd had a fight with her sister, and now Meg was making her pay for her sharp words, giving Lennie all the worst assignments. That day she'd been put on kitchen duty and she'd had to scrub the ovens. Then she'd been sent to a suite where a bachelor party had taken place the night before. She took off her white maid's apron and threw herself down on the bed beside Frieda.

"Human beings are pigs." Lennie lay on her back, one arm over her face. "Why can't they clean up after themselves? People leave their condoms on the floor. Used ones, mind you! And they know some poor maid will have to clean up after them. How do they live with their disgusting selves?"

"Listen to this." Frieda propped herself up on one elbow. "Forget about condoms. Just close your eyes."

In another world she and Lennie would have never met.

Frieda would have had university friends, but none of them would have understood her the way Lennie did. The room was hot but there was a breeze coming in through the window. They could hear the girls gathered in the street chanting.

"Shut up, you idiots," Lennie grumbled with her eyes closed. "He's not bloody registered here. I asked my sister and she said it's some guy named Lemming."

"Block them out and listen to me."

Frieda pulled down the shade so the room darkened and the noise was a little less annoying. She settled in to read "The Ghost of Michael Macklin" aloud. She read it slowly, as though her life depended on it. When she was done she threw herself down on her back beside Lennie.

"You wrote that?" Lennie said. Her eyes were open now.

"I did."

"It's fucking amazing. Jesus, Frieda. What are you, a poet in disguise?"

"They're song lyrics," Frieda said.

"Well who would have guessed? You're very surprising. You're a freak of nature if you really want to know. What can't you do? I will never understand why you're working as a maid when you're fucking brilliant."

"You really think it's good?"

"It's better than 'We all live in a yellow submarine,' I'll tell you that. It's wonderful. It reminds me of something, not in the words so much, but in the feeling."

It was "Greensleeves"; Frieda knew that's what it was. And that was just what she'd wanted, the kind of song that could come up behind you and grab you with its sheer emotion.

"If John Lennon ever did stay here," Lennie mused,

"maybe I'd say I have a friend with a brilliant song for you, Mr. Lennon." She was falling asleep. "She pretends to be a maid but she's a fucking poet. You need to rescue her from the Lion Park Hotel, Johnny boy."

Lennie was asleep in no time. Frieda never bothered to tell her that she didn't want to be rescued. If anything, it was the other way around. She was her father's daughter still when it came to matters of life and death. You never knew who you might save in this world.

Frieda was on the late shift, so she left Lennie sleeping and had her dinner with some of the other girls in the kitchen. The staff at the hotel was given dinner five days a week, meals consisting of whatever the restaurant hadn't sold out of the day before. Frieda wore her black dress under her maid's smock. She'd washed and straightened her hair and had painted on her Cleopatra eyes. She caught a glance of herself in the mirror set into the highboy across from the long table where the staff ate. She looked surprisingly attractive. She didn't look like a girl who didn't mind mice and dead bodies and illness.

"Don't you look dressy?" a gossipy girl named Vicky said to her. "Hoping to run into some famous musician?"

"Lennon isn't staying here, you twit," Frieda gleefully informed Vicky. "It's someone named Lemming."

It was Jamie whom Frieda had been thinking of when she dressed up. She'd gone past his room in the afternoon and knocked at the door, but there'd been no answer. She actually went down to the front desk to ask Lennie's sister if he was still registered.

"You know I can't tell you," Meg said. "Privacy issues. I'd lose my job. We're known for our discretion, aren't we?"

"Mr. Lemming is probably hoping so. Imagine if all those groupies descended upon him and he's probably just here to have an affair or dress up in women's clothes."

Meg raised one eyebrow; she might have laughed if she wasn't in charge. "Why do you want to know about 708?"

"It's personal," Frieda said.

"Personal is always a mistake. Trust me on that."

All the same, Meg left the book open when she went to the file room for a customer's bill. Frieda thumbed through till she came to his name. He was still registered. Room 708. He hadn't gone.

Frieda worked fast that night; she didn't clean the rooms as well as she might have, but she frankly didn't think the clientele at the Lion Park would notice. They were more concerned with privacy and locked doors. She turned down the beds and emptied the rubbish and left it at that. If she vacuumed, most of the guests wouldn't even notice. All they wanted were a few clean towels and to be left alone.

She went up to his room as soon as she was done. She felt silly and embarrassed and her pulse was wild. She stood in the hall thinking. Was it a mistake to make this personal? To think she was anything more than a maid? The hallway was especially cold and Frieda had little bumps up and down her arms. Before she could decide what to do, Jamie opened the door. He was going out to meet Stella. He was already late. He'd been shooting more heroin every day. He never thought he'd be one to get hooked, and if he was—so what? He was dreamy and loose. He felt like anything could happen. He wore his purple jacket and jeans and a white shirt and cowboy boots he'd bought on West Fourth Street the last time he was in New

York. He was feeling washed-up and his career hadn't even begun.

"Hey," he said when he saw the maid in the hall. Heroin was like the bed in Stella's house, all feather down, white and waiting.

"Hello," Frieda said. She was still wearing her stupid smock that she'd forgotten to remove. "It's me again."

"I'm just on my way," Jamie said. "I'm late."

"Sure. I understand."

Frieda blinked her Cleopatra eyes. She looked right at him in a way most girls didn't. Square on in some strange way. Not at all self-conscious. She acted as though she thought she was somebody. It was a little confusing.

"But I could have a drink first." Jamie had a little time, after all. He wasn't that late. Truth was, he'd like to stay in bed dreaming, half in reality and half somewhere a million miles away. It was so hard to get anything done in this world; there were so many interruptions. But this girl was a welcome distraction. She was like a doorway to another place. Jamie had known such people in the past—some of the nurses who'd cared for him when he was in the hospital. They had opened up time and space and let him step out of his pain. They were magicians, really, and when they left and he was there all alone under the white sheets and cotton blankets, his leg throbbing, in agony, he wondered how they'd managed to make him forget it all, even for a minute. Jamie had been avoiding the here and now for so long he looked for any portal out. He thought this girl might help him and he never said no to an offer.

They went into his room. Jamie didn't even think to be

embarrassed by the mess. She'd seen it before, and what was the difference really? He'd be out of here soon.

The room was so rank Frieda laughed, then went to throw open the window. "Good lord. It smells like there was a fire."

Creative men were disorderly and untidy and filled with ideas. Frieda wasn't surprised to see that the ashtray was overflowing with burned paper. There were ashes on the carpeting and some black singe marks as well. Frieda thought she'd move the desk a few inches and cover it up and no one would ever be the wiser.

"My song," Jamie said when he noticed Frieda looking at the ashy mess. Some water had been sloshed over it, which had only made more of a mess. "Or it was."

"Didn't work out?"

He looked so broken, and Frieda had always been drawn to broken things. She noticed needles in the ashtray. Her father had always told her to be careful with sharp objects, to wrap them in tissue so no one would get hurt. She looked more closely at Jamie as he poured their drinks. His hand was shaking. He was an addict. Frieda's father would have intuited that in a flash, as soon as he'd seen him. All the signs were there: dilated pupils, scabs on his arms, the pallor of his skin. Frieda hadn't seen it before and that puzzled her. She was usually so clear about things. She picked up on small details, and she'd missed this entirely.

"I never really finished the song," Jamie admitted. "I got fed up."

"My good fortune." Frieda had no idea how she came to be so brazen. What was wrong with her? She had the urge to open the top bureau drawer and see what was inside. She wanted to know him completely. "Now I suppose you owe me," Frieda said.

Jamie looked at her, not understanding.

"We bet the purple jacket, not that you have to give it to me, but we did make a bet and I do believe you lost."

Jamie nodded. "You're right." Though it pained him to lose it, he took off the jacket and gave it to Frieda. It was laid across her lap. He'd bought the purple jacket after his first paying gig in New York. Other than his guitar, it was his favorite possession. And his cowboy boots. He couldn't live without them. He certainly wasn't about to let those go. "Consequences and all that, right?"

"You don't really have to give it to me," Frieda said, though she wanted the jacket desperately. She ran her hand over the fringe. The other girls would die of jealousy.

Jamie bowed. "It's all yours. A real man pays his debts."

Frieda took off her white maid's apron and put on the suede jacket. She stood on a chair so she could get a look at herself in the mirror. Was that really her? The girl from Reading all done up like a dolly? If she saw herself walking out on the street, she would have thought she belonged in a magazine standing alongside Jean Shrimpton. Frieda laughed out loud and her laugh was so pure Jamie felt something go through him. Before he could stop himself he invited her out with his friends.

"We're just going to a club. You probably wouldn't be interested."

It was a private nightclub that Stella and Marianne belonged to, right behind a hotel in Mayfair. You wouldn't guess it was there if you didn't know about it; no number outside, no name.

It was called the Egyptian Club and every drink cost double what it would in a decent pub.

"I'm interested," Frieda said.

Maybe it was the purple jacket, maybe it was something else, but she just didn't want to let him go. They went out to get a taxi. Just that one drink had done something to Frieda. She was like another person. Jack Henry and Meg at the desk didn't even recognize her as she left. Not with that purple jacket and the black dress with Jamie guiding her past the crowd of girls still stationed outside. When the fans saw Jamie they started screaming. It was his long hair and the girl with the Cleopatra eyes who accompanied him that jump-started the screaming— they looked like they were somebodies. They sprinted for the taxi and jumped inside, laughing. Frieda felt like an impostor, but she didn't care.

"I didn't think anyone would know who I was," Jamie said. He'd only played a few gigs in London, the ones that hadn't gone so well. People had been chattering the whole time and the applause had been sparse. They wanted something louder than what he'd given them; something to shake their souls. "I don't even have a record yet. They couldn't possibly know me. That was weird."

Frieda smiled. She knew those girls were looking for John Lennon, but willing to settle for anyone. Well, she was some-body, wasn't she? She was happy to be where she was, away from the winding roads that led to her father's patients. Away from home. She had had a letter from her mother that day. It was not a normal letter. It was more of a list. It even had a title: When He Leaves You. It was all about practical matters, how to tie up loose ends, going to the bank, for instance, dividing possessions into boxes and cartons, returning gifts he gave you or selling them at auction for the best price. Things had not been going well for Frieda's mum. She couldn't give up on the doctor, even though he was living in a cottage in that little village with the toll bridge and the willow trees. He'd told Frieda that life was complicated. She of all people would understand that a person had to live it to the fullest. She had seen what he'd had to deal with over the years. The Angel of Death who'd come to sit in the backseat of his car. The dark country roads at night. He needed some time alone to reassess his life. It took Frieda a while to realize that her father wasn't alone, he was with that woman, the one who'd cried. Well, maybe Frieda needed to be selfish as well. Maybe she needed to reassess, too. She hoped her father remembered that when he was unhappy with her. This, after all, was her one and only life.

At the club the Ridge sisters belonged to, customers and their guests had to have their names on a list, and Jamie did. "There are my friends," he said. He pulled Frieda through the crowd and no one questioned her right to be there. Jamie's hand was big and callused and Frieda's hand fit inside his perfectly. She felt that she was burning, that she'd wind up like the carpet in his room, scorched by his touch.

There were so many people at the Egyptian Club, Frieda didn't have time to feel awkward. She wasn't beautiful like most of the other women, or rich; she wasn't anything much, she supposed. But she'd ridden with the Angel of Death, maybe that was where she'd gained her courage. She didn't feel intimidated, even here where she didn't belong. When they got to the table of Jamie's friends, Jamie shook hands with Nick, then went to kiss Stella hello. Stella let herself be kissed, but she was staring at Frieda. Her lips were pursed. She took a drag of a cigarette.

"That's your jacket," Stella said.

"I lost it in a bet. Sit down," Jamie told Frieda. Frieda dropped into the closest chair. Her black dress really was short. "This is Frieda. She's my muse," Jamie explained to Stella.

"Are you kidding?" Stella said. "I'm supposed to be your fucking muse, Jamie, not some stranger." Stella's hair was almost white and she was wearing a filmy blue dress. Crushed into a corner was a coat made of python. She had a hurt look on her face.

"A muse isn't something you choose. It just happens, Stella. It's called art," Jamie said.

Frieda felt herself flush; she felt like the other angel her father had always spoken of, not the ones who rode with them, but the one who walked among men and women. She felt as though she had a duty in this world, to be there for Jamie, to inspire him.

"This is Stella and Marianne and Nick," Jamie told Frieda. He signaled a waiter over and ordered champagne. Möet. It was going on Stella's account. He ordered two bottles. Stella never minded; she liked him to spend money. It was her father's, after all. Somebody had to get rid of it. She wasn't so pleased tonight, however. "You'd better make certain she's not a muse you're fucking," she said.

Stella had a strand of what looked like sapphires and diamonds around her throat. The stones were huge; the chain was twenty-two-karat gold. She reached out to take Frieda's hand. Her skin felt extremely cold. Frieda noted that her pupils were dilated. Her nails were long and painted ice white. "So what is

it you do other than steal people's jackets and amuse them?"
She pressed Frieda's hand so hard that Frieda's bones hurt.
Stella seemed dangerous, the way the wounded often are.

"I work in a hotel." Frieda withdrew her hand. She felt
as though she'd been bitten by a snake. She felt violated. She
thought of saying, I wash toilets and pick up rubbish and take
people's dirty sheets off their beds. Instead she smiled. She
should have known Jamie would have a girlfriend. There was
no reason to be shocked or stunned or disappointed. But a girlfriend wasn't necessarily permanent. That had been on her
mother's list of things to know about love and marriage: Nothing lasts forever.

Marianne was leaning against Nick's shoulder and nodding
out. She had long black hair down to her waist and ten gold
bangle bracelets on each arm. Her fringe was nearly over her
eyes, which were a surprising green, whenever she bothered to
open them. Her skin was as white as Stella's; Frieda could see
the veins running up and down her arms. She had abscesses,
too, red and black against the white. She had enough energy to
say to Frieda, "Don't think you can win against Stella. She's
much smarter than you'd guess. She's definitely smarter than
me. She certainly was last night."

Stella and Marianne laughed. They had a hundred private
jokes.

"What about you?" Frieda asked Stella. "What do you do?"

"Whatever Jamie wants me to," Stella said. "When he's not
being a total ass."

When the champagne arrived Frieda ordered a beer—she
was already tipsy from the whisky and she knew champagne
was dangerous. It tasted too good; she might go on drinking

and wind up doing something she would regret. Beer was simple.

People were dancing; the music was so loud it got inside your head. A friend of Jamie's, some record executive, asked Frieda to dance. Her first impulse was to say no; the man was much older and Frieda didn't like crowded dance floors. She preferred to observe. Then, of course, there was Jamie. She didn't really want to leave him in Stella's clutches.

"Go ahead," Stella urged Frieda. Her sister hadn't been kidding. She looked like a featherweight, but she was smart and strategic. "We wouldn't want you to be lonely," she purred. "There's nothing worse than being a fifth wheel."

Stella and Frieda assessed each other.

"I know what you're trying to do," Frieda said.

"So glad to hear that. I love a fair fight, if that's what you think this is." Stella looked right at her; her eyes were cloudy and blue. "Just so you know—we're not even in the same universe."

All at once, Frieda had the sense that Stella was right, that she wasn't quite human and that Frieda would never win a battle against her.

Jamie had been talking to the older man. Now he leaned over to whisper to Frieda. "He's the guy who's recording me."

"Don't worry," she whispered back. "I'll tell him how wonderful you are."

While she was out on the dance floor, Frieda felt lost; her head was pounding. There were so many people and the lights kept changing color and the fellow she was with was a terrible dancer. He was embarrassing really. He was almost as old as her father. Before the song was over, Frieda saw Stella and

Jamie get up from the table. Jamie helped Stella out from the booth. Frieda thought she should probably leave the club, go find Lennie, and head out for a drink with someone who really knew her at a pub where they could have fun. She didn't belong here, and what was more she didn't want to. But she stayed; she had a drink at the bar with her dance partner, the A&R man who worked for Capitol Records in the States and told a long story about his divorce. He must have thought Frieda was interested in how his wife had never been there for him when he needed her and how she gave their kids all of her attention. He must have thought she gave a damn. But at last, he spoke about something that did interest her: Jamie. He told Frieda that Jamie's recording date had been moved up to the following week. They were very excited about him. They had been looking for a singer-songwriter, someone like Dylan. All he needed was a band to back him. Yes, the concerts hadn't gone very well, but that was because he wasn't playing his own material. Once there was a record of original songs, that would change. All in all, they thought Jamie had something special.

"Oh, he does," Frieda was quick to agree. "He could probably use an advance like all creative artists, though. You wouldn't want to lose somebody as talented as Jamie because you didn't pay him enough."

The A&R man gave her a look. This girl was smarter than he'd expected, despite those Cleopatra eyes. She reminded him of some agents he'd worked with; you thought you were out having a good time with someone, then it turned out they'd had an agenda all along.

"Don't worry about Jamie on that score. He's got a girlfriend with a pile of money. I guess it doesn't matter if she's got a famous heroin habit."

"I've got to work in the morning," Frieda said. "Nice to meet you."

The record rep slipped her his card, which she dropped on the floor on her way to search for a ladies' room. She had to ask three people before she found the ladies' lounge, and when she got there, there was a long line out the door.

"Why can't people get high before they get here so a person can piss in peace?" the girl in front of her said crossly. There were perhaps twenty women on line. At last the door opened and Jamie and Stella tumbled out. Jamie had his arm wrapped around Stella and she looked limp, very rag doll, very beautiful and incapacitated, light as air.

Frieda felt herself hating Stella, something she rarely felt. Then she hated herself for feeling jealous. She had become sour and small, a nobody. From her place in line she could see them make their way back to the table. They slid into their booth, so close together you could hardly tell where one ended and one began. Stella curled up against Jamie. They looked perfect, really; they fit together.

"I'm not going to wait here all night," Frieda told the girl in front of her in line.

"Good for you," the girl said. "Piss somewhere where you can piss in peace."

Frieda left the club and started walking. She didn't have enough money for a taxi. She felt hot and stupid. She thought about her mother's letter. Always know what's yours and what's his. Don't become dependent. Have your own bank account. Once he's left, clean out all the closets. A mess never helped anyone.

It was always the doctor who was the center of everything, whom Frieda admired. Her mother nagged and worried, but now Frieda wondered if she shouldn't have listened when her mother spoke, at least occasionally; she might have learned something.

Frieda cut through the park and hurried through the dark. She was glad she hadn't had any champagne. At least she wasn't drunk. She didn't care if the park was dangerous at this hour; she wasn't in a caring mood. She started running. She'd been a runner in high school and it felt good to let go. There was cigarette smoke in her hair and it drifted off into the night air while she ran. Little gatherings were taking place all through the park and Frieda could smell hashish. She felt as though she was the only person alive. She felt as though Jamie had been carried off and was so far away she would never be able to get to where he was.

She crossed lawns and trotted across the grass, then ran along the bridle path. She would have done better to have been a horse, a white horse standing in the countryside in the dark, beneath a twisted, black apple tree. She'd spent too much time with the Angel of Death. She knew things she shouldn't, but she still didn't understand human beings. They lied and cheated and stole and loved the wrong people. There was no way to fix that, was there? No little pill that could make someone want you the way you wanted him.

When Frieda got to the hotel, she leaned down to catch her breath. She hadn't run this far in quite some time. She heard a man coughing. There was Teddy Healy, the drunk from the hotel, sitting on the pavement, his back against the wall.

"You again," Frieda said.

Teddy Healy stared at her. Then he turned his head and coughed terribly. Could it be the first stages of emphysema? Frieda wondered. Of course he didn't recognize her.

"You were thrown out drunk and I helped put you in a taxi." Frieda tried to refresh his memory. "Remember?"

"Sorry," Teddy said. "At least tonight I could walk out of my own volition before I collapsed."

"What does being drunk do for you?"

"You are young, aren't you? It allows me to be as close to dead as possible while still being alive. It's a lack of courage. Isn't that obvious? I lost something and I can't get it back."

"Maybe you should stop thinking about yourself and start doing something for other people. Maybe that would snap you out of it."

Teddy Healy actually laughed. "Are you telling me how to repair my life?"

"No. I'm saying save someone else's."

Frieda thought about her own advice as she went inside. It was exactly the sort of thing her father would have said. Well, he'd be right on this account. The more you gave, the more you got back. Frieda was convinced of it. She would think of this night as a bad dream, one she had escaped from. If she ever had sapphires she wouldn't need them to be so gaudy. If she ever had Jamie, she wouldn't treat him so carelessly.

She changed out of her black dress into jeans and an old shirt. Lennie wasn't in bed. After thinking it over, Frieda took her keys and went up to the seventh floor. It was quiet and no one was around. Frieda went into the maid's closet and got her basket and some linens. She walked down the long, cold hall. She simply wasn't the type to give up. She let herself into Jamie's room and locked the door behind her. It was dark and for a moment she stood there unable to make out anything. She remembered that her mother had written something about cleaning up messes in order to see what was right in front of you.

Frieda switched on the lights and surveyed Jamie's disaster, then she got to work. She stripped the bed and gathered all the dirty laundry and towels, which she put into the wash down in the third-floor laundry room to run while she was cleaning. She did a fabulous job; she even scrubbed the bathtub and polished the furniture with lemon oil. She thought she heard a man yelling while she was vacuuming and maybe she was making too much noise, but then she realized it must be the ghost across the hall. It was ten-thirty. She quickly opened the door, but no one was there. The door of 707 was closed and the Do Not Disturb sign was hanging from the knob, so maybe someone was staying there. Maybe it really was John Lennon or some other musician who wasn't afraid of spirits. Anyway, if anyone would have ever seen a ghost, it would have been Frieda's father, he'd spent so much time with the dying and the dead. But Dr. Lewis had never said a word about ghosts. Once a person had passed, what was left was the body, nothing mystical there. Except for that one night when they'd gone over the toll bridge into the village with the willow trees. When he'd called that woman's dead husband by name.

Frieda went back to her cleaning. She was actually enjoying

it. She thought of her mother, packing up all of her father's clothes into cardboard boxes and driving them out to the cottage and leaving them on the lawn. If she and Jamie were over before they'd even begun, well at least the end would be orderly. When Frieda had finished and was waiting for Jamie's clothes to dry, she sat by the desk and opened the drawer. There were vials of pills, a container of marijuana, a small pipe, and several waxy envelopes. She opened one of the envelopes and stuck her finger inside. White powder. She tasted it and it made her mouth go numb. She understood that people tried to ease their pain and that sometimes they destroyed themselves without even trying. She thought about riding in the car with her father; he never judged his patients. That wasn't in his nature, and it wasn't in hers. The only people they judged were each other.

Frieda put everything away and closed the desk drawer. Then she opened it again and took out the sheaf of Lion Park writing paper and a pen and started another poem or song or whatever it was. She wrote down stray words. She poured herself a glass of whisky—she knew the glass was clean now, for she'd washed it.

White powder. The way I love you. The way I shouldn't. Riding late at night. Who is behind me? Who is in front of me? Who is waiting for me? No one's on the road. No one's going where I am. How will I know who the angel is? How will I recognize his face?

Frieda was writing so fast she wasn't even thinking. She was so hot she had started to sweat; there was a line of perspiration down her back and her chest. She felt the way she had when she was writing the other lyrics, transported somehow, out of time and space.

He's not the angel in the backseat of the car. He's not the one who's driving with me. But he knows my name. He knows my game.

At the top of the page Frieda wrote THE THIRD ANGEL.

She sat there and finished her drink; she still felt hot, but it was a good feeling. It was not unlike the way she felt when she'd been running and then had reached her destination and could finally stop and take a deep breath.

Frieda went to fetch Jamie's laundry from the third floor. As she was going up the stairs she ran smack into Lennie.

"Jesus, Frieda, what the hell are you doing here?"

Lennie looked a little drunk herself. She was wearing her best dress, a silvery mini she had gotten in a sale on the King's Road, and heels so high she wobbled. Her hair was uncombed. She had on a lot of makeup. She looked guilty, as though she'd been caught pilfering.

"I'm doing laundry," Frieda said.

Lennie shook her head as if she didn't believe it. "Right. Now tell me you're from Mars."

"All right, it's Jamie's laundry. I'm overly involved, I agree. I know I shouldn't be washing his clothes, so shut up."

"I won't tell anyone," Lennie said. "I won't even tell you what an idiot you are. That's what friends are for. We'll ask no questions and give no false answers. Not either one of us."

They stared at each other. Frieda had a strange feeling, as though she had run into an alternate Lennie, not the girl who had become her best friend. Lennie looked tired; her eyes were small. She smelled like drink and her lipstick was smeared.

"I'm going to bed," Lennie said. "Forget you ever saw me here, Frieda."

Lennie was acting as though she were embarrassed at being found out, but at what, Frieda had no idea. Was there some fellow Lennie had fallen for? Could she really have been as foolish as Frieda and become involved with one of the guests? That just didn't seem like Lennie, who was careful enough to always look after number one.

"I'll be in soon," Frieda told her.

"You don't answer to me," Lennie said. "I don't need to know your private business. You're a big girl, Frieda, as am I."

Well, that was the policy of the Lion Park, wasn't it, at least for guests, so the same was surely true for the help. Privacy at all costs, no questions asked and none answered; secrecy even among friends.

Frieda brought Jamie's laundry back to his room, folded it, and left it on the chair. His T-shirts were worn and thin. He had two paisley shirts, one blue and green, the other different hues of red, orange, and yellow. Both needed ironing, which was really no bother. Frieda was a capable person. She liked ironing; it allowed her mind to wander. She wondered if that's why her mother never complained about housework.

When she was done, and everything had been neatly put away, Frieda felt she had accomplished something. This is what her mother must have meant, the true purpose of housework. To set things right. The room smelled nice now. Like lemon and soap. She'd given Jamie extra pillows and one of the good blankets, a silky coverlet usually reserved for famous guests. Well, he would be famous someday, so it was just as well. She hoped the A&R man had listened to what she'd said about talent.

Frieda lay down on the bed for just a moment. She thought

about the wild look in Lennie's eyes, as if she'd been caught at something really horrid when all she'd been doing was taking the stairs. Frieda's father had told her most people had secret lives, but usually they were secrets no one wanted to know. She thought again of the list her mother had sent her. Always use bleach to wash the bedding you used with him, or better yet, throw it all away and buy new sheets. Frieda fell asleep already dreaming that she was in a car with her father, on a dark lane. There were lights turned on within the houses they passed by. Every light is a life, Frieda's father told her in the dream. Every one is as worthwhile and as easily damaged. Frieda woke up because in her dream someone sat down in the back of her father's car; she could feel his weight and all of a sudden she felt cold. She wondered which angel it was. She wondered if she should look, or if in his glory and his terribleness, the Angel of Death would take her right then and there if she faced him. Frieda started to cry in her dream, even though she could feel herself waking. She opened her eyes and there was Jamie beside her on the bed, staring at her. He smelled of smoke and alcohol.

"What a nice surprise," he said.

Frieda hid her face against his chest so he wouldn't know she'd been crying, but he knew.

"I understand," Jamie said. "This world is a hard, cruel place, Frieda."

He told her all about his leg, about the months in the hospital, about the pain he carried with him always. He had fought his disability as though going into battle; he was a hero, really, one who refused to bend to his genetic flaws, that damned leg, all that torture of braces and surgeries and ridicule. By the time he got to the part about heroin, there was, in Frieda's mind, nothing he could do wrong.

"You could see a doctor about the drugs," she said. "Get help."

Jamie laughed at that. "I've seen too many doctors in my life. I know how to deal with my pain. But I think it's the thing that makes me unable to write. I give everything to my dreams when I get high. It knocks me out, takes every part of me. I have the songs inside of me, but they float out when I'm in pain and I can't catch up with them."

Frieda took out the paper on which she'd written "The Third Angel." She'd meant to give him "The Ghost of Michael Macklin," but that song was too much; it seemed to tear a person in two. She would try this one first. It was a solemn moment really, and if she hadn't been Frieda, with her brand of confidence, she would have been shaking. She read it to him, and when she was done Jamie stared at her as though he were suddenly completely awake. He hadn't really seen her before.

"Holy shit, Frieda," he said. "I didn't know that was in you."

"I know something about pain, too," Frieda said. "My father is a doctor. I used to go on calls with him when I was little."

"I thought you were going to write me a song about a ghost, but instead you wrote a song about me," Jamie said. "I'm honored."

They spent the night together, even though it was expressly against hotel rules, even though Frieda was fairly certain there was only one person who was falling in love. But you never could tell about these things. Time had the power to alter everything; her mother had written that in her list. Even love. It was worth it to be with him no matter what. Being with him was a dream, hot and intense, as if they were somewhere outside of the rest of the world. He made her feel things she hadn't expected, and she did things she hadn't even known about, found parts of love that were deeper, more urgent. She knew he'd been with so many women, but she didn't care about that. She was the one in bed with him, and it wasn't one kiss she gave him but a thousand.

Jamie told her no other girl could be to him what she was. She would be his muse, not just now but always. When the morning came around, Frieda could hardly stand to leave him. She had never understood how people could be in denial, how, for instance, someone with a terminal diagnosis could get up and get dressed and make breakfast and not think about dying every second of the day. And yet she was like that about Stella. For Frieda, Stella didn't exist; she had faded into blond nothingness; she might as well have been living in the sky above them. The reality was here, at the Lion Park. The two of them in bed. The angel that watched over them. The song that had appeared like a dream.

Frieda herself was dreamy that morning. She overslept and had to sneak out of Jamie's room and run down the stairs to the second floor. She quickly got ready; she was on the morning shift, as was Lennie. It wasn't easy to be up half the night, doing things you shouldn't be doing, and then report to work. Frieda and Lennie both were exhausted; they drank black coffee in the dining hall. Of course they were too late for breakfast. Lennie didn't look at Frieda or speak to her, but then again she was in a rush.

"Where were you all night?" their third roommate, Katy, asked Frieda as they were collecting their baskets of cleaners and sponges and mops. "Don't tell me you're moving into Lennie territory?"

"Actually, I fell asleep in a room I was cleaning. It was embarrassing. Thank goodness it was an empty room."

"Well, good," said Katy, relieved. "I'd hate to see you fall into the easy money like Lennie. Not that it's so easy if you ask me. The guys who are paying her certainly aren't Mick Jagger, if you know what I mean. She must just close her eyes and count to a thousand and pray for them to be done."

Frieda laughed. "You're mad. What do you mean?"

"I mean that's how she makes her money. You don't think she's shopping on the King's Road with the wages we earn here? Your father's a doctor, you don't have to worry about money."

"I worry about things," Frieda said. For instance she was thinking now about venereal diseases and the risks a girl could run when sleeping with strangers. She was thinking that perhaps she didn't really know her closest friend.

"You don't have to worry like us," Katy said. "Not like Lennie."

In the afternoon, when the first shift was through, Frieda looked for Lennie, who seemed to be avoiding her. Lennie's sister, Meg, said Lennie had gone to the park, to have lunch. Frieda went after her. Hyde Park was huge, but Frieda knew Lennie's favorite place, down by the Serpentine. Lennie was there, smoking a cigarette. The weather was cool and most of the golden leaves of the trees in the park had been shaken off by an early-morning rain. Everything felt damp and gray.

"Are you following me?" Lennie asked.

Frieda sat down on a bench beside her friend and snitched one of Lennie's cigarettes. Her father had made her promise that she would never smoke. He did so on a night when they went to visit a man who was dying of emphysema. It was one of the worst things Frieda had ever seen. She was ten years old. The man was in his bed, struggling for air. Save me, he'd whispered to Frieda's father, who slipped an oxygen mask over the patient's mouth. That was when Frieda realized there were some people you couldn't rescue no matter how you might try.

"Look, I'm not going to explain myself to you or anyone else," Lennie said. "So fuck off, Frieda. What I do is none of your business."

"All right," Frieda said.

Lennie looked at her friend and laughed. "That's it? No lectures about how I'm ruining my life? How sooner or later one of these fellows is going to murder me? How I'll get syphilis or I'll get pregnant and be left to beg on a street corner? That's what you think, isn't it?"

"You're Lennie to me no matter what you do," Frieda said. "As long as you're not on my street corner," she joked. But in a way she was serious; if you loved somebody you were honest with them, weren't you? You told them the diagnosis, just as the doctor always had. What have we here? he might have said of Lennie. A girl who does whatever she pleases no matter the consequences?

"Oh, I'll be there. I'll show up wherever you live." Lennie

grinned. "I'll come with a tambourine and a little monkey that screams outside your window all night. You can throw me down a few pence and a bar of chocolate. Dream on."

"You're my friend. Whatever you do I support."

"Well," Lennie said. "That's a relief." She stubbed out her cigarette and became quite serious. "I need the money. That may not be an excuse for the things a person does in life, but I don't give a damn. I'm not planning on being a maid here forever. Meg is the one who sets it all up and I give her half. In two years we plan to have our own place. A bed-and-breakfast. Maybe I'll hire Katy to be the maid."

They both laughed at that.

"Wouldn't she be Mrs. Mick Jagger by then?" Frieda managed to choke out. That notion sent them into near hysteria.

"That would be like you, thinking something lasting will come of you and Mr. Rock Star-to-be."

Frieda shut up then. She was not at all amused.

"No!" Lennie said when she saw Frieda's expression. "I thought you were a fucking pragmatist. I thought you saw people for who they truly were."

"We're not telling each other how to run our lives. Remember?"

"He is a lost cause, Frieda. Anyone can see he's on drugs. You need to know what you are to him: the girl who cleans his room. Or maybe you're the girl he takes to bed whenever he's got a free minute and can spare you the time. Then you clean his room. That's it, isn't it?"

"Shut up," Frieda said. "You don't know anything."

"I know you've got as much chance with him as Katy does with Mick Jagger. Actually, less, because your fellow is hungry, so he'll do whatever he has to in order to make it. And that doesn't mean marrying the maid."

"You're not one to give advice," Frieda said. "Not with who you're spending nights with."

"Oh, now it's me," Lennie said. "Turn on me why don't you?"

"Did I judge you?" Frieda asked.

They sat there on the bench, mulling things over.

All that day Frieda thought about what Lennie had called after her as she was leaving the park. In the end, people always show you who they are. That's what Lennie had said. You just have to be able to see it.

She met Jamie again that night. They ran into each other in the lobby and he told her to come up when she was done with work. Clearly, he was interested. Lennie really didn't understand anything at all. When she was free, she went upstairs, but no one answered in Jamie's room. Frieda let herself in with her key, the skeleton key that fit every room in the hotel. She had a moment of thinking, He won't be there, I'll just walk away, but he'd fallen asleep waiting for her. She took off all her clothes and got into bed beside him. She wasn't going to think about anything. She wasn't going to worry the way she always did. She was just going to be. She was Frieda, here in his room, nothing more.

"I thought you'd never get here," he said to her when he awoke.

He wasn't the first man she'd been with, and that hadn't been Bill back home either. It had been a boy she met on holiday when she was fifteen. She had decided it was time for her to have sex, the way someone else might decide it was time to get a driver's license, and she'd gone ahead with it. Pragmatic, that's the way she'd always been. This was entirely different. It was as if she'd imagined Jamie; that's how thoroughly she felt she knew him. The rest of the world was slipping away, which was what Frieda wanted. No one else existed. So this is what it was when you fell in love. It was so deep, so vast, Frieda was amazed. She had put away the list her mother had sent her. She never wanted to read that advice again. She just wanted to be herself.

While they were still in bed, arms around each other, Jamie said, "I want to play the song for you."

Frieda had nearly forgotten.

"I think you're going to like it," Jamie said. "I hope to God you do."

He got up for his guitar, then came back to her.

"It's rough, you know," Jamie said. "Unfinished."

Frieda loved unfinished things. Finished was over and done with; she liked process, she liked moving things: rivers, clouds, heartbeats.

Jamie's voice was so sweet, very clear. It seemed to come from a place other than inside him. Even he seemed a little surprised by the purity of the tone. He sang "The Third Angel" and it became something else entirely, much more than the words Frieda had written down. It became the story of a man chased by demons and by drugs. His story.

Jamie finished. He put the guitar down on the floor, then lay beside her again.

"Utterly wonderful," Frieda said. "I love it."

"I told you you were my muse. What would I have done if I hadn't met you?"

When Frieda told Lennie the next day, Lennie laughed out loud. "You wrote the damned song, did he ever mention that? Or did he just claim it as his own?"

"It is his own. He wrote the music. When he sings it it's changed. I'm doing another one for him. A really good one."

"At least I get paid for what I do, Frieda," Lennie said. They really weren't so much alike after all; they had both begun to see that. Ever since they had professed not to judge each other, something had gone wrong. "I'm just being honest with you, Frieda, and maybe you don't like that. But you wrote the song. It's yours."

Later in the week, Frieda learned that her father was coming to London for a conference and he was planning to see her. She hadn't expected him to be in touch, but there really was no way to avoid him once he telephoned. She hadn't been answering the letters from the doctor that her mother forwarded, but when she received a phone message from Meg, she felt cornered. Frieda hadn't told him where she was working, but somehow he'd found out. She'd phoned him then, out of desperation really. She didn't want him to see where she worked. It wasn't that she was embarrassed, not really. She simply didn't want her separate worlds to crash into each other there in the lobby of the Lion Park. And then there was Jamie. She couldn't even imagine the two men in the same universe. Best to keep the doctor away at all costs.

She agreed to meet her father at an Italian restaurant that he recommended off of Bayswater. She was a little late because she kept changing her outfit, trying to decide whether to look serious or carefree. In the end, serious fit the occasion. She wore a plain skirt and blouse that would have been perfect back home in Reading. But she wasn't giving in entirely; she wore her short black boots with the buckles. She wasn't about to go back to sensible shoes. And a bit of eyeliner; not Cleopatra, but Frieda Lewis all the same. Herself still.

Her father was waiting when she got there and had been for some time. She was more than half an hour late, even though she had hurried. She was dreading their meeting, and it was worry that had slowed her down. She was usually on time, early as a matter of fact. At least until today. Dr. Lewis was looking at a newspaper when Frieda came inside the restaurant. Seeing him, Frieda felt her love for her father; but she thought about how he'd betrayed them and love didn't seem quite so important. She gave him a kiss on the cheek when he stood to greet her, maintaining a cool demeanor.

"I thought you'd disappeared off the face of the earth," he said.

"Oh, no." Frieda ordered pasta and salad. The doctor was a vegetarian, and although Frieda wasn't as strict in such matters, she found herself following his diet most of the time. This evening, however, she thought she probably wouldn't eat. She had no appetite. That was how this whole thing started. It was how Frieda had come to leave home in the first place. She wanted to be in London, but she was also reacting to her father. She didn't owe him her life or her future, did she? Not after the way he'd left home. She didn't owe him anything at all.

"Look, Frieda, I think you're overreacting. True enough your mother and I are no longer together, but that is not the end of the world."

"It is for her." Frieda wanted to say, It is for me, but that complaint seemed childlike and selfish.

"So to punish me, you run off and instead of going to university you're working as a maid?"

"Who told you that?" Frieda was livid that he had managed to find out so much about her life and worse still that he knew she was reacting to him.

"Does it matter how I know?" the doctor said.

As soon as he refused to tell her, Frieda knew it was her mother. How could she have aided him?

"She told you? I didn't think she would even speak to you."

"Who does this kind of behavior hurt the most? You, Frieda, that's who. It's your life that you're ruining. Being a maid. There's nothing wrong with it, but it's not for you."

"I'm not ruining anything. I'm having fun," Frieda said. "I'm living my life. I don't owe anyone anything and if I want to be a chambermaid for the rest of my life, I will be!"

"Bill comes by once or twice a week." Now he had to throw up Bill when he'd always said Frieda was too young to get serious with anyone. "He's very confused about why you won't see him, Frieda. It's affecting his work at the university. He's taking a very difficult course of studies, you know. Frankly, you should be right there with him. You're at least as smart. You're as smart as anyone. You were meant to be a doctor and we both know it."

"I remember her clear as day," Frieda said. "Crying. Terrified."

Their pasta had come and the doctor ordered some wine.

"I suppose you drink now?" he said to Frieda.

"I'll have a beer," Frieda said to the waitress. When the waitress had gone, Frieda turned back to her father. She wasn't the only one who could be accused of ruining things. "She's the woman you're with, isn't she?"

"Her husband had died of bone cancer, Frieda. Surely you can understand that she was upset."

"I was fifteen and I wasn't afraid."

"You were always different," the doctor said. "You were like me."

It was so long ago, that night when the Angel of Death was right behind them in the car. Frieda thought she saw him once, in his black coat with his hat pulled low. She had opened all the windows, hoping a gust of wind would blow him away. But he just stayed put until they got to the house with the white horses. Now her father was living there with that woman, Jenny. He walked out into the field every morning, bringing oats to the horses, and Frieda wondered if they ran to him when they heard the back door open, if they waited by the fence.

"I'm nothing like you," Frieda said. She sounded more certain than she felt.

"Love is more complicated than you might imagine, Frieda."

"Well, thanks so much for the instruction." Frieda threw down her napkin and grabbed her purse. "Don't call me again," she told her father. "Don't contact me at all."

"Frieda," the doctor called.

He sounded hurt, but Frieda didn't care. She didn't think about the roads at night, or the songs he sang, or the way people looked at him when there was so much suffering and he was their only hope. She didn't care that he still wore two watches so he would always be on time. She had always believed he was the one person in the world she could depend upon, but she'd been wrong. Maybe if she'd been more afraid he would have stayed on with them, if she'd been a frightened little girl who screamed at the sight of mice, who feared death and fled from the angels.

That night Jamie was gone. Frieda knocked on the door of 708, then let herself in. It was dark, so she turned on the light. She opened the window for a bit of air. She tidied the room, and afterward sat at the desk and wrote down random words. She didn't even bother to think; it was like automatic writing. The words were horrible recriminations. It wasn't a song. If anything it was a list like her mother's, and Frieda didn't want to feel that way. Unlike "The Ghost of Michael Macklin," which she kept for herself, she threw this poem away. It wasn't possible to make art out of unbridled fury.

Frieda left Jamie's room and went down to the lounge to use the phone. She called her mother.

"I got your letter," Frieda said. "About men leaving."

"Well, I've tried it all and none of it works," Violet said. "So forget I ever wrote it. I'm not going to sit around and die because he went to some other woman. I decided to get my act together."

Frieda's mother had been doing volunteer work at the hospital, in the style of a proper doctor's wife, but she'd given that up. Instead, she was taking art classes at the university. She was living for herself now, something she'd never tried before. Frieda hadn't even known her mother liked art. Her mother had also changed her name from Violet to Vi. "It's more modern," her mother said. "More me."

"He came to see me," Frieda said. "I can't believe you told him where I lived and that I was working as a maid. Really, Mother."

"Well, aren't you?"

"And you gave him the phone number? You helped him reach me when you know I don't want to talk to him?"

"He's your father," Vi said.

"It doesn't seem like he is. I left the restaurant. I didn't even eat."

"Is he happy?" Frieda's mother asked.

"I didn't stick around long enough to find out," Frieda said, but they both knew the answer.

"You can't make someone love you," Vi said.

"Thanks for the advice."

"Are you all right?"

"Of course I am," Frieda said. "I always am."

When she got off the phone, Frieda went to the bar and asked the barman if she could have a drink.

"Against the rules," he told her. Hired people couldn't drink at the bar.

"She's my guest," a man said. It was Teddy Healy, getting drunk. "She'll have a glass of red wine."

"A beer," Frieda said. She sat beside Teddy Healy. "You're going to wind up with cirrhosis, and once you do damage to your liver, it can't be undone. A liver is irreplaceable."

"Doctor's daughter or hypochondriac?"

"Very funny." Frieda raised the beer set before her. "Cheers." She took a sip. "Doctor's daughter. Not that it's any of your business."

"I thought about what you said," Teddy said. "I might take your advice."

"Great." Frieda had no idea what he was referring to, but it was probably good that something had gotten him thinking. Her attentions were elsewhere. She recognized a group in the lobby. Jamie and Stella and her drug-addled sister with her good-looking silly boyfriend along with another couple. Frieda took a few gulps of her beer. Stella looked beautiful, even from a distance; she was wearing a pale fur coat the same color as her hair and high beige suede boots that buttoned up the side. She would bring him to ruin, Frieda thought, or if she didn't bring it, if he ruined his life all by himself, Stella wouldn't be able to pull him back. She'd be asleep or gazing into a mirror or she'd be too drugged out to get up off the sofa. She'd be perched someplace thinking about herself and her needs. She would never understand him.

Maybe Frieda was looking for trouble, maybe she just didn't know what her place was in the world, but she left the bar and headed straight for the elevator where Jamie and his friends were. They were all high, she could see that. The glassy eyes, the exhaustion, the pallor. Jamie nodded at her and grinned, nothing more. He was wearing a tux, but he looked disheveled. He had on his cowboy boots.

"Well here she is," Stella said. "The muse."

"Hello," Frieda said. To Jamie, not to Stella.

Stella turned to her sister. "Could you tell her? I don't have the heart."

The others got into the elevator, but Marianne stayed behind. She was a little unsteady on her feet, but she had a smart, sly little face. She had on earrings made of feathers. Her eyes were ringed with kohl and she was wearing her bangle bracelets and a huge green gemstone ring the same color as her eyes. Maybe it was emerald; maybe it was tourmaline.

"Look, I don't want to hurt your feelings," Marianne began. Her expression said otherwise. She was wearing a black-and-white quilted coat over a black satin dress. She had a dozen little braids in her long hair; when she moved her arm all those gold bangle bracelets sounded like birds chirping.

"You won't," Frieda said. "You don't have to worry about that."

"Okay. Right. Fine. Well, then. Here goes. They got married yesterday."

Frieda noticed that the brass hadn't been polished on the lift doors, and that the lift had already reached the seventh floor. It was an old model, with a lacy brass outer casing and glass doors, but it was still in good working condition. The staff, of course, was asked to use the stairs.

"Did you hear what I said?" Marianne asked. "We all went to the register office, the clerk did the deed, and then we drove to Nick's house in Wiltshire and drank champagne all night. A minister came this morning and married them again, for the religious part to be fulfilled and just for fun. We had a party that lasted all day at our place today, then we called the parents and informed them. And that's the end of the story. Mr. and Mrs. Dunn. Face it," Marianne went on, "he was never going to take you seriously. You're not from our world." She cast a gaze around the lobby. "You're from here."

"That's why you seem drunk," Frieda said. "You've been celebrating. Well, all that drinking added to no sleep is terrible for the dermis, you know. The skin," she added when Marianne looked puzzled. "One day you'll wake up and instead of being fresh and young, your skin will be hanging off and you'll look like you're a hundred years old. I can see the lines already."

Frieda turned and took the stairs up to her room. She ran, as a matter of fact. Once inside, she closed the door and wedged a chair in front of it. She wasn't about to cry over this. A broken heart was a physical impossibility, she knew that, and yet she understood why people referred to it as such. It felt that way. She got into bed and curled up, her knees drawn to her chest. She thought about her mother's list of things to do when he left you. Then she stopped thinking and rocked back and forth. Love wasn't rational; there was no proof that it even existed outside of people's imaginings. Frieda counted the cracks in the wall. She fell asleep and she dreamed of nothing, just blank space and heat. Her chest felt as though it were being crushed. She tried to wake up, but she couldn't; not until Lennie was knocking at the door, which was immovable because of the wedged-in chair.

"Jesus, you had me worried," Lennie said when Frieda finally came and pulled the chair away so Lennie could enter. "I thought you were in a coma."

"You don't have to worry about me," Frieda said.

Lennie looked at her, eyes narrowed. "All right," she said. "I won't if that's the way you want it."

They really had nothing in common anymore.

"I'm fine," Frieda insisted. The mark of her pillowcase on her skin made her face look crumpled.

"I see that," Lennie said. "I'm glad that you woke up and saw him for what he was. He's gone, you know. Checked out."

Just to make certain, Frieda went to his room that night. There was no one in the hallways. The only sound was of water in the pipes as someone ran a bath. She used the skeleton key and went inside. Everything was gone. Someone had already cleaned the room. They'd probably had to send up a crew of maids because of the way he'd left things. Frieda opened the desk drawer, to make certain there weren't any forgotten drugs that could get him in trouble. Everything was in order. She noticed a pad of hotel writing paper. IT SHOULD HAVE BEEN YOU had been scrawled in ink. Frieda tore off that page, folded it, and put it in her pocket. She felt those words imprinted upon her. She could not think of any words other than those. She lay down on the bed they had shared and tried to think, but she couldn't. Just those words. She couldn't get past them.

Soon enough it was ten-thirty, the haunting hour. Frieda could hear the racket in the hall, the man's voice beginning, the panic in his tone, as though he'd been so betrayed he could barely speak. Frieda got off the bed and went to the door. She could hear the man out there more clearly. "I thought you loved me," he said.

Frieda could feel the echo of her pulse in her ears. She felt as if anything could happen. She slowly opened the door. She thought she saw a man in a black suit standing there. A young, handsome man standing right in front of the door to 707. She thought perhaps he was crying.

"Michael Macklin?" she said, but the figure or whatever it was didn't hear her. He was there but he was also somehow far away. Frieda stood in the doorway and watched until the figure disappeared. A hand and a foot. A suit jacket and the back of his head. It happened so fast; she blinked and he was gone and all that was left was a tiny globe of light, like the floaters that appeared behind a person's eyes when they were developing cataracts; a white orb hanging in the air for a moment before it disappeared. Everything was gone. Frieda went back to her room and slept in her clothes. In the morning, she packed up her belongings.

"You're not leaving me alone in this craphole, are you?" Lennie asked.

Frieda hugged her. "I'm not going to be here to tell you what to do," she said. "You're on your own."

"Good, because I never listened anyway."

They laughed then. It had been a perfect friendship that could only exist in that bubble of time. Had Frieda stayed any longer, things would have disintegrated between the two; the differences between them would have made it impossible for either to understand or even appreciate the other. But for now, they were sniffling.

Before she left, Frieda stopped at the desk and asked Meg for one last favor. She asked for the forwarding address Jamie had left when he checked out.

"It would be my job if I got caught," Meg said primly.

"But you don't mind doing other things that are against the law and you don't mind putting Lennie in danger. Isn't what you do called pimping? Or is it just sisterly guidance?"

"Why don't you shut up? You grew up privileged; you know nothing about having to fend for yourself."

"Give me the address, Meg, and then you can do whatever the hell you like."

Meg wrote down an address in Kensington. "Don't say you got it off me."

Frieda went there straightaway. Her suitcase wasn't very

heavy. She didn't own much. She had left most of her belongings in Reading. The road where Stella lived was lovely, shaded
with trees, very exclusive. The sisters lived in a beautiful
Edwardian town house that looked like a wedding cake. White
limestone, five stories, across from a private park where two
little black dogs were chasing sparrows. Frieda sat down on a
bench in front of the wrought-iron fence that surrounded the
park. The fence was so old yellow moss had formed over it and
was as hard as brick. There was a small pond inside the park
and some children were playing. Their voices were sweet. The
light had changed. It wasn't the blue of summer, or the deep
indigo of September. Frieda's father had told her that people in
the grip of a mortal disease tended to hang on through fine
weather and that more deaths occurred during heat waves and
snowstorms than anyone might imagine. Even more deaths
took place right after a holiday or a major life event; the birth of
a grandchild, for instance, or a wedding.

People have amazing strength, the doctor had said. They
hang on beyond the bonds of what anyone would think is
humanly possible.

A dark green Mercedes pulled up and the driver got out
and leaned against his car to smoke a cigarette. He was young
and wore a brown suit. Frieda decided to watch him, biding
her time.

The driver waited a good half hour, then the front door of
the town house opened and Stella and Marianne came out, all in
a rush, laughing. They were wearing short silk dresses, one lilac,
the other blue; clothes too skimpy for the season. They were
laughing, their arms around each other. The driver hurried to
open the car door for them; they ignored him completely and

slipped inside. The driver caught sight of Frieda and as he went around the back of the car he waved to her, as if he knew her. Frieda waved back—they both needed some assurance that they were also human beings, worth something in the grand scheme of things.

When the car took off, Frieda crossed the street and went up the granite steps. She realized she was holding her breath. A stupid thing to do, it caused hyperventilation. She rang the bell, then knocked on the door for good measure. She'd never been shy. You never knew what you might receive if you didn't ask.

A woman came to the door, a pale blonde in her fifties who looked very much like Stella would someday if Stella didn't kill herself with drugs first. Very stylish, very attractive, and very busy. She clearly wasn't pleased to have been disturbed.

"Sorry to bother you," Frieda began.

"Well then don't," Stella's mother, Mrs. Ridge, said. "I just got back from a long trip and all the help has quit in my absence. Everything is a total disaster. The house is a mess and my life is falling apart. So tell me what it is quickly."

"I'm here to see Jamie," Frieda said.

Daisy Ridge stopped going over a sheet of paper in her hand. It was her to-do list. She looked at Frieda quite closely. "Are you?"

"For a minute," Frieda said. "I won't be long."

"If this is a delivery of some sort, just go around to the back door. The only remaining housekeeper is there doing God knows what. Planning on quitting, I presume."

"It's not a delivery."

Frieda was wearing black eyeliner and her black dress underneath her raincoat. She looked very competent, someone who knew what she was doing. She had her suitcase balanced on the step. Mrs. Ridge gazed at the suitcase. It was an old one that had been torn and neatly repaired with packing tape.

"Well you're welcome to take him home with you if that's what you're here for. He's all yours, really, if that's what you want." She often wished she had told her sister that when they'd argued over the same man.

Frieda looked past Mrs. Ridge. The entranceway floor was black-and-white marble. The walls of the sitting room beyond were painted red, then glazed to a shiny patina.

"Could you tell him I'm here? I'm Frieda."

Mrs. Ridge opened the door wider. "Tell him yourself. He's up on the third floor. Second door on the left. In bed, where I gather he spends most of his time."

"Thank you." Frieda stored her suitcase in the corner where there was an ornate mirror and umbrella stand. The stand was gilded with the head of a swan on each corner. "I'll just leave this here."

"He didn't wrong you in any way, did he?" Stella's mother asked. "Because I'll have the police here in an instant if he did. Frankly, I'd be happy to do so. I could help you out, you know. I could have him arrested."

"You needn't bother." Frieda wasn't the sort to confide in people, and she certainly wasn't about to tell this woman anything. Not that Mrs. Ridge was so easily dissuaded. Clearly, she wanted to be rid of her new son-in-law, no matter the means.

"Did he leave you pregnant?"

"No, but even if he had, that's not a crime, is it?"

"I'm sure if we look carefully we'll be able to find several crimes associated with Jamie."

"Does your husband hate him as well?" Frieda asked.

"My husband hates everyone equally. He's not very discerning."

"Well, I won't be long," Frieda said.

She'd heard enough. She went up the stairs. The carpet was gold with a pattern of silver leaves. Frieda kept her eyes down until she reached the third floor. Everything inside the town house looked like a wedding cake. The cornices, the molding, the doors. Frieda knocked on the second door. It was painted cream and gold. It looked heavy enough to withstand the police, should they ever be called in. There was no answer, but it was quite possible that the door also stopped sound. Frieda thought it probably took three or four maids to keep a house like this in order.

She opened the bedroom door. Nearly everything was blue inside: the walls, the canopy over the bed. It was like a gorgeous birdcage. The rug was Persian and very thick; the furniture was mahogany decorated with some sort of gilding. Jamie was indeed in bed. Frieda looked at him for a moment. He looked beautiful to her, and very far away.

Frieda sat in a chair by the window. The chair was blue-and-gold silk damask. The room smelled like jasmine and citrus; she assumed it must be the scent Stella used. It was possible to see the park down below, the gold trees, the blue sky. From up here the world looked like a different place, very far away, very small.

After a while, Frieda went over to the wardrobe and opened it. It was a walk-in wardrobe with huge built-in shelves; there were scores of dresses and pairs of shoes. There were tiny Mary Quant outfits, dresses from Biba in shades of white and cream

and yellow, and a row of sheer Victorian blouses with pearl buttons. There were three leather jackets, one black, one pink, one
white-and-tan stripes. There were gypsy dresses and Chanel
suits. There was the python coat Frieda had seen Stella wearing
at the Egyptian Club, hanging carelessly on a hook, and several
furs, one of them dyed a pale apricot. There were two pairs of
white Courreges boots and dozens of ballet flats in every color.
At the rear of the closet were the fawn-colored suede boots with
the buttons Frieda had admired. Frieda took off her short black
boots and pulled on Stella's. They fitted her perfectly. She went
back to the bed and sat on the side, her legs over the edge. It was
a very tall bed with down coverlets. Jamie opened his eyes and
smiled when he saw her.

"Where am I?" he said.

"I think you're in your marriage bed."

Jamie sat up and wiped the sleep from his eyes. He was
fairly sober, but he wouldn't be for long. He had a massive
headache and his leg was killing him. "Did you get a job here?"
he asked Frieda.

She laughed out loud at that. "I quit being a maid," she said.

"That's probably good," Jamie said. "It's a nowhere job."
He paused. "I don't know what happened. Things just moved
on. I wanted to say good-bye."

"Well now you can," Frieda said.

She noticed a used needle on the marble night-table
top. There was an ashtray filled with butts and a small hashish
pipe.

"Or we could still see each other," Jamie suggested. He
brushed back his hair, which was almost to his shoulders. He
had decided he would never cut it. He didn't have to sacrifice

himself. To hell with that. "I mean we only have one life in this world, so we have to follow our desires."

Jamie kissed her for a while, then Frieda pulled away. He felt cold in a funny way, as though he'd just stepped out of the rain. She remembered him as being different. He'd been hotter; he'd made her burn.

"I'm fucking freezing," Jamie said.

"How did the recording go?" Frieda asked.

Jamie took a cigarette from a pack on the night table and gave her one as well. He grabbed the matches and lit both.

"Great," he said. "Unfortunately, the guys at the label said 'The Third Angel' is the B side. I still need the hit song. It's never enough for them."

"Do you love her?" Frieda asked. "I mean, I hope you don't mind me asking, but I'd like to know."

Jamie looked at her and smiled. "Well, it's not always about that, Frieda."

"Isn't it?"

"Not for people like us," he said. "People who've ridden shotgun with the Angel of Death." He turned on his side and studied her face. "Stella would never have to know about us. Or even if she did know, it wouldn't really affect us. It wouldn't have anything to do with the thing that we have between us. That's something rare."

Frieda wished she'd known him before he'd been ill, when he was a little boy who hadn't yet seen any angels or made a vow to follow his desires, no matter the cost. He'd been different then, she was sure of it; a boy who had everything in front of him, a future worth living.

"Did you miss a great deal of school when you were grow-ing up?" Frieda asked.

Jamie laughed. "You came here to talk to me in my mar-riage bed and that's your question?" Frieda laughed, too. "I missed three years," he told her. "I could never make it up."

It may have seemed a funny question, but Frieda knew pre-cisely why she'd asked; she'd asked so she wouldn't hate him.

She went back to the chair by the window while Jamie got up to go to the bathroom. He rooted around in the night-table drawer for his works. He took a waxy packet from a black-and-white wooden and ivory box.

"I'll be right back," he said.

He reached for a bathrobe.

"I've seen you naked," Frieda reminded him. "You don't have to be shy."

"Right." Jamie grinned and went off to the bathroom.

Frieda watched the leaves, then went to investigate the dressing table. It was a beautiful piece of furniture, painted white, very old and inlaid with mother of pearl and abalone. There were three mirrors. Frieda was surprised to find that her reflection was different from what she might have expected. She was nearly beautiful. She took one of the lipsticks on the table and put it on. A pale shimmer. She looked at herself, then wiped off the lipstick with a tissue. Not her color. She used Stella's tortoiseshell brush. The next time Stella brushed her hair she would see dark hair among her own pale strands left between the bristles. She'd wonder, for a moment or two at least, who had been there. Who had climbed up into a world where she didn't belong.

After about twenty minutes, Frieda went to the bathroom and opened the door. Jamie was on the bathroom floor. It was black-and-white marble, like the front hallway. Frieda went to kneel beside him. She took his wrist and measured his pulse. It was slow and even. He was alive.

"Jamie," she said.

He murmured something. His head was leaning against the side of the tub. She could see his ribs, his arms; she knew all of his body, but it had changed. He was much thinner. There was a blue mark, like a plum, on his forehead.

"Are you all right?" Frieda asked.

"Yep." He nodded. Or tried to. "Just give me a minute," he said.

Frieda went back to the bedroom and got her purse. She opened it and took out the first song she had written. She hadn't wanted to give him everything all at once; she'd been hoarding it, waiting to see if he was worthy of it, perhaps, or maybe just waiting to see what would happen next. Now she knew.

She left it on the bed, on his pillow. "The Ghost of Michael Macklin." She could have gotten him a blanket or a coverlet to try and make him more comfortable on the bathroom floor, but Frieda didn't really think he would have known the difference. He'd be cold either way.

Frieda went out and closed the door behind her. She made her way downstairs and retrieved her suitcase from the front hall. Her footsteps echoed on the marble tiles. This is what Frieda knew for certain, this is the list she would have made: She would never stand by and watch him take his life into his hands so carelessly. She would never be silent while he threw the door open to the Angel of Death, while he called to him and begged him to come inside. She would never be on the outside of his life while he followed his desires. Frieda didn't want anything in return for her songs. What she'd wanted she couldn't have. She knew that. She felt she had what some people called a broken heart, but it wasn't anything physical, and it certainly wouldn't prevent her from carrying her suitcase down to the train.

Stella's mother came out from the parlor as Frieda went to the door.

"Are you done with him, or shall I tell Stella about you?" she asked. "He is your boyfriend, isn't he?"

Mrs. Ridge was a very tall woman. She looked as though she might have been a model once. She appeared softer than she had before, as if she was missing something and didn't quite know what it was.

"Tell her whatever you'd like," Frieda said. "She's your daughter. You're the one who cares about her."

Frieda already knew she would never be done with Jamie. She knew it as she carried her suitcase to Kensington High Street. The boots she had taken from Stella's closet were high heels, but they felt comfortable. It was as though she'd always owned them.

A couple were getting out of a cab, so Frieda got in with her suitcase and asked if the driver could go along Hyde Park on the way to the train station. It seemed the end of the yellow trees. Leaves were fluttering down. She would always think about the way they looked from Stella's bedroom window.

* *

FRIEDA WOULD NOT be there in the winter as she had hoped. She received a letter from Lennie in December about how the park looked like diamonds after an ice storm. Ajax, the manager, had quit, and the second-floor rooms were undergoing a renovation because some of the girls had started a fire with their cigarettes.

I hope you're not worrying about me, Lennie wrote to her. My plan is going strong. I'll be gone from here in under two years.

But when Lennie and Meg were found out over Christmas week, they were both fired by the management and threatened with police action, and Frieda never heard from Lennie again. By then, Frieda was married. She had considered it before she'd run off to London, and now she'd followed it through. Bill was the sort of man who would stand by you, no matter what. He was honest and loyal and maybe that was what she was looking for. Frieda and Bill Rice had a quiet wedding in early December; they went to the register office, and afterward had a luncheon at The Swan, just their immediate families and a few friends. There was cold salmon and champagne and Bill's father, Harry Rice, made a long toast that left everyone in tears.

Except for Frieda; she was not a crier. She looked elegant with her long dark hair wound up, wearing a pale beige suit and the high-heeled suede boots. Even her father, the doctor, had tears in his eyes, something that totally surprised Frieda. She had never seen him cry, except for once, when they went to visit a little girl in an apartment in Reading who'd been going through chemotherapy. Frieda was nine, grown-up enough to be his helper, but she had to wait in the hall that time; the doctor slipped on a mask and pulled coverings over his shoes. The little girl inside was susceptible to germs.

On that visit, Frieda hadn't even realized he was crying as they were driving back until she turned to ask him if he could help her with her math homework when they got home. She must have looked shocked.

"Everybody cries," Frieda's father told her. "Even me."

"Is she dying?"

"Well, we're all dying," Frieda's father had said. "Some now, some later." That was hardly comforting. "She is just a very sweet little girl. Not a complainer. Very much like you."

They were stopped at a light. Frieda remembered that night clearly; she had moved closer to her father. She always felt safe when she was with him. "I'm fine," she said. "I'm not going to get sick."

The doctor had laughed and kissed the top of her head.

He didn't do that often. "Thank you," he said for no reason, maybe because she wasn't that little girl dying inside her bedroom, maybe because she knew that even he needed a word of comfort now and then. Or maybe it was simply because she was his daughter and he loved her.

Frieda invited him to the wedding even though she knew it would be difficult for her mother. As for the doctor, he was decent enough to leave his new wife at home. Vi did quite well in her ex-husband's presence. Everyone was civil. Frieda appreciated that. She understood the reason for manners; they were a survival technique.

"So now you're a married woman," the doctor said to Frieda at the luncheon. It was a buffet. Frieda liked things simple. "You would have been a great doctor, my girl. You had the knack."

"No heart?" Frieda said. "Isn't that the prerequisite?"

Her father looked at her. "Did you think I was heartless?"

No matter what he'd done, Frieda had to be honest.

"No. I thought you were brave. I'm the heartless one." Frieda waved at Bill. Her husband was an extremely nice man. He was in his second year at Reading University, in the chemistry department. Now that they were married they would be living in a cottage on his parent's property, paying rent, of course, but at a reduced rate. He had his graduate studies to think of, after all. "Anyway, being married doesn't mean I'm dead. I'm starting nursing classes. I'm going to specialize in oncology."

The doctor was delighted. "You'll be using your talents. That's what I like to hear."

When Frieda realized that she was pregnant during her first term of training, Bill was over the moon.

"Oh stop." Frieda grinned. "It's only a baby."

"Only!" Bill said. "Only?"

It was spring and Frieda finished out the term. She was a good student, a little less good at being pregnant. She was tired and cranky and she didn't feel much like eating. On Saturdays she always made time for her mother. They went for long walks in the country. Frieda's mum seemed to have aged; she was often confused. Still, Vi was passionate about things she'd never mentioned an interest in before and had joined the local environmental club. "If we don't save the earth, who will?" she asked Frieda. She'd become a rabid bird-watcher and she didn't keep her feelings in check as she had before. She was freer somehow. Once, when they were walking across a field, Frieda's mother turned to her and said, "You won't believe how much you'll love your child."

"Well, of course," Frieda said. Didn't everyone?

Her mother grabbed her arm. "I mean it, Frieda. I don't want you to be shocked. Nothing else will ever matter. You have no idea."

Frieda embraced her mother, then they resumed walking, looking for birds. Vi kept a notebook of the varieties they'd spied: dove, hawk, blackbird, sparrow, wren. Frieda was occupied with other matters as they rambled through the countryside. As always, she was thinking about Jamie. She had left him in that town house in Kensington, but she hadn't given him up. She had taken him back to Berkshire. Jamie might as well be sitting at the table every night at dinner while Frieda and Bill discussed their day. He might as well have been right there in bed with them. Frieda felt like a liar far too often; she played the good housewife, but at night, when she sat in the kitchen looking out the window, she was wishing for another life. Sometimes she gazed down the long gravel drive, still expecting Jamie Dunn to arrive, after he'd searched half of Berkshire for her in a taxi or a limousine. She had the purple jacket folded away in the closet, along with some old sweaters and the black minidress, things she would never again wear but couldn't bring herself to throw away.

That spring, when Frieda was seven months pregnant, she heard Jamie on the radio. She was at the kitchen table with the radio switched on. Thankfully, she was alone. She had fixed a pot of Russian tea and a muffin with jam. She was famished all the time. Outside everything was green. Bill's parents house was known as Lilac House, and their cottage was called The Hedges because it was surrounded by boxwood that had to be trimmed back each year. She actually loved living in the countryside. She who had longed for a city life had become a bird-watcher. She even went to those Save the Environment meetings with her mother and had gotten involved with all sorts of local green issues.

She was perfectly happy, and then, all at once, there was his voice. Frieda truly felt that she'd been shot, as though something had gone right through her, lead or ice or sorrow or love. She sat down. It was "The Ghost of Michael Macklin." It was as if she'd never written it, as though it had been formed whole from the power of Jamie's voice. It was different in some ways; there were electric guitars now, and more of a beat, a pounding one, but inside it was the same song.

When I walk down this hallway, everyone thinks I've left you, but I'm here in my black coat, I won't ever be gone.

Frieda listened to the radio all day long, longing to hear it again, and then, just before Bill came home from university, she found a pop station that was playing it. This time she was more prepared, less stunned by the sound of his voice. She listened as a critic might, and was won over again. It was his first release as a single and the radio station said there was a lot of excitement about his album, *Lion Park,* due out at the end of the week. The single was already number five with a bullet. A bullet must be good; a bullet meant it was getting to people, through the heart, through the soul.

That night, Frieda couldn't sleep. She felt she'd been trapped in an alternate universe, one in which she lay beside Bill in bed and went to visit her mother on Saturdays. She belonged somewhere else, no matter what Stella had said. She belonged with him.

She continued her routine, as if in a dream. But when she went to visit on Saturday, Frieda found her mother was too ill to walk.

"It's just a headache," Vi said, but it seemed like more. She had to lie down. Her head was throbbing. She asked Frieda to close the curtains because the light hurt her eyes. Frieda phoned her father from her mum's back hallway. He said he'd be over in fifteen minutes, but he was there in less than ten. He must have been speeding. Their house was a suburban brick row house with a pretty yard. .

"I was probably stupid to phone," Frieda said. "It's probably nothing."

"You were right to phone." The doctor went upstairs to what had once been his bedroom. Frieda followed behind.

"Not you," Vi said when she saw him.

The doctor laughed. "You know I'm the best doctor in town. Even if you hate me, admit it."

"Fine," Frieda's mum said. "Still wearing two watches, I see."

"Wouldn't want to be late for you," the doctor said. He turned to Frieda. "Can you get a glass of water and two aspirin tablets?"

It wasn't until Frieda was halfway down the stairs that she realized that was what her father did whenever he wanted to get rid of a patient's family member; whenever he thought a diagnosis might be bad.

In a panic, she went into the kitchen and ran the water. She thought she saw someone in a black coat standing outside the window. Her heart flew up, thinking it might be Jamie and then she knew all at once it wasn't Jamie at all. Jamie would never be here in Reading. He would have never come after her. It was the angel who'd sat in the back of the car; the one who waited outside the window until the time was right to come inside and take whatever he wanted. It was the one you didn't want to see at your door.

Frieda's dad called an ambulance and he and Frieda followed along in his car. It was twilight and all the birds were singing. The ambulance didn't have its siren on. Frieda knew that was a bad sign. She'd told her mother everything would be all right when the medics came to get her, but her mother's eyes were closed and she didn't answer. Frieda and her father were silent as they drove. Frieda had begun to cry. She'd thought it might be a stroke, and that her mother would recover, but the doctor told her it had probably been an aneurysm.

"Oh, Frieda," he said. "I wish I could make it turn out differently. I wish I had the power."

Then she knew for certain. It was the tone he always had when there wasn't any hope, when the angel in the black coat had already come and gone and the other two angels were nowhere to be found.

The funeral was small, her mother's closest friends, a few people from the environmental group, Bill and his family, and Frieda's father. The service was held at the graveside because Frieda's mother never had liked anyone making a fuss over her. It was a warm day and Frieda stood in the shade. Her stomach felt huge and her feet were swelling and she thought she might faint. She could not believe that her mother would never know her grandchild. She could not believe this was the way her mother's life had turned out.

After the service, Bill's mother made a luncheon at Lilac House, cold meats and cheese and crusty yellow bread that the bakery down the road was known for.

"You all right?" Frieda's father said. He had come out to the porch to where Frieda was sitting. She could not stand the pleasant chatting going on inside. She couldn't bear to be polite.

"Not really."

"No. Of course not. I don't know if this makes it better or worse, but when I sent you in the kitchen that day she said the best thing that ever happened to her was you."

Frieda's throat hurt and her eyes burned but she didn't cry again. The more she didn't cry the worse she felt. The more she cried the worse she felt. There was no difference, so she might as well not feel anything. That afternoon, when everyone had left, she asked Bill for the keys to the car. She wanted to run some errands to take her mind off things. She drove to the music store in Reading. She wandered around until she found the new releases. There it was. *Lion Park*. Frieda stood there with her head bent. She couldn't stop herself from crying then. It just poured out. A clerk came up to her, a young woman with straight blond hair, wearing jeans and a flowing Indian floral blouse. She probably wasn't more than a few years younger than Frieda was, but she seemed a mere girl. Maybe Frieda had seemed that way when she first went up to London. Like the world was open to her. Like she deserved something more.

"You all right?"

Frieda nodded. She held up the album. "I know him," she said of Jamie.

"Cool," the girl said. "I love that record."

Frieda went and paid for it. He'd taken credit for her two songs, but then she'd always thought he would. The album was dedicated to the nurses who had helped him survive as a child and to his wife, the angel of his life, Stella. Frieda drove home. She kept the record in the china cabinet, and only took it out when no one was at home. She sat by the window and looked at the leaves moving in the hedges and the sparrows nesting there and she listened to Jamie's voice. She still felt the same as she had the first time she'd heard him, and she felt ridiculous for feeling that way. She started taking walks with her father on Saturdays, as she once had with her mother. It was a way to mourn her mother, but after a while she simply enjoyed the doctor's company. They were a good deal alike, after all.

They went on long rambles, through fields, in and out of gates, to villages they'd only passed by in the car. They'd driven to see the doctor's patients in most of these places, but they'd usually been in a hurry. Everything was so different close-up. They saw bluebells, tricklets of streams, little frogs, pollen floating in the air; occasionally they'd spy a family of foxes, a male, along with the vixen and their cubs. The sight of them made Frieda feel like crying all over again, they were so joyous running through a field, but she kept herself in check. She was only twenty, too young to think about crying all the time.

By the end of the spring, Frieda was slowing down. She had gained too much weight and she felt like an ox. All the same, she was starving nearly all the time. They'd begun to take a rucksack of picnic food along on the Saturday walks because

Frieda was so often famished. She'd never been so hungry in her life. They sat in meadows and ate cheese sandwiches and pickles and didn't talk much. When they did, they discussed her father's most interesting and puzzling cases. The woman who was poisoning her own daughters with little balls of mercury taken from a thermometer and calling in to the doctor's office every day. The man who ate nails and suffered from traces of metal in his blood. The baby who couldn't feel pain and kept banging his head on the bars of his crib.

"Medicine is solving mysteries," the doctor said.

"Isn't all of life?"

They agreed that it was. Frieda had brought along a thermos of tea and she now poured two cups. The air smelled sweet, like grass.

"I feel the same way as your mother, you know," the doctor said. "I know all lives are supposed to be equal, but nothing has mattered to me the way you do."

"That's a mistake. I'm quite nasty," Frieda joked. "I've been having cravings for mayonnaise and egg sandwiches and I belch a lot. I'm revolting actually."

"No one but you," the doctor told her.

By then, Frieda had learned to be sociable to the doctor's new wife, who was a pleasant enough woman. Frieda not only remembered the night when Jenny was crying, after her husband had died; she now remembered driving over to that house with her father several times afterward, and having him tell her to stay in the car, where she read until the light disappeared. She saw through the window once. They were having tea. He sang on the way home, and Frieda had wanted to believe everything was the same, but it hadn't been.

The baby came at the start of summer, a little boy they named Paul who'd taken three days of horrible labor before he arrived. At the end of those three days, Frieda thought she might die and she didn't much care if she did. She hated her own baby and herself and the whole world, and then all at once he was born and everything changed. She wondered why no one spoke the truth about birth; it was so close to dying you could see the angel before you, right there, standing on the linoleum floor. Actually there were two angels, the Angel of Life and the Angel of Death, both beside the window, waiting. One was in shadow, one was in light; it was difficult to determine which was the one you wanted to watch over you. And then there was the Third Angel, the one her father had spoken of, the one right in the middle that could fall either way, the one you have to try to rescue, if you can, and that was when the baby was born.

The moment she saw her child, Frieda became another person.

"Can you believe we made this little man?" Bill said. "He's perfect. All fingers and toes." It was the first time Frieda had ever seen her husband cry.

She fell madly in love in that instant. She wasn't even listening to Bill. The baby seemed to be staring at her with his clear gray-blue eyes. He was looking right inside to the deepest part of her. Love of my life, Frieda thought. Angel of angels. She sobbed as though her heart was breaking and everyone thought it made sense that she needed a sedative after the labor she'd been through. She deserved a rest, after all; she was entitled to spend the rest of the summer enjoying the baby.

She didn't go back to nursing classes in autumn; she'd wait

a year before she returned. She wanted the autumn to last forever. The green turned to that golden color she'd always loved, of ash trees and oak. She and her father took the baby on their walks now, bundled into a backpack the doctor had fashioned into a papooselike creation.

"You should patent it," Frieda said. "Women all over would want to carry their babies this way."

Paul wasn't in the least bit fussy. His eyes had stayed blue and he had great powers of concentration, on this the doctor and Frieda agreed. The baby seemed to be able to tell the difference between the songs of a magpie and a sparrow. He preferred the magpie, oddly enough, and let out a squeal whenever one called out. Paul also had perfect pitch when he cooed his little baby songs, perhaps because Frieda listened to Jamie's album so often when they were alone. She played it while she nursed him in a chair by the window and while they took their rests at midday. Once she swore Paul was humming "The Ghost of Michael Macklin," the chorus, which was so mournful. The words had been sad enough when she'd written them, but the music took the sorrow to an unspoken level. Frieda felt a chill across her back when she heard the baby humming, and then of course she realized she must have been mistaken. No baby could be that spot-on musical, not even hers.

Still, she had the feeling there were great things in store for her child, and she was humbled to be the one lucky enough to raise him. She was well aware that most mothers might feel the same way about their children, but that didn't lessen her sense of possibility. She felt as though she had known Paul forever, as though he'd been her destiny all along, what she'd been running to when she hadn't even known she was on the run.

"You were wrong," Frieda told her father as they walked back across the meadow to The Hedges at the end of one of their rambles. They were wearing boots and sweaters and they'd wandered especially far that day. The baby was sleeping in his papoose backpack, tied onto the doctor's back. Frieda had never been happier. "Love isn't complicated," she said.

SHE HEARD ABOUT Jamie's death one afternoon after she'd gone to buy apples for a fruit crumble. The baby, now three months old, was with Bill, and Frieda had gone to a farm up the road; Frieda bought the apples, then put the sack in the backseat of the car and switched on the radio. Jamie's album had been a big hit and he'd been touring all through the spring and summer. But to her horror, she now heard that he'd been in a car accident in France a month earlier. Frieda had been so busy with the baby, she'd stopped listening to the news. She'd never even heard about it. Jamie Dunn and his wife and her sister and the drummer in his band were gone. He'd been out of the world for more than thirty days while Frieda had been going on with her life, taking care of the baby, going for walks, not knowing. The broadcaster announced there had just been a memorial service at the Chelsea Town Hall where Jamie had given his last concert in London earlier in the year. Mick Jagger was reported to have sung "The Ghost of Michael Macklin." It was said that a thousand candles had been lit outside the town hall, and that fans were collecting the wax from the pavement as a keepsake.

Frieda sat there in the lot for a while, then she drove out onto the road. Instead of taking the first turn at the roundabout that would lead toward home, she took the second exit and went south, heading toward London. When she stopped to refill the car's tank she phoned The Hedges. She told Bill that an old friend had died and that she was driving to London; she'd be back as soon as she could.

"Someone from the hotel where you worked?" Bill asked. It was a time they rarely spoke of.

"Yes," Frieda told him. "We were friends."

"You're all right?" Bill said.

"I think so," Frieda said. "I will be."

She hated driving in the city, but she made her way. She was afraid she wouldn't find parking, so she left her car on Kensington High Street. She remembered where the park was. It had seemed much larger last time but it was only a pretty neighborhood park ringed with a Victorian iron fence covered with moss. She was not as sure of the house; they were all Edwardian town houses, not identical, but all equally graceful. Then Frieda remembered it had looked like a wedding cake, all white; the one with the arched windows facing the park. She went up the stairs and knocked and a housekeeper answered.

"I'm sorry," the housekeeper said. "Mrs. Ridge isn't accepting any visitors."

"Of course I am." Stella's mother was in the hall. She came closer. "Do I know you?" she asked Frieda.

"Not really," Frieda said. "We met a while back. I knew your daughters, and Jamie."

Daisy Ridge studied Frieda. "The girl with the suitcase," she said.

"Right."

"Come in."

Mrs. Ridge asked the housekeeper to bring them tea. She was wearing a black suit and high heels and Frieda felt dumpy and out of place in jeans and walking shoes and an old Burberry jacket that had belonged to her mother. There were burrs stuck to the fabric, all along the cuffs.

The Ridges' marriage had ended before the girls died, and now Daisy Ridge was alone in the house. She had lost everyone who had ever mattered to her. In the mornings she couldn't believe she woke up, as she had no reason to do so. She thought maybe her sister had been the lucky one to pass so early, before she'd had time to become too attached to the world, before she had too much to lose.

"You have a lovely home," Frieda said. The tea was brought around. There were scones and jam and a pot of green tea that smelled like weeds and honey. When the housekeeper left, Frieda said, "I just wanted to come and say how sorry I was."

"For what? Because you didn't take Jamie away from my daughter? I assumed that was why you came that day. I wish you'd been more successful. Maybe they'd all be alive if you had been. He was driving, you know. When a drug addict drives, what can you expect?"

"In all fairness, he wasn't the only one."

Mrs. Ridge stood up and Frieda thought perhaps she was about to be asked to leave; perhaps she'd insulted Stella's memory even though she'd only spoken the truth. But no, there was something more Mrs. Ridge wanted to show her.

"You never saw the rest of the house. Just Stella's bedroom," Mrs. Ridge said. "I was rude to you. I made assumptions."

"I did come here for him that day," Frieda admitted. "I

wanted him terribly. I was crazed with it. But he didn't love me. I realized that. I wasn't in his world."

"Love," Mrs. Ridge said. "Is that what led to this?"

"They were right for each other. He'd have to be crazy not to have fallen in love with her."

Mrs. Ridge turned her face away. She had been crying for weeks, stopping and starting. She'd suddenly feel a wave of heat across her chest, up along her throat and face, and there she'd be. It happened when she least expected it, when she didn't even think she was feeling anything. She quickly composed herself—she was good at that—then she turned back to the girl who was visiting her. Ordinarily she wouldn't even have spoken to a girl like this—a stranger she had no interest in. Now she couldn't seem to stop herself. She was lonely, she supposed. She didn't see many people who had known her daughters as anything more than two spoiled, selfish girls. Yes, they took drugs, but they were so much more than that.

"Marianne was supposed to spend the weekend in the country with me. At the last moment she changed her mind. They were inseparable, you know. Best friends, watching out for each other. Stella phoned her, invited her along on tour. It would be fun to go on a trip with the band, much more fun than being with me. One was bad enough. Two is destruction. I don't know if I can bear two."

"They seemed to take care of each other. Even I saw that."

Mrs. Ridge looked up. "Yes," she agreed. "They were always together from the time they were little girls. I couldn't separate them, even for a nap."

"I have a little boy," Frieda said. "His name is Paul. That's why I came here. I didn't come here because of Jamie. I came because of you. Because I'm someone's mother, the same as you. And I'm so sorry."

Mrs. Ridge looked at her. Frieda wasn't at all what she expected; she hadn't been back then and she wasn't now. She was smart and she was honest. She looked like an ordinary girl, but she wasn't. Mrs. Ridge saw that now.

"If there's anything I can ever do to help in any way, I'm here," Frieda told her. "You can call me, and I'll drive to London."

What she didn't say was that she'd also come because she felt lucky, and her luck had filled her with guilt. It wasn't her father who was the one who'd been left bereft. The deepest truth was that she had come because Jamie hadn't loved her, because she hadn't been the one in the car with him, so crowded with people and musical equipment and suitcases heaped with clothes, that the Angel of Death must have had to squeeze in to fit between them. Frieda was here in this house in Kensington because she hadn't been wanted, she'd been the loser at the time and now somehow she had won. She was still here, still the owner of the stolen beige suede boots, the ones she put on whenever she and Bill went out, which wasn't very often these days. They only went out when Bill's mother would stay because Frieda didn't trust a babysitter with her child. Not yet. Maybe not ever. She would probably turn him into a mummy's boy, her darling child, but she didn't care. He'd probably be the sort of man who called home every Sunday and who argued with his wife about always inviting his mum to holiday dinners. He'd be a man with perfect pitch, who liked to walk through the countryside, who knew the difference between the song of a sparrow and the song of a dove. Just thinking about what she would do if she should ever lose Paul made her eyes start to tear.

"I'll show you something," Mrs. Ridge said. "You'll understand."

They went to the back of the house into the conservatory. The curtains were drawn and the room was darkened, but there were so many windows and a skylit dome that bands of sunlight managed to stream through. There were tall ferns and orchids in majolica pots. Mrs. Ridge opened the glass doors that led outside. There was an enormous garden behind the house, astonishingly large for the city. They stepped out. It was so overgrown it was like entering a jungle. Everything was golden, a jumble of vines and shrubs that should have been cut back. Bramble, ash tree, tufted weeds. And then there were surprising varieties for a London garden: belladonna, thorn-apple, hemlock, black nightshade. These things had never been planted; they had arrived on their own in the past thirty days, ever since the girls had gone. Everything poisonous had flourished.

"My mourning garden," Mrs. Ridge said.

She had lost her daughters and she felt as though she was never going to let this garden be cared for again. It was grief that fed this garden, nothing less. In summer it was green, and now it was gold. In a few weeks it would be black as satin, and then at last it would be white. For months it would stay that way, pure white.

Frieda stood there in the cool shadows. There was a beautiful herringbone path made of brick and cobblestones. There was a plum tree whose fruit had fallen, left to rot on the ground. There were white roses, overgrown as the weeds, falling into pieces, dropping from twisted black canes. In the branches of an apple tree there was a dove in her nest, roosting out of season. They could hear the chirping of her fledglings, even though it was bad timing, the absolute wrong season. It would be cold before they knew it. They stood there and worried for the birds in the nest, for the coming winter, for all that could and would happen in due time. At that moment Frieda understood all there was to know about love. It was all very clear, as though the truth had written itself in the air. Everything was yellow; everything was moving so fast. Frieda took Mrs. Ridge's hand and stayed outside with her until it grew dark.

III.

The Rules of Love

1952

LUCY GREEN COULDN'T STOP READING. She was a secret reader and the trip across the Atlantic had given her all the time in the world to be secretive. Her stepmother, Charlotte, thought she was unsociable, perhaps even pathological, but Lucy stayed in her tiny stateroom and read *Anne Frank: The Diary of a Young Girl* three times. Sometimes she felt as though she lived in that attic, that she had Anne Frank's dreams. She was motherless and she had the look that motherless girls sometimes have, uncared for in some deep way, hair unbrushed, socks mismatched.

She only came out of her stateroom for meals and to walk around the deck with her father in the evenings, during which time they did not speak, except to occasionally mention the shape of the clouds or the color of the sea. The ocean was endless and terrifying and beautiful. There was no need for words when you were on the deck of an ocean liner, when the world seemed so vast, and you were only a speck of flesh and blood.

Anne Frank: The Diary of a Young Girl had just been published in the States in June and Lucy's stepmother thought her too young for such material; she nixed it and suggested Lucy stick to Nancy Drew. Frankly, Charlotte wasn't much of a reader, and she thought books could be dangerous if placed in the wrong hands. But Lucy was twelve, old enough to read what she pleased; she didn't care what her stepmother thought, or her father, either, for that matter. She didn't care that she was on a ship crossing the Atlantic, and that all of her friends at home in Westchester were jealous that she was going off to a wedding in England while they led their boring lives back home.

What did she care about adventure and festive occasions? Lucy was the sort of girl who thought a lot about why people were put on earth, and spent her time wondering how she might right the wrongs of the world. She did not believe that sitting at the captain's table and ordering shrimp cocktail would help her along this path. She didn't want to sprawl out on a deck chair or talk to the other children on board, as her stepmother continued to suggest. Lucy was not sociable and she wasn't a great fan of traveling. For one, she had a turtle named Mrs. Henderson that she'd had to leave with the next-door neighbor who didn't even like turtles, and she worried about

Mrs. Henderson's well-being. Secondly, on her only other trip away from home she had gone to Miami with her father and Charlotte—whom she was supposed to call Mom, but whom she called nothing at all—and she hadn't enjoyed the trip one bit. She'd been shocked to discover that the golf course her father was so excited about down in Miami did not allow Negroes to play, except for Mondays, caddy day. There were so many wrongs out there in the world; so many people mistreated. Plus, Lucy didn't even believe in marriage as a valid institution, not since her father had married Charlotte at any rate, so going to the wedding of her stepmother's sister seemed pointless, even if it was in London.

The boat docked in Liverpool, and after they collected their luggage there was a taxi to the train station. Lucy sat on a bench while they waited in the station and continued reading the diary. She was wearing a skirt because her stepmother insisted that slacks were for tomboys, and were totally unacceptable wear for travel. Lucy's father, Ben, had winked at her, but he went along with what Charlotte said, so there Lucy was, uncomfortably dressed in a frumpy skirt. Lucy thought she might be a pervert, actually. She certainly had weird thoughts: That her mother had died because of something she had done wrong. That her stepmother was slipping arsenic into her iced tea, which Lucy poured into potted plants all through the voyage over rather than drink. That her father would be better off without her, his life simpler and easier. That it wasn't possible to fight off all that was wrong in the world and that it took too much to get through each day and probably wasn't worth the effort. Lucy was disappearing and no one even noticed. Every day she was slipping farther away.

"You doing all right?" Lucy's father asked in the train station.

It was sooty and hot. The beginning of August. Ben Green was a lawyer and a Democrat and he said he was glad to leave the States for a month because Eisenhower and Nixon had just gotten the Republican nomination. He'd prefer to be standing in a sweltering train station in Liverpool, hauling around his wife and daughter's luggage, than forced to read the *New York Times* back in Westchester and be hit with the news that charted Ike's progress.

"I'd rather be home," Lucy said. "Anne Frank didn't go outside for over two years. She didn't have to travel to know about people. She understood things from the inside out. She wanted to be a writer."

"The whole world wants to be a writer," Ben Green said. He'd written a novel at college and thrown it in the trash. "You'll be the prettiest girl at the wedding."

"Unlikely." Lucy kept reading, but she felt herself blush. She knew she wasn't pretty. She noticed that one of her socks was brown and the other was gray. She crossed one foot over the other to hide her mistake.

Her father kissed the top of her head, and then it was time to get on the train. They had their own compartment, which was sweltering and dim. Lucy curled up with her book. She pretended she was at home.

"She'll get eyestrain reading in the dark," Charlotte said to Lucy's father when they were on their way.

Despite her reading, Lucy was eavesdropping. She was very good at it.

"Leave her be," Ben said. "She's in mourning."

That was when Lucy realized that she was. Even though

her mother had been gone for two years, she was still in mourning. There was no point trying to escape that. Whenever she stopped reading, she started to think about her mother. Sometimes she imagined the last day they had spent together, the most perfect day in the world. They had gone for a walk in Central Park and they'd seen something no one ever saw in New York City. A blue heron in a pond in the Ramble, the wildest part of the park, filled with brambles and bird nests. Since that time, nothing had seemed interesting or worth paying attention to. Except for books.

Lucy closed her eyes and slept all the way to London. It was pitch-black and very humid when they got there. They gathered their luggage and got off the train with the rest of the crowd. And then something unexpected happened. As Lucy stared up at the chaos of Euston Station, she felt the way some people did when they fell in love. London had won her over despite herself. She actually felt a quickening of her blood. Outside it was even better—darker and more bustling. The streetlights were yellow and Lucy felt she was in a dream. She could vanish into the hustle of London and yet still be herself. There were probably thousands—no, millions—of books she hadn't yet read in this city. There were bookshops and libraries and bookstalls and publishers and guided tours of places where writers had made up whole other worlds out of nothing but words. Every person who passed by was most likely a writer, or at the very least, a story waiting to be told. Lucy wanted to visit each bookstore; she wanted to walk through the streets, to look into people's faces and guess what had happened to them. The way that Lucy felt surprised her. It shocked her, actually. It had been a very long time since she'd wanted anything.

They took a taxi and went to their hotel. Charlotte's entire family would be staying at the Lion Park, and Charlotte was aggravated because they were the last of the Evans wedding party to arrive. She blamed bad luck and Lucy's dawdling. Plus this was not the hotel she would have chosen; it was plain and homey and that was not Charlotte's style. Lucy fully expected to hate it as well, but first she had fallen for Euston Station and now she was mad for their hotel. Everything was so unpredictable and charming. The lobby looked out onto a garden in which there was a stone lion rumored to have been stolen by a knight during the Crusades. The statue was faintly mossy and green and surrounded by bluestones. The lobby itself was even better. There was rose-covered wallpaper and fresh white woodwork. Best of all, there was actually a huge rabbit sitting behind the front desk. Lucy loved London.

"Is that real?" she asked Dorey Jenkins, the girl who was the night clerk. The rabbit was as big as an extra-large Persian cat. It had long white hair.

"Oh, yeah," Dorey said. She turned to the rabbit. "Show us your bunny hop, Millie." The rabbit came hopping over and Dorey gave her a bit of lettuce kept in a drawer along with the paper clips and rubber bands. "She's our mascot. She wandered in off the street one day. We think she found her way over from the park, but now she lives under the desk."

"If you followed her she'd probably lead you to another dimension in space and time, and you'd be just like Alice," Lucy said. "You'd see worlds of wonder. You'd have to struggle to get back."

"Nah, she'd lead me straight to the bin in the kitchen. She

likes to look for potato peelings. She's crazy about them. And she likes to eat wallpaper as well, which gets her into trouble."

"I don't mind trouble." Lucy felt excited and alive just being in London.

"There you are," Dorey said warmly. "You and Millie are two of a kind."

LUCY DIDN'T WANT to be traveling with her father and Charlotte, but at least she had her own room on the seventh floor. It was stuffy, with a vanity right there in a bureau beside the bed, and there was a bathtub instead of a shower, but at long last she had some privacy and could go more than ten minutes without someone getting in her business, informing her that everything she did was wrong. As if she didn't know that.

Lucy unpacked her clothes, washed up, and read the diary until she fell asleep. She liked the way London sounded, traffic and birdsongs both. The noise put her to sleep and when she dreamed she dreamed she was following a rabbit down a hallway. Because her internal clock was off, Lucy woke up early, before she could get to the end of the hall in her dream. When she woke Lucy felt shortchanged, the way she would if she'd lost a book before she'd gotten to the end of the story. Maybe she'd dream that same dream some other time and find out what happened. She got dressed and went downstairs to the restaurant. It wasn't officially open, but the cook said he'd make her tea and toast, so Lucy sat down and read from the diary. A good-looking man came in and glanced around.

"This place is dead," he said.

He had a New York accent and great Irish looks, dark hair and light eyes. From then on, Lucy always preferred men with that coloring. He had an incredible smile, as well; even someone who was twelve could tell that.

"Seems like you're the only living person in London," the man said. "Mind if I sit down?"

Lucy nodded. She kept reading. She didn't mind being rude when she needed to be.

"Anne Frank," the man mused. "I saw her house in Amsterdam."

Lucy put down her book. "No you didn't. You're just saying that."

"Swear to God." The man held up his hand as though he was a Boy Scout. "I've been traveling around and I was there last week. Stood outside and said a prayer."

"Really?" Lucy said, not quite believing him.

Her tea and toast came. She put marmalade on it, but when she took a bite, she wasn't sure whether or not she liked it. It was bitter, but maybe she'd get used to bitter things. She was somewhat embarrassed to be chewing in front of the man who'd sat down across from her. Thankfully the handsome man was hungry, too; he ordered eggs and bacon.

"Give me three sunny-side up," he said. "Make that four."

"Tea and toast," the cook offered. "We're not open yet, you may have noticed if you've bothered to look around."

"Great. Fine. Make it toast. Give me anything. Jesus, you'd think I was asking for a gourmet meal." The man lit a cigarette. Lucky Strike. "So what are you doing in London?"

"I'm here for a wedding, not that I believe in marriage."

"Ah. Marriage."

"It's a load of crap actually," Lucy said.

She raised her chin, expecting him to react the way most adults did and tell her that girls with foul mouths were unattractive, but he didn't.

"Utter crap most of the time," he agreed. "But not always." The man stuck out his hand. "Michael," he introduced himself.

"Lucy."

"I see we have something in common, Lucy. We're not big believers in things."

"Why should we be?" Lucy said.

"Love exists," Michael informed her. "Believe it or not."

"Not." Lucy had finished her tea and toast just as Michael's order arrived. She sat there anyway and watched him refuse the marmalade. Despite their differing opinions on love, they were quite alike in many ways.

"Love brought me all the way from New York. Through Paris, through Amsterdam, past Anne Frank's house, right to here."

"My stepmother brought me here," Lucy said. "I could be home reading. Instead I have to go to some stupid wedding."

"What makes it stupid?" He sounded genuinely interested. Grown-ups were usually bored with a child's opinion, but Michael was different.

"I don't even know the people involved," Lucy explained. "It's my stepmother's sister, Bryn. I hope for her sake that they're nothing alike."

Michael grinned. He nodded to the book on the table. "That's the diary Anne Frank wrote?" When Lucy said yes, he asked if he could borrow it. Lucy didn't usually like to lend books; people never returned them and besides, she'd gotten used to reading the diary all through the day.

"Unless you don't trust me," Michael said.

Lucy looked up at him. It wasn't easy to say no to him.

"You'll give it back?" she asked.

Michael crossed his heart with his hand, making an *X*. "Hope to die," he promised.

LUCY WAS A little lost without her book. She stood at the front desk and asked the day clerk if she could see the rabbit. But the day clerk was a middle-aged man who was studying accounting and disliked children. He was nothing like Dorey Jenkins.

"This is a place of business," he told Lucy.

She spied the rabbit in a wire hutch in the rear office. For some reason that made her feel like crying. She wandered into the courtyard and sat on the base of the lion. The stone smelled damp and mossy.

"That is a statue, not a bench," the day clerk called.

Lucy went through the lobby, out onto the street, where she asked a woman who looked like a grandmother how to get to the nearest park. She was directed to Hyde Park, only a few blocks away, and when she arrived she was shocked by how enormous it was. There were probably hundreds of rabbits living in the hedges. Her mother had always told her when in doubt about a city, visit a park.

On the trip over, Lucy had met a woman who practiced fortune-telling. She was the maid who cleaned the staterooms, and she told Lucy that she'd been fortunate enough to be born in the year of the rabbit in the Chinese calendar; so maybe she was lucky, if she could ever make herself believe in anything as stupid as luck. Now it was the year of the dragon, which probably meant anything could happen. As she walked through Hyde Park, Lucy had the same weightless feeling she'd had in Euston Station. She was still in love with London. She walked on until she stumbled upon the Peter Pan statue in Kensington Gardens. Then she sat down in the grass. It was a lovely place to be. For the first time in two years she was without a book, and that was very strange indeed. But her mother had been right; parks revealed the inside of a city, the greenest, sweetest piece.

There were two young women staring at Lucy and clearly talking about her. The grass was perfect and it didn't even smell like a city. Every once in a while it was possible to hear the drone of a bus in the outside world, but that was it. The young women were still talking about her.

"Don't be rude," Lucy called. They were tall blondes who looked very much alike; they reminded Lucy of swans, with their long necks and their pale hair. She thought perhaps there was a rule about not sitting on the grass, or she had crossed onto private property. Or maybe they just didn't like Americans. "Come and talk to me if you have something to say."

Lucy would have never been so forthright back in the States, but it was different here. No one knew her. No one knew that after her mother died she locked herself in her bedroom and didn't eat for a week. She drank water, though, and the water had developed a strong taste after her first three days of not eating. It tasted like wine, or what she imagined wine to be. Sweet and dark and rich. At first she'd thought it was the start of a miracle, water turning to wine and all, and that if she left her room she would discover that her mother was still alive, working in the garden or fixing French toast. But it had only been water in her glass and her mother was gone. Her beautiful mother with the long black hair who wasn't afraid to take off her shoes and wade into a pond in Central Park when she saw a heron.

That was when Lucy stopped believing in anything. She came down from her room and fixed a sandwich and started eating, giving up her diet of pure water. Her father thought her reappearance meant everything was fine again, but he'd been wrong.

The English women wandered over; their names were Daisy and Rose. They were sisters, but also best friends, and they held hands. They were wearing blue pleated skirts and white blouses. "We were looking at you because you look like Katharine Hepburn. She's our favorite actress. She's brilliant. We thought you might be related."

So it wasn't something horrible, something she'd done wrong. Lucy smiled. Daisy and Rose were grown-ups—Daisy had two little daughters at home—but they spoke to her as though she were an equal. They were so excited to meet her that she suddenly felt important.

"My aunt," she said. It was an outright lie, but a good one. It was so nice talking to people who thought she was a somebody that she didn't want them to go away disappointed. "Katharine and my mother had the same grandmother. We see her all the time."

Daisy and Rose wanted to know all about Katharine Hepburn and Lucy kept them in thrall throughout the afternoon. At Kate's house, she told them, there was lemonade and ice cream for breakfast. Kate had a chauffeur who was a magician who could call doves out of the sky. Miss Hepburn asked Lucy to read all her scripts before she made a decision about what part to play next; she depended on Lucy, actually. People didn't wear bathing suits in Hollywood; they all had huge swimming pools and they went swimming at night, in the moonlight, naked as fish. They drank champagne as soon as the sun went down and they wore their party dresses only once, then threw them in the trash.

"I'm going to Hollywood," Rose announced. "I need to start a new life."

Her sister looked surprised and said, "You can't go that far away!"

Daisy and Rose walked Lucy halfway back to her hotel; when it was time for them to part, they hugged each other as though they were the best of friends, and Lucy said if they were ever in the U.S.A. they should look her up. She'd have Kate's chauffeur pick them up at the airport and drive them all over town.

When Lucy got back to the Lion Park, her father was in the lobby with a policeman. As soon as Ben saw Lucy he ran over and grabbed her.

"Where on earth were you? The clerk said you were in the restaurant talking to a stranger and then you disappeared." Lucy's father was so upset he looked as though he might smack her, something he'd never done. He didn't believe in things like corporal punishment or the death penalty and he certainly didn't believe in hitting his own child. He just looked that way, as though he could explode.

"I was just in the park," Lucy said. "I met some English women who wanted to know about America."

"Good God, Lucy, you're a little old to be behaving so

irresponsibly. Don't you understand how worried I was? I thought you had disappeared. We're in a foreign city and I turn around and you're gone."

"I'm sorry." Lucy felt idiotic and small. Now Charlotte would have another weapon to use against her. She was irresponsible. One more flaw that could be added to the list. Unsociable. Unsophisticated. Unappreciative.

"WE SHOULD HAVE left her home," Charlotte said later when she and Ben were alone in their room. They'd gone out to dinner with Charlotte's family, and Ben had wanted to bring Lucy along, even though she would have sat there reading the entire time. Charlotte had to beg him to leave her at the hotel, and then she had forced Lucy to sign a contract vowing she would not leave the hotel without informing her father. Now Charlotte was brushing her hair, which was long and honey colored. She had brought three suitcases along on the trip, one for purses and shoes.

"For a month?" Ben said. "Lucy will be fine. Kids can adjust to anything. Look at Anne Frank."

"Do not mention Anne Frank, Ben. I mean it! I can't stand hearing about her all the time. I don't even want to hear the word *frankfurter*."

Ben laughed. He was in bed watching Charlotte. He had fallen hard for her. She was ten years younger. He'd been so sick of being alone and she had been so beautiful and that was that, a whirlwind of heat, and then marriage.

"Maybe we should have skipped the wedding," Ben said. "Gone back to Miami. Had some fun."

"In August? And Bryn is my sister, despite her mistakes. I was not going to miss her wedding."

Bryn was set to marry an Englishman she'd met in Paris and her family had come to help celebrate. Everyone was overjoyed, and for good reason. Bryn Evans was only twenty-three, but she hadn't had an easy time. Only a very few people knew the truth about her, and all of them were related by blood. Outsiders, including Ben Green, had no idea that Bryn had a secret history. She had been married before, to a wildly inappropriate and dangerous man of whom everyone had disapproved. No one had actually met him, but they had read the police reports. That was more than enough. He was actually some sort of con man who robbed widows of their fortunes or something like that. Anyway, the family had taken care of things and there'd been an annulment. Bryn had been sent to Paris, where she'd met Teddy Healy, a banker who would surely be a good influence on her. Teddy was a good choice, a man the family approved of. At last, a logical decision, unlike most of what Bryn did. Still, despite having Teddy in her life, Bryn seemed shaky and moody. On top of that, she had begun to drink.

Tonight, for instance, their dinner had quickly gone wrong. There were three nights before the wedding and that seemed a good enough excuse to celebrate at every opportunity. Charlotte's whole family—her parents, Carl and Mary; the eldest sister, Hillary; and her husband, Ian; along with Teddy's brother, Matthew; and his wife, Francie—had joined in for the festivities. Teddy and his brother had been orphaned early on, then raised by an aunt who'd passed away; each boy had been the other's rock, two dependable, serious boys who'd grown to be dependable men.

Halfway through the meal, Matthew started to have his doubts about his brother's choice. Bryn had two glasses of wine before the main course was served. Bryn wasn't only the youngest sister, she was the prettiest as well, and she'd been spoiled. She was stubborn about foolish things; she refused to cut her pale blond hair, for instance, which hung to her waist. That night at the restaurant she wore it up, twisted into a French knot; even so, it was her best feature. She wore a cornflower blue silk dress. Teddy had given her a huge square-cut diamond, set in platinum. On her small pale hand it was impossible not to notice the ring.

"This old thing," she had said when her sisters complimented it. "It weighs a ton."

Halfway through the entrée, Bryn was sloshed. Charlotte asked if she'd like to come along with her for a breath of air, which in truth meant taking a cigarette break during which time Charlotte would attempt to sober her up. The two went downstairs to the ladies' room. Bryn nearly fell down the steps.

Charlotte got out cigarettes for them both.

"Stop drinking," she said. "You look like a fool up there."

"You always think you can tell me what to do. For your information, I'm not drinking. Not seriously." Bryn took a drag of her cigarette. Her face was flushed and hot. "Not yet."

"No one's going to be here in London to watch out for you," Charlotte said. She had always worried about her sister, whose bad decisions Charlotte believed were due to youth and naïveté. "You're going to have to start being responsible for yourself."

Bryn smoked her cigarette and stared at herself in the mirror. When she narrowed her eyes she looked as though she had disappeared. A blur of blue and blond and smoke. All of it fad-

ing into the ether. She actually despised her engagement ring.
She felt as though she were wearing handcuffs.

"Did you ever hear of love?" Bryn said. "Or are you totally
cold-blooded?"

"Love," Charlotte said dismissively. "That's the way a child
approaches marriage. You're as foolish as my stepdaughter."
Charlotte had had enough of such nonsense. It was not a crime
to be a realist, was it? It didn't mean you were any less of a person. "Next thing you'll be telling me you're reading the diary of
Anne Frank. Grow up, Bryn."

"At least Anne Frank died for something important and
worthwhile!"

"Listen to me: Anne Frank died because there are horrible,
awful people in this world and for no other reason. Everything
is a botch and a mess, and you have to set your own life straight
if you get the chance. She wasn't able to, but you are not in a
war. You're in London with a huge diamond on your hand. So
just stop it."

Bryn put out her cigarette. She had already decided that she
wasn't going back to the dinner upstairs. She had a particular look when she was about to be defiant, not unlike the
expression Lucy had whenever she opened a book. Bryn's lips
were pursed and there was a slight tremor beneath one eye, as
though she were a bomb set to explode.

"You're going to fuck it up, aren't you?" Charlotte said.
"We all came over for this wedding. Teddy is a great guy who's
crazy about you. This is your chance to have a real future with a
nice, normal man."

Bryn laughed. She opened her handbag. Charlotte thought
she was getting another cigarette; instead, she pulled out a pair

of cuticle scissors. When she'd lived her secret life, Bryn had been settled in an apartment in Manhattan right off Ninth Avenue. It was hardly the best address, but she really didn't care. She'd stopped going to classes at Barnard; she'd stopped all contact with her family. She had never known anyone who lived with a man without being married. Because she was uncomfortable with the situation, the man she was in love with married her, down at city hall, even though he didn't believe in society's rules and regulations. He was a socialist and a free-thinker, but he did it for her. He would have done anything for her; he never complained or told her she was spoiled and stupid and worthless. Bryn didn't even have sex with him until their wedding night. It was funny to hear him say he would wait, he who had been with a hundred or more women, but he said she was worth it.

A detective had found her. When he and the girls' father jimmied the lock on the apartment door and walked in, they could hear her singing. They followed the sound. They were both practical, wary men who felt as if they'd stumbled into a dream. Bryn had a beautiful voice, sad, a little like Patti Page. Her voice echoed as though she'd fallen down a hole; but actually it was reverberating off the black-and-white tiles. She'd been in the bathtub, in steaming hot water. When Bryn saw her father and the detective, she'd stood up without even bothering to cover herself. "No," she had cried. "Go away from here."

Bryn was thinking about that moment as she pulled the pins out of her hair and let it fall down her back. She moved so quickly Charlotte didn't even understand what her sister was doing at first. Later, Charlotte had the sense that it was almost as though someone had committed suicide in front of her, as though Bryn had stood there and pulled the trigger without giving her sister time to react. Charlotte sat there in shock while Bryn began to hack at her hair. She held the length of it in one hand like a snake or a rope. With a few quick clips, she cut it off right there in the ladies' room.

"Jesus, Bryn." Charlotte rushed over but Bryn just kept snipping, shorter and shorter until the floor was littered with clippings. Charlotte backed off; she wasn't about to fight Bryn for the scissors. She knew how headstrong her sister was. "Are you happy now?" Charlotte asked when Bryn finally stopped. There were pale blond threads all over her blue dress. Bryn was silent; she'd run out of steam. The strange part was, she was even more beautiful.

"If this is how you want to look when you get married, fine. I'm going up to finish my meal," Charlotte said. "You're your own worst enemy, kiddo. No one's going to feel sorry for you."

"Then feel sorry for Teddy," Bryn said. "It's not fair for me to marry him and you all know it. Considering I'm already married."

The man she had married four years earlier, when she was only nineteen, was Michael Macklin. He was the one who'd taken vows he never thought he'd say and certainly never thought he'd believe. He was now drinking at the bar of the Lion Park Hotel. He'd had dinner there as well, some fairly awful stew and a salad. He was hoping to see the little girl, who he knew was his best chance. Lucy hadn't been invited to the adults-only family dinner. She'd signed that stupid contract Charlotte had shoved in front of her just to shut Charlotte up. Anyone who knew Lucy knew she wasn't the sort to get into any real trouble, and in fact she had fallen asleep while reading a guidebook about London. She dreamed about the ravens at the tower. She dreamed Hyde Park was filled with snow and white rabbits, huge rabbits that were as big as dogs. They would come when called, but you had to ask nicely. You had to say, O rabbit, I beg of you.

Here is a secret, one rabbit said to Lucy. It's all pretend.

When Lucy woke up she didn't know where she was. She had to look out the window at the lights of passing cars on Brompton Road before she remembered. She was relieved not to be at the dinner with the adults. She wished she still had the diary of Anne Frank and hadn't lent it away. When her stomach started growling, Lucy realized she had missed dinner; she came down to the restaurant at nine, famished.

"Hello," she called when she saw Michael, who was on his second drink.

"Skip the beef stew," he called back. "I don't recommend it."

Lucy ordered macaroni and cheese and an apple tart for dessert.

"Oh, and tea," she told the waiter. She had become a tea fanatic in the short time since she had arrived. In a way she already felt like a different person from the one her friends knew back home. She probably looked a lot older; she probably sounded a little like Katharine Hepburn.

Michael came over and sat across from Lucy. He was wearing a black suit and a blue shirt. He had a lot of style.

"I started the book," he said. "Anne Frank had courage. I can see why you admire her. You don't find much of that in this world."

"Most of the time you find crap in this world." Lucy looked

up to see if he was shocked by her language this time. He wasn't.

"I need you to do something for me," Michael said. "Well, actually, for love."

Lucy stared at him. "I'm not an idiot," she said. Her food had arrived and she started to eat. "You want to use me in some way to get something you want. Right? Otherwise you probably wouldn't even bother to talk to me."

Michael Macklin smiled. "You're smarter than most people."

"That's exactly what a person would say when he wanted someone to do some dirty work. Do I have to shoot someone and say the gun went off by accident?"

Michael took out an envelope. "It's a letter I want delivered. Simple. That's all you have to do."

"Did you know there was a rabbit living in this hotel? Her name is Millie. She's actually huge. I've never seen such a big rabbit before."

"Did you know rabbit is a popular dish in restaurants in France?"

Lucy put her fork down.

"And by the way," he added, "I would have talked to you anyway. You're the only interesting person in the place."

Michael Macklin was the handsomest man Lucy would ever meet in her life. She didn't think that's what people should look for in a husband, however. They should look for soul. But at the moment she was here, sitting across from him, dazzled. She realized Michael Macklin was more than handsome. When she looked in his eyes she saw something she didn't usually see. He seemed real in some way adults never did.

"Go on," she said.

"Ah, the poor rabbit. They call it *le lapin* and cook it with onions and wine."

Lucy laughed in spite of the gory details. "Not about the rabbit."

"It really is love. I want you to take this letter to your stepmother's sister Bryn."

"The bride-to-be?"

"She can't be engaged. She's already married." Michael leaned forward and Lucy did, too. "To me."

"Why should I?" Lucy felt sick to her stomach and a little too young for the conversation. She already knew it was hard to turn Michael down when he wanted something. Still, she was interested in hearing his argument. It was simple and effective.

"Because deep inside you believe in things," Michael Macklin said. "Just like me."

At eleven o'clock Lucy was sitting behind the registration desk feeding Millie the rabbit a carrot that she'd gotten from the hotel cook, who was in love with Dorey, the night clerk. Lucy liked being in a hotel late at night. She was overseeing things while Dorey and the cook had a cigarette together out on the street, or so they said. Lucy noticed that Dorey was right. The rabbit liked to eat wallpaper as much as she liked carrots.

"That's not good for you," Lucy said, not that the rabbit listened.

After a while the rabbit hopped into Lucy's lap and fell asleep; Millie shuddered. Bad rabbit dreams.

"Thanks for watching over things," Dorey said when she returned. Her hair was messy and her mouth looked puffy, but she was cheerful and she treated Lucy as though they were friends.

"Are you in love with the cook?" Lucy asked.

"Of course not," Dorey said. "I need a ring on my finger before it's love. A diamond. And not some little bitty thing." Dorey got out a packet of chocolates and shared them with Lucy. "I see Millie likes you. She's a good judge of character."

Lucy went upstairs and got ready for bed. Her father would never know that she was wandering around the hotel at such a late hour. He didn't need to know that Michael Macklin had asked for her help. She put the letter in the desk drawer. When Lucy fell asleep she dreamed of rabbits. It had become a recurring dream; she almost looked forward to it. She was in the park and she came upon a lake. She thought she should jump in and swim across but then she realized that the lake was a mirror. One touch and it would shatter. She stood on the edge, uncertain as to whether or not it would be safe to cross. She noticed that the rabbits were only shadows, not flesh and blood. They were just black shadows made out of soot. Lucy's mother was standing in the lake, the way she had on the day they saw the heron. She looked so real Lucy tried to run to her, but there was water everywhere in her dream, too deep to cross.

She gave Bryn the letter the next day at the dressmaker's. She'd been dragged along since Charlotte didn't seem to want to give her any time alone with her father. But this time it served Lucy's purpose. Charlotte and the other sister, Hillary, were out by the mirrors with the tailor having their hems taken up, complaining as usual. They didn't notice when Lucy wandered off. Bryn was in the dressing room in her slip, smoking a cigarette. She looked up and saw Lucy staring at her.

"What?" she said. "My hair?" Bryn ran a hand through her feathery pale hairdo. "Am I ugly?"

"Anne Frank had all her hair cut off," Lucy said. "Not by choice."

"Who has choices in this world?"

Lucy sat down on the bench next to Bryn, who seemed utterly weird and mysterious.

"You'd look pretty with short hair," Bryn told her. "A pixie cut. You should get one. I'm sure Charlotte would hate it."

Lucy didn't like her long dark hair. It tangled and made her hot. She was interested in the idea of pixies. She was interested in Bryn, who seemed so different from anyone she'd ever known, so moody and self-centered and beautiful.

"Are you in love?" Lucy asked.

"Personal, aren't you?" Bryn took a drag of her cigarette. "Yes, but with the wrong man. You?"

"I don't believe in it. I'm never getting married."

Bryn laughed so hard she doubled over.

"I'm glad you think I'm funny," Lucy said.

"You're smart," Bryn said. "Smarter than anyone in my family. Fuck them all," she added. "They think they know everything."

Lucy sat up straighter. She was not accustomed to hearing grown-ups curse. "I see," Lucy said, mostly because she couldn't think of a response. For some reason she had a wave of missing her mother. She wondered what her mother would have made of Bryn. Bryn must have been psychic or something; she could tell Lucy was sad. She took Lucy's hand and held it. They sat there for a little while, not saying anything, just feeling sad together. They could hear Charlotte and Hillary talking to the tailor. Their bridesmaid dresses were pale peach silk. Lucy hated the color.

"He wanted me to give you a letter," Lucy said quietly. "I don't know if I should, I don't even know if you want it—"

Before she could finish her statement, Bryn squeezed Lucy's hand so tightly her skin turned white. Her bones felt crushed.

"Give it to me," Bryn said.

Lucy reached into her pocket and took out the envelope.

Bryn let her go. She shoved the letter into her purse. "Did you read it?"

"Of course not. Who do you think I am? Charlotte?" Lucy rubbed her hand. It still hurt. "You didn't have to squeeze me."

"If you were Charlotte you wouldn't even believe in love. I'll show you what love is." Bryn grabbed Lucy's hand back and put it to her chest. Bryn's flesh was hot and Lucy could feel her heart pounding. She felt her own blood rush to her head. Everything seemed heightened and fast and wild. "Now you know." Bryn cast Lucy's hand away. "Don't forget it."

MICHAEL MACKLIN HAD done some bad things, it was true. He continued to do them, using a child to get his letter to Bryn, tracking her down, changing his room to the one across from Lucy's so he'd have access to Bryn. Well, that was who Michael was. He'd lied about everything in his life, and he wasn't going to stop now when it really mattered. He'd lied so often and so well he sometimes got confused about the facts of his own life. In truth, they were simple: He'd been born in Manhattan to parents who meant well and did little. He was out to work at fourteen, then in the army, stationed in France, where he'd learned not only the language, but how to get what he wanted. He put his life on the line in France, and he hadn't even shivered. Some of the guys he knew said the only people who didn't fear death were those who had nothing to lose and he thought they were probably right. In battle, he'd felt alive. On the run, he felt he had something to run to. He liked danger, he liked the smell of it. He liked the feel of his blood running hot.

Michael was a thief, but he never stole from the poor. He'd seen *Robin Hood* with Errol Flynn when he was a boy, after all; he knew to look for people who could afford to lose some money, people who'd never even miss it. Michael resembled a dog in many ways: He could smell danger and he could smell wealth, he could stalk and quarry. He lived in the moment, for the here and now. He had gone through life without questioning much. The only time he ever felt connected was when he saw stray dogs. It had happened in abandoned villages in France and in New York City, down by the docks. It was a weird, visceral connection, like seeing yourself in the mirror and recognizing yourself even though you looked different from how you'd imagined, all fangs and fur and fear.

He'd come back to New York after the war and nobody gave a damn if he was a hero or a thief. Nobody knew him. Sometimes he went down past Tenth Avenue and he sat in the dark waiting for one of those dogs, desperate to be in the presence of a creature who would understand him. Funny how he'd felt that with Lucy, a twelve-year-old kid who couldn't possibly understand the kind of life he'd led. And yet she seemed to get him. She saw people from the inside out, and that was both a blessing and a curse.

Michael had met Bryn unexpectedly. He was walking down Fourteenth Street and she was walking ahead of him and he found himself following her. He had a strange thought, the strangest he'd ever had. He imagined that he had found an angel on earth and that he needed to protect her from people such as himself. Would anyone from his previous life believe he had fallen in love? Unlikely. He was a user, out for numero uno; everyone who knew him knew that much. They would never have believed he had spent all his money to court Bryn, or that he waited to have her in bed until they were married, or that he meant it when he said it was forever.

Walking down Fourteenth Street on an ordinary day he had changed. It was as though his cellular structure had been rearranged. Now he could feel things, and he understood why he hadn't for such a long time. It made sense to be a dog in this world. To keep moving and have a nose for trouble. He should have done that again after Bryn was taken from him, cut his losses, forgotten he'd been in love. Instead, here he was in the Lion Park Hotel, having tracked Bryn to Amsterdam and then to Paris and now to London. He was waiting for a twelve-year-old girl to rescue him. She didn't fail him. Lucy knocked on his door and slipped an envelope underneath.

"I am not doing this again," he heard her say while he scrambled to retrieve the letter. He didn't even bother to open the door to thank the kid. He read the letter from Bryn greedily, so fast he missed some words. So he read it again, and again. He'd been sitting there waiting, nearly drunk, in wrinkled clothes, almost ready to give up. Now he took a shower and sobered up and put on a clean shirt. Lucy was his angel. He had needed help, and she had given it to him. He had needed someone, anyone, to have faith, and she had.

He sat down at the desk to write. He'd thought it wasn't possible to put one's soul into words, but it was. He wrote down all the evil things he had done. He wanted to be known. It was like thirst or hunger, maybe even stronger. He thought of the dogs in New York City and how he'd thought he'd known them, but he'd been fooling himself. He hadn't known anyone, least of all himself.

He stayed up most of the night writing the letter, and in the morning he was already waiting in the restaurant when Lucy and her family came down for breakfast. He hadn't slept because he'd been waiting for this moment. Lucy looked at him, then looked away. Her father and Charlotte were taking her to see the Tower of London even though Charlotte thought it was a waste of time and would be terribly crowded. Lucy's father had insisted that they needed one day to be tourists because Lucy hadn't seen much more than the inside of a hotel room.

They sat down and ordered eggs and fried tomatoes and coffee. Lucy wanted tea and toast. She was developing a taste for marmalade.

"That is not nutritious," Charlotte said. "You need the five food groups."

"Chocolate, pizza, cereal, soda, and French toast," Ben and Lucy said at the same time.

Lucy grinned. It was a private joke they used to share before Charlotte came into the picture. A list of their favorite things.

"Is that man over there staring?" Charlotte said.

They all looked over at table by the window. Michael Macklin was stirring his coffee. He really was handsome. He put down his spoon and saluted Lucy. Again, she looked away.

"Do you know him?" Charlotte asked.

"I wouldn't say that," Lucy hedged. "I lent him *The Diary of a Young Girl,* by Anne Frank."

"This Anne Frank thing is not normal," Charlotte said to Ben. "It's an obsession."

Lucy raised her eyes. "Do you think most people detest you?" she asked Charlotte. "Or just the ones with brains?"

"Lucy," her father said. "That's no way to talk!"

"Well, then tell her that," Lucy said. "She just can't talk about me while I'm sitting here. I'm not a piece of furniture."

"I didn't mean it that way," Charlotte said. "You're taking it much too personally. I just meant there are more cheerful things to think about in the world other than Anne Frank."

"Hey there." Michael Macklin had come over. He looked like a movie star, like someone Katharine Hepburn would be in love with, and then lose and have to win back again. "Nice to meet you." He shook Lucy's father's hand. "You've got one smart daughter. I'll tell you. She's a brain, that's for sure." He took the copy of Anne Frank's diary out of his jacket pocket. "I learned a lot," he said to Lucy. "I want to thank you for lending it to me. I don't think I'm the same man anymore, thanks to you."

Lucy took the book and put it on her lap. There was so much wrong in the world she couldn't bear it. Was it really possible for love to exist?

"Well, have a great day here in London," Michael Macklin said.

"New Yorker, right?" Ben Green said.

"Aren't we all?" Michael shook Lucy's father's hand again.

In the taxi, on the way to the tower, Charlotte insisted they drive past Buckingham Palace. Elizabeth had been Queen since February, called home from Kenya suddenly when her father died.

"There it is," Charlotte said.

Lucy was paging through Anne Frank's diary while she looked at the men standing guard behind the gates. She thought they must be terribly hot. She felt the edge of an envelope in the middle of the book. Immediately, her heart begin to race. She put her hand on her chest. She hadn't even thought she had a heart, but there it was, thumping away. Michael Macklin was smart, all right. All through the tour of the tower, Lucy was aware of the letter in her pocket. It seemed to weigh more than paper should. There was a lot of talk of beheading and wives locked away. For some reason Lucy felt like crying as they went along with the crowds to see the Crown Jewels behind glass. Her mother loved art and she and Lucy often went to the Metropolitan Museum. She missed her mother and her father and the self she used to be. She missed it all.

In the taxi, on the way home, Lucy said she had left her glasses with Bryn. She was supposed to wear them for distance, but she never did. The taxi pulled up in front of Teddy Healy's flat—that's where Bryn was staying while Teddy bunked with his brother until the wedding.

"I'll run," Lucy said. "I'll be right back."

"We can't wait here all day," Charlotte called after her.

Lucy went inside the building, then up to the second floor. She had to bang on the door before Bryn came to answer.

"Where is it?" Bryn was wearing a bathrobe even though it was the middle of the afternoon.

Lucy handed over the letter. She'd have to tell them she'd been mistaken if they asked where her glasses were. They were actually on the bureau in her room at the Lion Park Hotel.

"I have to write back," Bryn said.

"Are you crazy? They're waiting for me in the car."

"Okay. Okay," Bryn said. "Then just tell him to meet me at the Church of the Apostle on Westbourne Grove. Everything is all set for tomorrow at ten. You won't forget?" Lucy promised she wouldn't. Bryn leaned down and kissed Lucy, right on the lips. "I want you to be my witness. Will you do that?"

Lucy nodded.

"Well then go!" Bryn told her. "Before they come to search for you."

They didn't even ask her about the glasses when she got into the taxi. They appeared to be in the middle of a fight.

"How did Bryn seem?" Charlotte asked on the ride back to the hotel. "Normal?"

Lucy wanted to laugh out loud. She looked at Charlotte quite carefully. She didn't give a damn what her stepmother thought.

"Perfectly normal," she said.

LUCY SLIPPED A message under Michael's door that evening. In the morning she sneaked out early, while her father and Charlotte were still asleep, leaving them a note that she was going to see some English people she'd met who wanted to show her the town, maybe take her to the zoo. She knew she wasn't supposed to go anywhere, but she'd be quick, and no one need ever know where she'd really gone. She met Michael on the corner and they took a taxi to Westbourne Grove and were exactly one hour early. The church was old, made of red brick, with a pretty spire. There were stained glass windows and statues of saints.

"I think this is a Catholic church," Lucy said.

"Smart as always. Are you sure you're only twelve and not forty? She said ten o'clock, right?"

Michael was nervous. He smoked three cigarettes in a row and walked back and forth.

"Ten o'clock," Lucy assured him. "Don't worry. It will all work out." It wasn't like Lucy to be comforting, but she felt compelled to calm him down.

"Oh, yeah, sure. Just like everything else. Did everything work out for the Jews in Nazi Germany?"

"She'll be here," Lucy said.

"Expect nothing and be grateful for everything, that's what my mother told me," Michael said.

"My mother said she was afraid to die." Lucy had never admitted that to anyone. It gave her shivers to think back to that moment when she sat with her mother in her darkened room near the end. Usually that moment was blanked out in her head.

"Sounds like your mother was one of the few honest people on earth." Michael stubbed out his cigarette and lit another. "That's where you get it from, most likely. It's a gift she gave you. Your honesty."

But she wasn't honest. Not really. When her mother said

that Lucy had quickly said, You won't die. Even though it was obvious that she would. Lucy couldn't bring herself to tell Michael that part. She couldn't have him hate her for being such a coward.

"I'm not so honest," Lucy did manage to say. "I told my father I was going to the zoo today with some people I met in the park so he wouldn't find out I was here."

"That's not a lie, it's a cover story. You're honest about the important things, Lucy."

Lucy smiled. She thought, No wonder she's in love with him.

Bryn arrived at a little before ten. She got out of the taxi and started kissing Michael in a way that made Lucy look away. She had the feeling she shouldn't be seeing so much; that some things were meant to be private.

"My witness," Bryn said when she noticed Lucy.

They went into the church and Michael stopped to cross himself with some of the holy water from the font. The priest, along with an elderly woman as the second witness, was waiting for them, and they went right up to the altar. The air smelled like incense. Lucy stood beside the couple, and although she didn't understand the liturgy, which was surprisingly lengthy, she understood when the priest told them they were married in the eyes of man and of God. They kissed again, crazy kisses, and then Michael and Bryn had to say good-bye. Michael was off to get tickets to Paris, so Lucy went with Bryn to help her pack. Bryn threw clothes on the bed and Lucy folded. When they were all done, Bryn took off her diamond ring, the one Teddy had bought for her, and she gave it to Lucy. "For you. Keep it."

Lucy held the ring up to the light. The stone looked like a

huge ice crystal. It was quite beautiful. She put it in her purse while Bryn wrote out a last letter to Michael. She believed in love letters and in romance and in destiny. She wanted to let him know how much she loved him. She would come to the hotel for him, and then they would go far away and no one would find them this time. While she was busy writing, Bryn let Lucy eat as many chocolates as she liked out of a fancy box that came from Harrods. There were candies with caramels and others that were raspberry creams or milk chocolate with ginger fillings that made her mouth pucker. Lucy drank fizzy lemonade afterward. Lemonade soda and chocolates; two out of the five food groups she and her father had always preferred.

"Wish me luck," Bryn said as Lucy left to walk back across the park to the Lion Park.

Lucy hadn't the heart to tell her she didn't believe in luck.

The day was hot and breezy and the park smelled fresh and sweet; it made her think of those chocolates in a box. Lucy walked along the Serpentine and watched the families out on boats for hours. She liked the fact that nobody knew her. No one knew she had a diamond in her purse. No one knew her name. She imagined that people really could start over. She let herself think about her mother. Now that she'd told Michael about her, it was less painful to bring her to mind. Her mother had said something to the blue heron on their perfect day. She had gone right up to it, the water up to her knees. The heron had seemed to listen to her and then he flew away. Lucy and her mother had both waved to the heron. They'd jumped up and down and shouted out to him; then they had watched him disappear into the trees. Lucy's mother had climbed out of the pond then. The hem of her dress was soaked, her feet were bare. "I told him to watch over you," she told Lucy. That had been the last good day of Lucy's life.

Lucy took out the engagement ring and slipped it on her finger. If she ran into those young English women again she'd tell them that the ring had belonged to Katharine Hepburn. Clark Gable had wanted to marry her, but she'd turned him down flat and given the ring to Lucy instead.

When Lucy got back to the Lion Park it was past dinnertime. The entire hotel was in an uproar because Millie, the rabbit, had gotten loose. The maids and the porters were all looking for her. She'd left a trail of her droppings, and worse, wallpaper everywhere had been torn from the walls. She'd chewed on the phone wires so that the entire sixth and seventh floors had no service. Now something had gone wrong with the lift as well; Lord only knew what the rabbit had chewed up. Guests were advised to take the stairs.

"No good deed goes unpunished," Dorey said gloomily. She'd been called on the carpet and her position was in jeopardy. Usually she wore the gray jumper and white blouse that was her uniform; now she had on a flowery dress and heels and scarlet lipstick. She'd been all set to go on a date when she got the call about the rabbit. The cook who was in love with her had threatened to chop off Millie's head if he found her. He was walking around in his good holiday clothes with a meat cleaver, slicing through the air.

"Save me the foot," Dorey called after him. "That's the lucky part."

Lucy headed up the stairs. She had decided to count them and was up to eighty-one when she ran into Charlotte.

"There you are," Charlotte said. "Have fun at the zoo?"

"It was brilliant," Lucy said. That was a word those English women had used all the time. Lucy planned to use it quite often when she returned home. "There were twenty-three camels and one of them was an albino."

"You are such a little liar," Charlotte said. "You may have your father fooled, but I see right through you. Where have you been all this time?"

Charlotte might have said more, but suddenly she was staring at Lucy's hands. Lucy put them behind her back. She had forgotten to take off the ring.

"Where'd you get that? Oh my God! On top of everything else, you're a thief!"

"That just goes to show how much you know," Lucy spat back. "She gave it to me."

"She?"

Lucy shut up and turned to go up the rest of the stairs. She thought of the rabbit, hiding somewhere. She thought she probably had another hundred steps to go before she escaped. But Charlotte grabbed her. She wrenched Lucy's arm.

"Are you talking about Bryn? Did you take that ring from her?"

"Does my father know you don't even believe in love?" Lucy said. She should have felt trapped. Instead, she felt oddly powerful.

Charlotte yanked Lucy's hand up and forced the ring off her finger. "When your father hears about this you'll be seriously punished for once in your life."

What happened next was Lucy's fault. She pushed Charlotte and she never should have done that. Charlotte clutched onto Lucy to keep from falling and that's how the letter dropped to the floor. It was the sort of instant that lasts too long and then all of a sudden time speeds up and there's nothing anyone can do to stop it. It's much too late for that.

Charlotte bent down and picked up the letter. She recognized her sister's handwriting and Michael Macklin's name. She stared at Lucy as though she had never quite seen her before.

"That's mine, give it back," Lucy said.

But it wasn't, and they both knew it.

Charlotte tore open the letter and read it.

"It's mine," Lucy said again, hoping to convince them both.

"Then what does it say?"

Lucy couldn't answer.

"If it's yours you tell me what the hell it says, Lucy Green, you little liar! Go on!"

"It says I hate you," Lucy finally answered.

Lucy ran upstairs and knocked on Michael's door, but he wasn't there. When she turned, Lucy knew she had made a mistake. She shouldn't have gone directly to find Michael. Charlotte had followed her.

"Is this where he's staying?" Charlotte said. "He's the man at breakfast, isn't he? You've been planning this with him all along. You've been helping a criminal and a thief!"

Lucy had her key in her hand. She opened her door, then slammed it behind her and turned the lock. There was no peephole, so she couldn't look out to see if Charlotte was out there. But she didn't have to wait long for her answer; her stepmother began to pound on the door.

"You get out here right now!" Charlotte said. "Don't think you can just walk away from me!"

Lucy sank down onto the carpet, her back against the wall. She was never opening that door. She could feel her heart pounding, and the thrumming of her pulse echoed in her ears. She saw something across the room, under the desk. She thought it was a shadow, or a lost soul, or a rat, or the devil himself, but it was only Millie, the rabbit from downstairs. Lucy crawled across the floor and moved the chair away, then got under the desk with Millie, who was huddled at the back, next to the wall. It felt safe under there. Very hot and somewhat stinky, but safe.

Everything seemed surprisingly quiet when Charlotte finally stopped yelling and thumping on the door. It was hardly possible to hear the traffic noise from under the desk. Lucy curled up and closed her eyes. She listened to little puff-puffs of breath, the rabbit breathing, or maybe it was herself as she fell asleep. When she dreamed, Lucy dreamed about that last day with her mother. First they had gone to Saks, their favorite store, where her mother had bought Lucy a camel-hair coat. And then, at the last moment, her mother had pulled her over to a jewelry case and on impulse also bought Lucy a small gold watch with a black leather band.

It was October, and Lucy should have been in school, but her mother had said to hell with it all; she said some days were too perfect for school and that's when they'd driven into the city. After they went shopping, they had lunch in the Rainbow Room high above Fifth Avenue. The world below looked blue and gold. Lucy kept checking her watch and announcing the time, which made them both laugh.

"This is my forever day," Lucy's mother said.

They ordered shrimp and steak. Lucy had a Shirley Temple

cocktail and her mother had a martini, straight up, with five olives. She gave the olives to Lucy, then asked for five more. In real life, they went to Central Park and saw the blue heron and he flew away and Lucy's mother sat on the rocks and wept. In real life, Lucy's mother had cancer, and her face looked ashy, and she was wearing a heavy coat even though the weather was fine and her dress was soaking wet. She'd had beautiful dark hair that she'd worn long, but she was wearing a wig. She was thirty-six years old. She had looked at Lucy and then she'd said, I'm sorry. In real life, Lucy had taken off her new watch and dropped it in the water. She knew she shouldn't do it, and that she'd regret it, but she didn't want time to go forward.

Everything is either beneath us or above us, Lucy's mother said.

People started to shout in Lucy's dream. Maybe because her mother was standing close to the edge of a bridge in her dream. Below, there was a stream and a waterfall and huge rocks. People were screaming when Lucy's mother stepped off the bridge. Lucy was in a panic; her heart almost stopped—her dream heart and her real-life heart—but then she saw that her mother was in the air. The heron had been waiting, and she didn't need the earth at all. Everything was either below her or above her, just as she'd said. Lucy had to put one hand over her eyes to look upward; everything was blue and the sun was so bright it hurt her eyes.

Lucy woke up when the rabbit kicked her. She opened her eyes and heard the screaming in the hall. She looked at her watch. It was ten-fifteen. Everything was dark. The rabbit had hopped away and was shivering under the bed, startled by all the noise. Lucy went to the door. She opened it a crack. A tall man was in the hall. The door to Michael's room was open. The man went inside, still screaming. He'd been betrayed, that's what he said.

Lucy opened her door wider and slipped into the hall. She felt fuzzy, as though she were a sleepwalker. She felt drawn to the screaming; it was like a magnet. She could hear a woman screaming now. She knew the voice. She started to feel something like chills, the way she felt when she had a fever. Lucy looked inside the room. There was Bryn getting out of bed. Michael was there as well, pulling on his clothes. They looked far away, half-naked. The other man went to Michael and grabbed him and hit him in the face. Again and again. Michael didn't fight back. "Go on, if it makes you feel better," he said. "I deserve it." Blood came out of his nose. It was ridiculously red.

"Stop it," Lucy cried, but no one was listening to her. She was invisible. She was watching a dream.

"How am I supposed to forgive you for this?" the tall man said to Bryn.

"You're not! Don't forgive me, Teddy. I don't want you to. We should have never been together, so just let me go."

He didn't listen to what she was saying. The man called Teddy grabbed for Bryn; he was saying he was going to marry her for her own good. He looked like he was about to hit her, but Bryn managed to pull away and get past him. Then Michael hit him. He hit the tall man hard, but as he was doing so, Michael shook his head; he didn't like what he had to do, but it seemed he had no choice.

As for Bryn, she was like a shadow; she ran right past Lucy. She smelled like heat and lilacs. Inside the room, Michael realized she was gone; he stopped paying attention to the other man and went after Bryn. He was shoeless. Lucy could practically hear his heart thumping. He was drenched in sweat and there was still blood coming out of his nose, but he took off down the hall.

The other man, the one called Teddy, stayed where he was. He sat on the bed and looked down at the floor. There was blood on his face, too. He seemed stunned, but when he gazed up, he saw Lucy standing at the doorway. Lucy stared at him and then she ran. She ran as fast as she could. Her pulse was so loud she thought she'd gone deaf. She ran down the stairs and through the lobby and out into the street.

She was still in a dream, wasn't she? It was possible for things to go backward in dream time, to change and reverse themselves. That's what she counted on. She was running so horribly fast she thought her lungs would burst open. Lucy thought about blue herons, rising into the sky. There was so much traffic on Brompton Road, it seemed endless. Lucy wished they had those Walk/Don't Walk signs that had just gone up in Times Square.

She could see Bryn running through the crowd. In her slip, Bryn was so white in the dark night she looked as if she'd tumbled down from the moon. She looked to the left and then took off running, but she had not looked to the right. She crossed as she might have in New York, without thinking twice, and in an instant she was hit by a van. Even with all that traffic Lucy could hear the thud. Even worse, she could hear Michael Macklin. She would hear him forever. The sound of his cry, below her, above her, everywhere.

Lucy was sitting on the sidewalk when her father found her. It was Dorey the night clerk who phoned the authorities; then, because she'd seen Lucy race out through the door, Dorey ran upstairs to get Ben Green. There had been a horrible accident and his daughter had been right there in the midst of everything, Dorey told him. The young woman hit by a van, the man who walked into traffic afterward. The blood was already fading into the black road and the black night, but Lucy had seen it all. Those frozen moments right before, when she could have run out and stopped him if only she'd been faster on her feet. Michael had looked at her from the other side of the road. He had focused for one moment as though he was glad they saw each other and recognized each other. Then he stepped off the pavement like a man jumping off a bridge, as calm as a swimmer with an ocean out below. Lucy had known he was going to do it the instant their eyes met. She'd known what he intended because she would have done the very same thing if she'd had his courage. Nothing was going to break his fall.

The Greens checked into another hotel that night. Their luggage and all their belongings would be sent around. Dorey offered to do the packing. Charlotte was going to stay with her sister, Hillary, and see to the details of bringing Bryn home, so it was just Lucy and her father. Their new hotel was smaller, a family-owned place called the Smithfield, very comfortable. Ben Green got a suite, and he let Lucy sneak the rabbit from the Lion Park into their room. Ben wasn't usually one who approved of taking what didn't belong to you, but Lucy simply refused to leave without Millie. She'd gotten hysterical and had crawled under the desk. She kept saying people at the Lion Park were going to chop off the rabbit's head and cook it. Her father had to make a blood oath that he would protect the rabbit no matter what. Ben nicked his hand with a razor and made an *X* on a piece of stationery before Lucy would come out from under the desk. She took a Lion Park ashtray to use as a feeding dish.

The new hotel was on the other side of the park, not that far from the church where the wedding had taken place. Lucy remembered it, something Grove, as if there was woodland right in the middle of the city. To leave the Lion Park with the stolen rabbit, Ben wrapped it in his suit jacket, sneaking it out before anyone could see. The taxi driver looked in his rearview mirror when Lucy slipped off the jacket to make certain the rabbit was all right.

"I didn't see that," the taxi driver said. "If you've got any living creatures that shouldn't be riding around in a cab, don't tell me."

They didn't say a thing. They were all in shock, Lucy and her father and the rabbit. When they got to their new hotel suite, the couch in the parlor area was made up as a bed for Ben, and Lucy was given the bedroom. The hotel was quieter and the streetlights didn't glow through the windows, but Lucy didn't sleep. She picked up Anne Frank's diary, but she couldn't bring herself to read it. She didn't want to read it anymore. Lucy didn't sleep for three nights, and then she got sick.

She had started to shiver and now she couldn't stop. She was burning up and yet she was cold. Her mouth hurt and she didn't want to drink any water. There was a doctor staying in the hotel, in London for a conference, and the management called upon him to see to Lucy when her father asked for a physician to be sent up right away. Millie was sitting on the bed chewing on a woolen blanket when the doctor came in.

The girl's father had already told him that his twelve-year-old daughter was impressionable and sensitive and that she'd witnessed a horrible accident.

"What do we have here?" the doctor said. "A rabbit in a hotel room? Now that's something I wouldn't have expected."

Lucy didn't say anything. She liked the room she was in. She didn't particularly want to leave it. She didn't want to talk. She wasn't going to tell anyone that she couldn't sleep at night because she heard Michael Macklin's voice.

The doctor had been told that Lucy had stopped talking, and that the same thing had happened when her mother had died.

"Ever hear of the Third Angel?" he asked.

Usually that got a response, but Lucy didn't even glance at him.

"People say there's the Angel of Life and the Angel of Death, but there's another one, too. The one who walks among us."

He could tell that she was listening.

"He's nothing fierce or terrible or filled with light. He's like us, sometimes we can't even tell him apart. Sometimes we're the ones who try to save him. He's there to show us who we are. Human beings aren't gods. We make mistakes."

"That's not a very comforting thing for a doctor to say. You're supposed to cure people, not talk about making mistakes." Lucy hadn't spoken for several days so her throat felt scratchy and dry.

"I do the best I can," the doctor said. "I think you do, too."

"You don't know anything about me," Lucy informed him.

"I've got a daughter who likes books." The doctor had

taken note of the copy of Anne Frank's diary on the night table. "She's a big reader, too."

Lucy glanced at the doctor. His voice sounded sad; he had probably seen a lot of sick people. She noticed that he was wearing two wristwatches. That seemed very odd indeed.

"You're not a quack, are you?" Lucy asked. Her chest hurt her and she was coughing at night. She kept her face in the pillow so her father wouldn't hear her. She had worried enough people. She didn't intend to worry anyone anymore.

"As in duck?" the doctor said, puzzled. "That sort of quack quack?"

Lucy might have laughed, if she hadn't felt so dreadful. "As in lunatic," she said.

"Ah, the watches. One I use to take your pulse." Which he then did. "The other is to make sure I'm always on time. It's a time-traveling watch."

"Really." Lucy had never had a doctor quite like this one. She sat up straight.

"Mind if I listen to your lungs?" he asked.

Lucy shrugged. The doctor had an old black bag that opened when he pushed on a silver clasp. He took out a stethoscope and listened to Lucy's back, then her front. She could hear herself wheezing. When he was done she had one of her coughing fits. She covered her mouth up. She felt her ribs would shatter. The doctor waited politely until she had finished choking and had managed to catch her breath.

"The rabbit doesn't cough, does he?"

"She," Lucy corrected. "No. She's totally silent. Never a peep."

The doctor asked Lucy to sit on the edge of the bed and when she did, he tapped on her elbows and knees. She felt like a puppet. When he asked her to cough again, she did so and then couldn't stop. This time the rabbit startled and jumped down, then skittered beneath the bed. "What do you mean a time-traveling watch?" Lucy asked when she got her breath back.

"I set it an hour later, so when I get home and see my daughter I'm actually an hour ahead."

Lucy laughed, then wheezed.

"You know what I think?" the doctor said.

Lucy shook her head. There were certain things she hated now, ever since that night. Traffic, blood, the color red, sudden noises, the thud of her own heartbeat.

"I think you've got pneumonia. And some very serious asthma. Have you ever had an asthma attack before? Any huffing and puffing?"

Lucy shook her head. "We're taking the ship home soon. I'll be better by then." She realized she hadn't thought about her turtle, Mrs. Henderson, at all and she felt like a bad pet-owner and a bad person. For all she knew Mrs. Henderson had already died and no one had bothered to tell her. She had better get home right away. She wished she could leave that very day.

"I think you'd be better off if you went to the hospital for a bit," the doctor told Lucy.

"Well, that would be impossible, really." For some stupid reason Lucy had begun to cry. She had nothing to cry about. She wasn't Anne Frank after all. She wasn't living in an attic to be carted away to a death camp. She was in a comfortable hotel room with her father.

"Why is it impossible?" The doctor had written down the

name of a cough syrup for her father to get at the chemist so that Lucy could get some immediate relief. "Do you have something else you need to be doing that prevents you from going to the hospital?" He was listening quite carefully for her answer in a way adults usually didn't.

"I'm taking care of a rabbit," Lucy said. "Isn't that obvious?"

The doctor thought that over. He put away his stethoscope and the thermometer and his prescription pad, all back into his black bag.

"I'll take the rabbit home with me," he said.

"And eat it?"

The doctor recognized someone who had lost her faith. He had seen it before.

"I'm a vegetarian," he told her.

Lucy studied his face. He didn't seem like a liar.

"Actually, I wasn't thinking of keeping it as a pet. I was thinking of letting it stay in my house for the winter, and then setting it free in the field behind my house."

"She," Lucy said.

"She," the doctor amended. "She could still come and eat from the garden. We usually have lettuce and peas planted. She could sleep under the shed."

"I wish I could time travel." Lucy called to the rabbit under the bed, but it wouldn't budge.

"Any particular time?"

Lucy considered. "The moment before the bad things started happening."

"Well that would have to be before the universe existed. That would be blank and empty space I'm afraid. You really don't have to worry about the rabbit. I'll take good care of her."

Lucy realized how difficult it was to breathe. She didn't think the doctor was a quack anymore. "Yes," she agreed. "That would be good. Her name is Millie."

Lucy went into the hospital that night; she had to sleep in a plastic tent where warm wet air was circulated. She was far more ill than the doctor had let on. She was wheezing until she thought she might vomit and when she closed her eyes she saw things that weren't there, probably because of her fever. She saw black trees covered with thorns. She saw a man she thought she recognized and she wondered if he was the Third Angel come to visit her, the one who made mistakes. She saw a mourning dove that could no longer fly. The nurses were very nice and let Lucy change her nightgown three times in a row when she got too sweaty from being inside the plastic tent. They had to keep the air damp and warm to hydrate her lungs. Her father came to sit beside her bed. He wanted to hold her hand, but the nurses told him that wouldn't be a good idea; he'd let all the steam out of the tent. So he read the *London Observer*. Once he read a *Time* magazine with Katharine Hepburn on the cover; even through the plastic tent Lucy could see she looked nothing like her. Nothing at all.

Ben told her that Charlotte was going home on the ship, but that they would be staying for a while. He had rented a flat for the rest of August and September; Lucy could make up the work she would miss at school with a tutor whenever she was well enough to study again. While she'd been ill, Lucy's eyes hurt and she had no desire to read. When she got ready to go to the hospital on the night she saw the doctor with the two watches, she had given her copy of *Anne Frank: The Diary of a Young Girl* to the hotel library. It was really only a bookcase where guests left the books they had finished. Ever since she'd given the book away, Lucy had a lost feeling, as though she really were floating in blank, empty space.

After the first week in the hospital, Lucy's hair was so tangled and wet from the humidifiers and the damp air in the plastic tent she couldn't stand it. She begged the nicest nurse, Rebecca, to cut it for her. They went out to the sunroom and Rebecca spread out some towels. Rebecca cut Lucy's hair in a pixie cut. It was such a relief to be rid of her long hair; Lucy shook her head and there was no heavy weight.

"You look just like Audrey Hepburn!" Rebecca said.

"Not Katharine Hepburn?"

"Oh, no. Audrey." Rebecca sounded sure. "She has the same haircut and the same beautiful face."

When Lucy looked into a mirror she was surprised by what she saw. She looked older, like a teenager; she looked like the person she was meant to be.

Her breathing had gotten much better, and after two weeks, the hospital let Lucy go home to the flat with her father. Rebecca came by every day to check on her and have her breathe into some tube thing and listen to her lungs. The nurse often stayed through lunch—they were all worried because Lucy had lost a great deal of weight. Lucy was glad to have the nurse visit; she liked to listen to Rebecca and her father talking in the kitchen as they made tomato soup and cheese sandwiches; they laughed over silly things, English things Ben Green didn't know about. What a kipper was, how he wasn't to eat Ploughman's pickle straight from the jar, how to use the funny old-fashioned toaster with the holes in it that left a pretty brown pattern on the bread.

Sometimes when Lucy looked out at the street she still saw blood. She didn't tell anyone this. She knew it wasn't real. It was like the hallucinations she'd had when she was in the hospital. The man in the black coat who might have been an angel; the doves falling from the ceiling. She had asked her father to tell Charlotte that Michael and Bryn had been married and that they should be buried together, and he had; but Bryn's family didn't believe her. In their opinion, Lucy was a liar and a thief and they went ahead with the funeral arrangements of their choice. Lucy didn't know what had happened to Michael Macklin's remains; he didn't seem like a man who had a family.

One day when her father was out, Lucy went for a walk. It was the first time she'd been out by herself since the accident. She roamed around, feeling her way, and at last she found the church. She had remembered Westbourne Grove. She went inside and crossed herself the way Michael Macklin had done, then sat in one of the wooden pews. She couldn't tell if she believed in anything or not, but she prayed anyway. At least she thought it was a prayer. She said it for Michael. She wished that he and Bryn were together. She wished that love was real.

When she left, Lucy noticed a bookstore across the street. She went inside. She missed reading; she felt empty without it. It was a used bookstore, and it smelled of paper and ink. It was a very disorderly place but Lucy managed to find water-stained copies of *Through the Looking-Glass* and *Alice in Wonderland*.

"Good choices," the clerk said to her, and he gave her a discount. "Those two would see you through on a desert island, wouldn't they? They'd be books enough."

Lucy took her Alice books in their brown paper wrappings tied with string and walked toward the park. She'd grown so much that Rebecca had taken her shopping at Selfridges earlier in the week and they'd picked out new slacks and shirts. Rebecca was a fan of casual clothes. They bought sweaters and shirts and hiking boots and a new handbag. If those two English women she had met in the park that first week had seen her they would never have recognized her. They'd be looking for someone who resembled Katharine Hepburn and they'd be wrong.

It was September and the park smelled spicy. There were people riding horses on the bridle path and the air held the odor of horseflesh and fresh earth. Lucy walked and walked and then she crossed the bridle path on the far side. She had gone all the way across Hyde Park. She faced the street where it had happened. She hadn't thought it out, but somehow she found herself on Brompton Road. Now that she was here, she knew she had to go farther. She really had known it all along.

It was late in the day, nearing suppertime, but the light was still clear. People were rushing home from work. It had been so dark on the night when it happened; everything had been black and blue and red. Now everything looked normal. Lucy wondered how many people from America who weren't used to people driving on the left had stepped out in front of traffic. She held her breath; she didn't know if she could cross the street, but she managed to get to the other side. She just waited for a crowd and when the light turned she crossed with them. When Lucy reached the other side, she bent over and took a few deep breaths.

She made her way to the Lion Park Hotel and stood outside and looked up into the windows. She counted up seven floors, but she couldn't tell which room had been hers. There was the old stone lion covered with moss in the courtyard. She went into the lobby. There was the flowered wallpaper. A new young doorman called her miss and welcomed her to the hotel. Lucy went over to the desk. Dorey was there; she had been promoted to day clerk.

"Can I help you?" Dorey asked formally, and then she recognized Lucy. "Oh my lord! You look brilliant!!! What have you done to your hair?" Dorey came around to give Lucy a hug. "I adore it!"

"It's a pixie cut," Lucy said. She had been feeling guilty about taking Millie without a word, so now she told Dorey the truth. "Just so you know—I stole the rabbit."

"Well, I wasn't going to cry over a rabbit, even if it was Millie. I figured she found her way back to Hyde Park."

"I gave her to a doctor who'll take her out to the countryside."

"She'll be happy hopping around in the woods. It's only natural, I guess. But she'll probably miss eating wallpaper. She was a real wallpaper lover." Dorey took out some chocolates and offered Lucy her pick. "That was a bad time back then," Dorey said quietly. "We had news reporters and everything here afterwards. I was interviewed twice."

"I made it happen," Lucy said.

"You? You had nothing to do with it. The real culprit comes here every night and gets sloshed. As if that could help." When Lucy looked confused, Dorey added, "The groom. That fellow Teddy Healy. He should have found a woman who loved him back, that was the problem. You can't force things like that. She wanted Mr. Macklin, and who can blame her? It's chemistry, you know. There've been studies done and it's been proven. Love is ancient and mysterious and you can't mess with it. If you do it just backfires and you meet with disaster. That's a fact."

Lucy considered this. "He comes here every night?"

"I no longer work that shift, but that's what Miles Donnelly told me. Nights are his now. I've been promoted. I was the one who called the authorities and the hospital, you know. I handled the whole thing. And that room where they were, the one across from yours? We can't rent it. It's haunted. That's a fact as well. Every night at ten-thirty there's a racket of some sort." Dorey seemed relieved to have someone to talk this over with. "People think I'm crazy, but I saw the ghost myself. That's another reason I made them switch me to days. I'm not going to sit here alone at night with some ghost wandering about."

"Who is it?" Lucy's chest had started to feel funny, as though she'd soon have difficulty breathing, just like in the hospital. She had an inhaler she was supposed to use when she felt this way, but she'd left it on her bedside table.

"It's Michael Macklin, of course," Dorey said. She had never actually seen the face of the ghostly presence, but anyone could figure out who the most wounded party was. "It must be the moment when that car hit him. Ten-thirty."

Lucy shook her head. "I think it was ten-thirty when I went to their room. He must have died later."

Lucy looked shaken.

"Maybe you shouldn't think about that," Dorey said. She took Lucy into the restaurant where her boyfriend, who was still the cook, fixed the child some food.

"Look what he gave me," Dorey said of the cook. She

waved her left hand in front of Lucy's face. She had on a diamond ring. "After the incident we both figured life was short
and there was no point waiting around for things you really
wanted."

A group was checking in, so Dorey gave Lucy a hug and
went back to work. Lucy sat in one of the booths with her used
books on the table. The restaurant looked completely the same.
It was very strange being at the Lion Park. She felt as though
she'd spent most of her life there, as though Westchester and
everything that came before didn't even mean anything.

The waitress brought a steaming bowl of soup with bits of
celery and potato and a tall glass of ginger ale with cherry juice
added so that it had turned pink. Lucy realized she didn't have
enough money to pay. She was embarrassed, but the waitress
told her there was no problem.

"Dorey's treat," the waitress said. "Eat up."

Teddy Healy came in at about eight. Lucy had finished her
dinner. When she saw him she felt more shivery than ever.
Teddy Healy didn't look the same. He looked run-down and
skinny. He started drinking right away. His poison of choice
was whisky.

"Slow down," Lucy heard the barman say to him. "You've
got hours to go, man."

Lucy started reading her book. She really had to concen-
trate, but eventually the story won her over. She liked the way
Alice spoke her mind and didn't hold things back; she admired
that. The world dropped away when you went inside Wonderland. Before Lucy knew it, it was ten, and then a quarter past. At
this late hour, her father was probably worried sick, but Lucy
couldn't back away now. She just wouldn't think about that.

She'd explain herself. She had to come to the Lion Park one last time. Surely her father would understand that.

When Teddy Healy paid his tab and set out to leave, Lucy gathered her books together. He took the lift, so she took the stairs. Her legs felt heavy, almost as if they wanted to slow her down, but Lucy made herself hurry. She could see the lift rising on the wires the rabbit had once tried to chew through; the brass on the doors had recently been polished and shone like a mirror. Lucy let Mr. Healy get a little ahead of her and then she followed him. The hallway felt freezing cold.

Teddy Healy stopped, so Lucy did, too. She prayed that she would see Michael Macklin, that he would make his presence known. All she wanted was to ask for his forgiveness. I dropped the letter, that's what she intended to say. I never meant to, but I did. It's all my fault.

There was a footstep where there was no person. Lucy felt so cold she thought her lungs might freeze; they were still damaged, after all. Teddy Healy said "No" out loud. And then Lucy saw it, the thing everyone thought was the ghost. But it wasn't Michael Macklin. She would have recognized him, the most handsome man she would ever in her life see. The figure in the hallway was Teddy Healy the way he was that day, furious and in a rage, shouting at the open door. It was the part of him that had split off and been lost; the soul, some people might call it.

Lucy could feel her legs giving out. They felt as though they were made of string. She couldn't breathe either; she had that wheezing thing that took hold of her lungs and made it so difficult for her to take in any air. She made a noise and then she dropped to the floor. She saw the thing that wasn't Teddy Healy and the thing that was, which turned to her when she crashed down. She hit her head, hard, on the wall, and then she thought she heard someone yelling, although it was probably in her dreams, nothing more than that.

Lucy wasn't punished because of the circumstances, even though she refused to discuss what on earth she was doing halfway across town. She had a severe concussion and her asthma was considered to be a serious health risk. She had to stay overnight in the hospital again, under the plastic tent, until she could catch her breath. Ben Green was truly worried now. Perhaps he'd done everything wrong. He was a parent alone, a fool most probably, a man who'd surely made mistakes. When Lucy was released from the hospital, Ben telephoned Rebecca, and she came over and sat with Lucy while he went out to have her prescriptions filled.

"I don't know what to do to turn this around," Ben said to Rebecca before he left for the chemist's. "I'm out of ideas."

Rebecca brought a glass of milk and some cookies into the bedroom. She said hello, but Lucy didn't answer. Lucy lay in bed. She felt limp and used up. Now her short hair made her seem like a little girl. She had a big lump on her head that throbbed. She kept her eyes closed most of the time, even when Rebecca read to her from the Alice books in silly voices that might otherwise have made her laugh. Rebecca put the book down. Books wouldn't fix what was wrong.

"Are you very unhappy?" Rebecca asked.

"I don't see the point of things," Lucy said.

After that Lucy stopped talking. She liked Rebecca but there was nothing to say; not that day, not ever. If her father or the doctor who came to visit asked her a question, Lucy wouldn't even shrug. They'd tricked her before, but now she was done. It was as if she had forgotten how to form words, as if language was a mystery to her now. She was polite, but she did not speak.

"Just tell me what I can do for you," her father said. "Anything."

But because there was nothing she could think of, Lucy didn't answer.

Rebecca thought perhaps Ben should take Lucy on a trip, outside London, somewhere quiet and new and beautiful. She believed that travel was good for the soul, and that sometimes a person had to go away in order to recover from sorrow. She suggested Edinburgh, a city she loved. When Ben agreed, she made the arrangements. He asked her to go, but Rebecca said no. She said this was a trip for the two of them, father and daughter, and if he wanted to take her somewhere some other time, perhaps when he wasn't married, she might consider his offer.

They packed lightly, only one suitcase for the two of them, and they took the train at King's Cross Station. Lucy was relieved that her father didn't expect her to talk anymore. Once, he took her hand and she felt like crying, but she stopped herself. She wanted to make certain she didn't start crying again; once she started doing that there'd be no hope for her whatsoever.

There were smokestacks and the train windows became sooty, but once they were beyond the city the landscape was beautiful. Lucy looked outside and felt as though she could drown in all the burnt gold and green. She hadn't expected such a lush landscape. She fell in love with the colors of southern England. She liked the rhythm of the wheels on the track rever-

berating inside her head. They blocked out what she was thinking, terrible thoughts she didn't guess anyone in the world had,
except for Teddy Healy. He might want to block things out as
well.

There weren't many people on the train, but in the last row
there was a boy who was writing like mad. He hadn't looked
out the window once. He had a large book on his knees.

"Looks like a reader," Ben Green said. "Just your type."

But Lucy's father had no idea what or who her type might
be. Lucy gazed out the window. In time, she closed her eyes and
fell asleep. In her dream she was on the train with a very large
rabbit that was seated across from her. She expected the rabbit
to say something, but it was silent. She thought there might
be tears in its eyes.

The train shifted and Lucy woke up. Her father had gone
to the dining car to have a drink. Lucy raised her eyes and saw
that the boy in the rear of the car was looking at her. He waved,
so Lucy waved back. It was only to be polite. Then the boy
signaled her over. When she tried to ignore him, he waved
again so Lucy got up and walked down the aisle, holding on to
the backs of the seats. She was curious, after all. She still felt
dreamy. She might as well have been a million miles from
home.

"Looks like we're the only two interesting people on the
train. I saw you reading the Alice books. My favorites."

Lucy sat across from the boy. He was working on something
called "Anthology," which had a coat of arms on the cover—it
was a notebook filled with pen and watercolor and colored
pencil.

"It's a project for school. I'm illustrating my favorite poems.

Stuff like Robin Hood. Alice being the most favorite." He looked up. "You don't talk? Do you speak English? Are you deaf and dumb?"

"No," Lucy said. She felt tricked; he'd gotten her to talk. She hadn't done so for days. "Not deaf at any rate."

The boy laughed. "Ah. You're an American. So I was right. You don't speak English. You speak American." He was working on the coat of arms.

"Are you royalty?" Lucy asked.

"No. Not one bit. I'm a writer. And an artist. And a musician. I'm everything. And you?"

"A reader."

No one would ever have to know she'd spoken a few sentences to him. She could stop talking again any time she wanted.

"I'm John," the boy said.

"Lucy."

"I'm from Liverpool. I was just in London for a visit. I usually go to Scotland in the summer to visit my aunt, but I'm going up for a couple of days now. My mother's left."

"Mine's dead. And I saw two people die in London."

John didn't seem the least surprised. "Blood and guts?"

Lucy nodded. "It was over love."

"It's always over love," John said.

They both thought about that.

Ben Green came back from the dining car and waved.

"My father," Lucy said.

John waved hello. "Reader?" he asked.

"Major reader." Lucy bowed her head so her father wouldn't see that she was talking. "I wish I believed in something," she said.

"How about reincarnation? You'd come back again and again. You'd be a moth and a dog and a soldier."

"What if I came back as a pig or an ant or a walrus?"

They both laughed now.

John showed her his drawing illustrating Alice. It was the walrus and the carpenter. "The walrus always has the carpenter," he said. "The pig's got his sty. The ant's got ten thousand other ants that think exactly the same thoughts he does."

They looked out at the fields.

"A dog wouldn't be bad," John ventured.

"I'd better go," Lucy said. Talking so much probably wasn't a good idea. Her chest felt weird.

"Good-bye, Lucy from America. Keep reading."

"Good-bye, John. Keep doing everything."

Lucy went back to her seat. Her father had brought her a sandwich and an apple.

"Did you have a nice talk?" Ben asked.

With her hair cut short, Lucy looked so much like the woman she would grow up to be it was startling. Now that she was out of bed and stronger, she didn't seem like a little girl. Ben had the feeling they were starting from scratch, as though everything were new, even the words they used.

"Maybe I shouldn't be questioning you," he said. "You don't have to talk to me if you don't want to, Lucy."

After talking with John, it had gotten a bit easier for Lucy to speak. "Thank you for taking this trip with me," she said to her father. "It's beautiful here."

"It *is* beautiful here," Ben said, relieved to be granted a single sentence, let alone two. For the first time in years and years he wasn't in a rush. He wasn't thinking about Nixon or the *New*

York Times or Charlotte's phone calls that he hadn't returned. He was actually thinking of the day Lucy was born. The truth was, he hadn't wanted children. He'd been irritated with Leah for talking him into it. He wanted their life together to go on and on as it had been, and then there she was, pregnant, and he was annoyed. All through the pregnancy he'd worried he'd be a terrible father. Leah had insisted that once he saw the baby everything would be different. But when he saw her she just seemed like a wrinkled little alien who took up Leah's attention. He didn't feel anything at all until the day they took Lucy home. A car had cut them off as they were pulling out of the hospital parking lot and Leah had been propelled forward, the baby in her arms. For a moment Ben had been utterly panicked. What if I lost them? he had thought. How could I ever survive?

When they got to Edinburgh it was dinnertime. Lucy saw the boy from the train meeting his aunt; they waved at each other. She thought that some people were like stories rather than whole books—at least the ones you never saw again. With people like that, you never knew what the real ending was.

Lucy and her father took a cab to Hotel Andrews, where they had adjoining rooms. It was run by a woman named Mrs. Jones who looked like she must be someone's perfect grand-mother. There were two photographs, one of a boy, the other of a girl about Lucy's age, hung above the mantel near the registration desk, but the photos looked old, from another place and time. Lucy thanked Mrs. Jones when the landlady gave her a peppermint candy, but she didn't ask about the children.

Lucy and her father went out to dinner; they wanted to get the lay of the land. They walked past the castle, which was so amazing that Lucy had to stop and stare. She wondered if she was crazy or if anyone else had ever seen something like the apparition she had seen at the hotel. Maybe because the castle was so old people were trapped inside forevermore; maybe they'd turned into the sort of thing Lucy had come across in the hall. Lucy hadn't told the whole truth to that boy on the train. She did believe in one thing, something so vast and deep she couldn't bring herself to tell John, even though it was probably safe to confide in someone she would never see again.

She believed that people could lose themselves.

The sky in Scotland was inky and beautiful and the air smelled different. Maybe this is what that doctor who took the rabbit home was talking about, the blank space of the universe, so endless that people and their petty concerns didn't matter. They stopped in a pub so Lucy's father could have a drink. Lucy had a ginger ale and her father had a glass of port. They ordered cheese and pickles and a plate of haddock and potatoes.

"I think this thing with Charlotte isn't going to work out," Ben Green said while they were having their dinner. "I'm sorry I put you through that."

Lucy hadn't told her father that she was the reason two people had died. She never intended to tell him. He had no idea that Charlotte had called Teddy Healy because Lucy dropped the letter. He would never know that Lucy heard Michael Macklin's cry all the time, in the back of everything. She couldn't get rid of it for a second.

"If I'm being asked my opinion, I prefer Rebecca," Lucy told her father.

Ben laughed. "Me, too."

They remained in Edinburgh for four days before heading off to the countryside.

"We'll be back," Lucy told Mrs. Jones, who'd been teaching Lucy to knit. In the afternoons, after they'd been sightseeing, when Ben went to take a nap, Lucy had sat in Mrs. Jones's kitchen, where she learned how to do simple stitches: knit and purl, yarn over, knit two together. Mrs. Jones had given Lucy a skein of yarn that smelled like heather and salt, a purplish gray shade the color of dusk. Their landlady never talked about the children in the photograph, and there were no signs of children in the house, so Lucy never did ask. Mrs. Jones made jam tarts and Ovaltine so Lucy would gain back the weight she had lost. Once Lucy said, "My mother would have taught me how to knit if she was still alive." She didn't know what made her say that; it just slipped out. Mrs. Jones didn't even glance up, but she insisted that Lucy and her father stay for supper, and for dessert she gave them slices of sour cream and green pear cake, which sounded bad but tasted delicious.

Now that it was time to go, Lucy didn't want to leave the hotel.

"You'll be back at the end of your trip," Mrs. Jones said, and she offered Lucy some more yarn and a pair of wooden needles of her own so she could keep up with her knitting. This ball of yarn was even softer, the color of old leaves.

Ben rented a car and tried his best driving on the wrong side of the road. He made Lucy nervous. Once he nearly went into a stone wall.

"You're not going to kill us, are you?" Lucy said.

"Not if I can help it."

They drove around the city until he got the knack of it. Lucy was nervous, and then she wasn't. Her father was a good driver. He was practical and adaptable, and he was a patient man. In little more than an hour it seemed as though he'd always been driving on the wrong side of the road.

"North, south, east, or west?" he asked Lucy before they really headed out.

They were living that way now, day-to-day. Everything was up in the air. Lucy thought it over.

"Definitely north," she said.

TEDDY HEALY HAD not gone back to work or returned to his flat. His brother, Matthew, said there were things that happened in this world that people couldn't understand and certainly couldn't control; he suggested they go together to the church and talk to the minister, but Teddy had refused. Teddy had checked into a nearby hotel, one that had a view of the road where Bryn had died. It was morbid, but he didn't feel he was there for morbid reasons. He stayed there so that when he woke in the morning he could go to the window and remember. He was not going to pretend it hadn't happened. It had. There was no way to deny it. After a while, Teddy went to speak to the minister himself; the minister embraced him and told him it was not his place to question but to accept. Teddy shook the minister's hand, and he didn't go back to church.

The moment he most often replayed was not the one when Bryn's sister phoned, or when Charlotte met him on a bench near the Serpentine to hand him the letter his beloved had written to Michael Macklin; it wasn't even when he read it and discovered that Bryn loved someone else. It was when he'd first seen her, in Paris, sitting in the Tuileries, just across from the Musée d'Orsay. He had a meeting with a real estate firm in Paris, and if he hadn't, if Barry Arnold had gone from the London office in his place and Teddy hadn't taken off the afternoon and walked through the garden, he wouldn't have looked up to see a beautiful young woman with long, pale hair sitting in the sun. As it was, he'd watched her doze off, already falling in love with her. When she opened her eyes that was it.

Now Teddy felt like a science experiment gone wrong. What had attracted him to her? Her scent? The shade of her eyes when she looked up at him? The fact that the lilacs looked pink in the afternoon air? The sound of pigeons and of doves? His own metabolism? His own history? Paris?

He had asked her to lunch, where she told him that she was in love with someone. She tried to be honest with him, but he didn't want to listen. They ate sandwiches and olives and drank white wine. She was on a trip till the end of the year; she had gone to Amsterdam before coming to Paris, but she'd never been to London. She leaned over at one point, after she'd had too much to drink, and she'd said, I want someone to save me. That was the instant that had stayed with him more than any other. Another man might have run, but not Teddy. He and Matthew had lost their parents very early, in a train accident, and had been raised by an aunt. There was not a day when Teddy didn't think the situation might have been different if he'd been on that train rather than playing football at school. He might have heard the squeal of the brakes, he might have thrown open the window, helped his parents climb out of the wreckage. He might have done something.

He and Bryn spent the night together. She had cried at first and she'd said there was someone else, but she was lonely and in the end she was the one who asked him to stay. She came to

London because of that loneliness, because Teddy was the only one she knew in Europe and she didn't want to stay on in Paris alone, because he was kind, because he was so in love with her.

When her parents heard about him after her older sister Hillary visited London, they wrote Teddy a letter to say how happy they were that Bryn had found love; they insisted they would pay for the wedding. They hadn't discussed marriage, but after that letter from her parents Teddy had thought, Of course, we should get married, and he'd gone out to look for the ring. Bryn slept late and went to bed early, so he left the ring on the table before going to work and when he came home that evening the diamond was on her finger. It was much more than he could afford, but Teddy wanted his love to be obvious; he wanted her to know how he felt. He didn't notice when she took off the ring; they were no longer engaged and he'd never even known it.

Matt came to visit him at the hotel where he was living. It was called the Eastcliff and it had neither a bar nor a restaurant. Teddy brought his own liquor up to his room; he'd been drinking hard and he hadn't showered. He was twenty-eight years old. Matt was older by eighteen months, but Teddy now seemed like an old man.

"You can't let this kill you," Matt said. "It was terrible, all right, but unexpected things happen in life. No one knows that better than you and I."

Matt was an organizer; he worked at the same bank as Teddy. Now he went into high gear. Matt rented his brother a new flat, got rid of the old furniture, especially the things that would remind Teddy of Bryn, the bed for instance, and his wedding suit, and all those gifts that had arrived. He got Teddy a week's leave, and at the end of that week Teddy had been moved into the new flat near Lancaster Gate and was ready to go back to work, more or less. People approached him tentatively, as though he'd been through a grave illness and was still quite weak. He did his work, true enough, but on the way home he had begun to stop at the Lion Park bar. It turned out that he was weak. He began to drink in earnest.

When Teddy opened the door on the night he saw them together in bed, everything he thought he knew and believed in had shifted. In a way, he'd made it happen. He couldn't just walk away; it was exactly as it had been when he'd met her and he'd refused to listen. He had stopped at the desk when he arrived at the Lion Park and demanded the key from the night clerk, who seemed too confused by his request to deny him. Then he'd run up the stairs. He knew it was bad, knew it was over. Why had he needed to see for himself? Because he needed proof? Because he didn't really believe it? They were utterly tangled together, in the midst of making love; he barely recognized Bryn, it was her back he saw at first, long and white and beautiful. She hadn't even heard the door open.

He started shouting and he couldn't stop. Not when she turned to him, not when she stayed where she was, stunned, while the man she was with moved quickly to cover her with a sheet. He said she had betrayed him. That she was committed to him and had to marry him. He didn't recognize his own voice. Who would want a woman who didn't love him? Who would never really belong to him?

He grabbed her while she was hurrying to pull on her slip. She tried to explain it wasn't about him; she was already married when they'd met; she'd been wrong to make any promises.

He pulled her close and said something horrible. That was the instant he could never forget. That was what drove him to the bar at the Lion Park each night. You don't deserve to live is what he'd said. He'd turned on the man then, and hit him straight on, and that's how Bryn managed to get away. The other man, the one Bryn loved, had finally punched him back in order to go after her.

Teddy Healy drank his whisky neat, and sometimes the bartender would put a sandwich or a bowl of stew in front of him. Sometimes he ate and sometimes he kept to his drinking. One night, when he was good and drunk, Teddy Healy went upstairs. He had never done so before this night. It was raining and his bones hurt as though he were an old man. It was late September by then and chilly and the hotel was not as full as it had been over the summer. On the seventh floor there were strips of wallpaper torn from the lower wall from the time when the pet rabbit had wandered off. The hallway was down-right cold.

Teddy went to what had been Michael Macklin's room and knocked. There were no guests, so he opened the door. He smelled something. Lilacs. He backed away, but before he could leave he heard a man's voice. He leaned his head against the wall and the oddest thing happened: He saw himself in the doorway, shouting, in a rage. It was impossible and yet it was true. There he was.

Teddy went back downstairs to the bar and drank even more. Every night afterward he went upstairs at the very same time, and every time he found himself there, the man he used to be, the person he no longer knew, someone who'd believed in things.

"She's not here, man," the bartender said one night when Teddy could barely stand by the end of the evening, when he dragged himself off his stool in order to go upstairs at the appointed hour. "It's not her ghost up there, so you might as well stop looking."

"Have you ever felt that you lost something and you can't get it back? As though it's been stolen right out from under you?"

"Sure," the barman said. "It's called life."

There was only one person who could ever understand. The girl, Lucy Green, who had seen everything. That night Teddy had spied her in the doorway after Bryn and the other man had run out. He had seen the expression on her face. It was as if an angel had been trapped in a cage of blood and bones, torn apart from the inside out. She looked stunned; she shouldn't have been there. They stared at each other and in that instant Teddy felt something he had never in his life felt before: a total connection of thought and emotion. They were there in the same exact moment, having the same exact thought.

Then the girl turned and ran. That was the difference. Teddy stayed in the room that smelled like lilacs while Lucy fled. She had seen everything, all that ugliness. As for Teddy, he hadn't wanted to see anymore. He sat down on the bed where Bryn had been with that man, and he didn't even cry.

As a penance, Teddy joined a group that did clean-up work in parks throughout the city. He enjoyed working outside and was amazed by how much wildlife there was in London. He saw foxes in the middle of the city one morning, startled by his presence as he used a long net to collect trash from a fens. He was struck by the way the foxes ran off together, looking behind them to make sure he wasn't following them. Teddy sat down on the grass. He was wearing high rubber boots, a mac, and old paint-splattered trousers that he used for such chores. Sometimes Teddy thought about Lucy Green and what she had seen and he just couldn't bear it. The oddest thing would put him in mind of the look on her face, just as the foxes had.

The following Sunday, he went back to his church; he had missed it. He talked to his minister about the existence of a soul; he tried his best to understand. The goodness within a human being was what he'd thought it must be, the innocent spirit, but his minister had said no, it was the essence of a person. Pure and simple. The deepest, most complete part, the part that was called to God.

And without that a person goes to hell? Teddy had asked.

Without that you live in hell, the minister said.

TEDDY REALIZED THAT his life had been altered by a letter. The only letters he'd ever written were thank-yous to his aunts and cousins on the occasion of his birthdays when he'd been sent presents; the only ones he'd received were from relatives he'd never met in Australia, sympathy notes after his parents had died. But one letter written by Bryn had changed his life, and then in October came another. It arrived at the Lion Park with his name on it. It was actually several days before he received it. The hotel clerk was marrying the cook and everyone was in a tizzy. The wedding was to be held in the Lion Park restaurant and everyone who worked there was invited. One night when Teddy arrived the barman said, "Sorry Teddy, but we're closed for the evening. Private party." He handed Teddy the letter. "Dorey's been so caught up in her arrangements, she forgot to give you this. Lord knows why it was sent here."

The wedding party was going on inside the restaurant. White and violet satin ribbons had been hung around the bar; there were bottles of champagne set out and silver platters of sandwiches and fruit. The ceremony was over and the festivities were in full swing. The clerk was dancing in her white dress. There was the cook, her groom, toasting all his friends and telling them they had better drink up since the expense of the bar bill was being paid for by the hotel management.

By that time Teddy had a fear of letters. He sat in the lobby for a while, but the sound of the music and the partygoers was turning raucous, so he went down the street. He intended to go to the hotel where he'd stayed right after the accident, and sit in the lobby there, a dim lonely place, but instead he went home. He walked through the dark. He chose to go through the park to avoid seeing anyone. He was alone, after all; he might as well feel that he was. The park smelled like leaves. This used to be his favorite time of year. When the leaves looked yellow and the weather was still fine. Now he didn't care. He was half a person, really, and the half that he was didn't give a damn about things like leaves and weather. He went to the flat his brother had rented for him and got a bottle of whisky.

The letter had been written on hotel stationery from a small inn in Scotland. Teddy didn't recognize the handwriting. He opened the envelope with a knife and took the letter out and let it sit on his table for a while. It was probably another great trick of life. He was most likely being informed he had a disease, or he owed the tax man money. He had another drink before he started to read. It began: *Dear Mr. Healy, I am the girl from the hotel. My name is Lucy Green and I'm writing to you because I think you are the only person in the world who understands me.*

At first he thought it was a practical joke, but then he recalled the moment before she ran out of the room and he thought it might be real.

I was wondering if you could tell me if you've discovered if there's any reason to go on living. I have thought about this a great deal. Unlike Anne Frank, I do not still have faith in people. I think you may not either, but I'm not sure. I am traveling with my father. We are going to Loch Ness to look for the Loch Ness Monster, but really we are just driving until we figure out when we should go home and what we should do with the rest of our lives. We will be back in Edinburgh on the twenty-second of the month at the Hotel Andrews owned by Mrs. Amanda Jones. You can write to me there if you have an answer. If not, I am very sorry to have bothered you. Everything was my fault. She gave me the letter to give to her husband. You didn't do anything wrong, it was me.

Teddy couldn't sleep that night thinking about that letter. It would do no good for him to answer her; she was right, he had no faith in people. But he didn't want her to feel that way. If he stumbled upon some part of her that had been lost in the hallway of the Lion Park Hotel he would not be able to live with himself. She was a twelve-year-old girl, and she'd had nothing to do with it, really. There was no reason for her to be haunted. So Teddy did something out of character. He made a phone call up to the hotel where the girl would be staying again in Edinburgh. The Andrews. He spoke with the landlady, who was made to understand what Lucy had been through. He spoke only of the illness of course, not all the rest. Not the deaths and the road and the blood and looking into his eyes to see that he had lost himself completely. That was knowledge only for those who would truly understand. Someone such as himself.

LUCY AND HER father stayed at a bed-and-breakfast near Loch Ness for more than a week. They walked along the paths near the loch, through brambles. The ferns were turning brown and the air was cold. It was beautiful, wild country. Ben bought them woolen scarves and gloves in a little yarn store where the sheep were kept right beside the shop. He bought Lucy another skein of wool, tinted indigo, for she had become a fanatical knitter during her time in Scotland and had already used up everything Mrs. Jones had given her. They hiked for miles around the loch and they never once saw a monster. They went motoring on a boat with an old man who swore he would take them to the place where the monster had been sighted, but there were only some logs rolling around in the water. The water was deep and murky and Lucy felt drawn to it. She thought of Michael Macklin, the way he seemed to jump off a bridge into water when he walked into the traffic. Lucy leaned over the boat and trailed her fingers in the icy loch and dared the monster to come bite off her thumb.

One morning Lucy's father came down to breakfast and he said, "Well, now we really don't have to hurry back. They gave me the ax." He didn't seem particularly upset about being fired; in fact, he was cheerful and famished. He ordered both oatmeal and sausage with eggs. "I'll walk it off," he said.

Lucy looked at him. She immediately thought it was her

fault that he had no job, and that she'd have to beg down by Penn Station in New York; they'd have to live in the subway in a cardboard box.

"Lucy," her father said when she started to cry right there at the table. "There is such a thing as fate."

But Lucy didn't believe in anything, least of all fate. She thought they would probably wander forever. When they left Loch Ness, they drove back to Edinburgh; it was a long trip. They stopped at a bed-and-breakfast along the way for the night. From the parlor where there was a fire going, Lucy heard her father say to the innkeeper, "My daughter has been ill," and she realized that she had been. She sat down on a chair and warmed her hands. She had been too ill to go back to her life in Westchester.

She still dreamed about rabbits, but not all the time. Sometimes her sleep was filled with purple hills, blank spaces. When they were settling back into the Andrews Hotel, Mrs. Jones's nephew, Sam, mentioned that Mrs. Jones's children had died in a flu epidemic during the war. Lucy went to her parlor with one of the heather-colored scarves she'd made.

"You did a lovely job," Mrs. Jones said.

"I made one for you and one for me," Lucy said.

Mrs. Jones was an expert knitter, but she was kind enough not to mention any of the dropped stitches. She put the scarf around her neck. "Perfectly beautiful."

Lucy felt sick when she thought about leaving Edinburgh. She felt that if she took too many steps she would fall off the earth. Westchester didn't even seem real to her anymore; maybe everything had disappeared in her absence. Maybe nothing had survived.

And then on the day before the Greens were to take the train to London, Mrs. Jones said there was one more thing they had to see in Scotland. She asked her nephew to drive them out to a farm. Sam was more than happy to do so. It was beautiful country they drove through, the prettiest Lucy had seen. She was wearing one of the scarves she'd knitted herself, with a seed stitch and a lacy border. Mrs. Jones was wearing the other.

"Don't take a wrong turn," Mrs. Jones told her nephew. "You get us lost every time."

Mrs. Jones had brought along a blanket and a picnic lunch with a thermos of very strong tea for Lucy if she started wheezing. They soon arrived at a huge farm that belonged to friends of the Joneses, where there was a sheepdog trial. There was a line of trucks and cars and vans and a field that had been cut up into pastures and pens. There were dozens of baaing sheep.

"This is different," Ben Green said. "Where we come from dogs just sit in the yard and bark or they lie on the couch and beg for biscuits."

"Not here," Sam Jones said. "Dogs earn their keep here."

They went to watch with the crowd as the dogs and their owners worked together herding. The farmer would whistle or shout and the dog would respond as if the two were communing in a language all their own. Just the man and his dog and no one else in the world.

"You notice every whistle is different?" Sam Jones said to Lucy. "The dogs understand the meaning of every one. Go left, go right, fast or slow. Some dogs are said to know a hundred whistles. They're smarter than we are."

They had a wonderful time watching the sheep being

herded. One of the farmers came over to say hello. He was a cousin of Mrs. Jones's named Hiram.

"He's got the best dogs," Sam said. "He's sure to win."

"Come around to my van afterward," Hiram said to the Greens. "I'll show you something I bet you'd like to see."

Hiram's dogs were smart. They raced around the sheep and got them into the pen in amazing time, but in the end another herder won top honors that day. Lucy and her father cheered for every dog; they all worked so hard and with such passion it was hard to pick a favorite. The afternoon had turned cold and the sun was about to go down; Lucy couldn't remember when she'd been so happy and tired. She felt she could stay in this place forever, but everyone was packing up and gathering their dogs into their cars. Sam led them to the sheep pens, where Hiram was having a drink with some of the other men. They all seemed to know each other.

"Oh, here she is," one of the shepherds called out. "The girl from New York."

Lucy blushed as she and her father were introduced. They all seemed to know about her, they even knew that she was a knitter. The sky was purple around the edges. It looked like spilled ink spreading out on a page when darkness fell here. The end of the day seemed so natural and beautiful.

"Come on," Hiram said. "Follow me."

He had a van and his three sheepdogs were sitting in the front seat, jumping up when they saw him. They went around the back and Hiram opened the door and there was a young collie bitch curled up on a blanket.

"Oh!" Lucy said. "Can I pet her?"

Hiram nodded and Lucy scrambled over to sit on the bumper. "She's a bit shy and she may have to warm to you."

This collie was smaller than the others. She sniffed Lucy's hand.

"Hello," Lucy said.

"She was the runt of Rosie's litter last year. She's deaf in one ear, so she'll never be a herder. That's why she's going home with you."

Lucy felt something inside. It was like a shovel smacking against her chest.

"Well, that would be great, but we live across the ocean," Ben Green said. "So I don't see how that's possible."

"You'll take her with you," Hiram said. "That's no problem. She's well-behaved. She'll be the toast of the ship. She's been bought and paid for, so you can't say no."

Mrs. Jones sat down on the bumper of the truck with Lucy. "You can tell she's smart by the shape of her head."

Lucy looked at her father. She put her hand on the little border collie, who was shivering; she had never wanted anything more in her life. She didn't even have to beg; Ben Green went aside with Hiram and when he came back he had the dog's leash in hand. Maybe this was a sign of their lives changing from what they had been to what they would become. You never could tell. They drove back to Edinburgh with the little collie in the backseat settled between Lucy and Mrs. Jones. The collie had curled up on a blanket that smelled like sheep and had quickly fallen asleep. Its front paws twitched and Lucy wondered if it dreamed of rabbits.

"What will her name be?" Mrs. Jones asked.

Lucy thought about the photos of Mrs. Jones's children on the mantel in oak fames. The boy and the girl. She didn't know why they had to die young, she just knew they were gone and that Mrs. Jones was here beside her.

The sky was all ink now; the whole bottle spilled out.

"Sky," Lucy said. "Skyler."

Mrs. Jones leaned in close. She smelled of wool and peppermint. "There's a man somewhere who wanted you to believe in something," she said. "He's the one who bought the dog."

No one else could hear above the motor of Sam's car, an old Vauxhall that rumbled and strained on the steep pitch of the little roads, but Lucy had heard perfectly well. That man Teddy Healy was answering her letter; he was letting her know he still believed in something. Lucy and Mrs. Jones smiled at each other. This was their secret. The collie made puffing sounds in its sleep. There were stone walls on either side of the road and hedges that looked black in the falling night. Lucy gazed out the window. She wanted to remember this when she went home.

Acknowledgments

I am indebted to my extraordinary editor,
John Glusman.
Many thanks to Shaye Areheart for
championing this book and to Jenny Frost for
her support.

Thank you always to Elaine Markson.
Thanks also to Gary Johnson and to Julia
Kenny. And many thanks to Camille McDuffie.
Thank you to Alison Samuel and everyone at
Chatto & Windus and Vintage UK.

To my dear friend, Maggie Stern Terris,
always on my side.
To Tom Martin, for everything.